MW00379764

Dragonfly

a novel by

Robert W. Oliver II

Dragonfly Copyright © 2017 by Robert W. Oliver II. All Rights Reserved.

No part of this book may be used or reproduced in any manner whatsoever, including internet usage, without written permission from the author, except in the case of brief quotes in critical reviews.

FIRST EDITION

Library of Congress Cataloging Data

ISBN: 9781973480570

Edited by Carla Rossi

Story Consultant: Nikki Johnson
Illustration Photography by Marsha A. Bradford
Illustration Model: Amy Burgess

Pawnee language assistance provided by Laura Redish

Special thanks to Renita Boniak

Robert W. Oliver II
Cider Grove Media
a division of OCS Solutions, Inc.
PO Box 3355
Florence, AL 35630

https://jeweledwoods.com/
robert@cidergrove.com

Chapter 1

"I've been here before."

"That's unlikely," my father replied with the strangest expression on his face. He gave his apple core from lunch to one of our horses, then pointed to the wagon. "We need to get back on the trail."

The scenery hadn't changed much since we left Independence, Missouri. The gentle rolling plains of the Kansas Territory offered a vast canvas for the imagination, yet I knew with certainty that sensation was not simply an artifact of my mind. Every sense was intensely familiar. The green fields that stretched as far as I could see, the numerous, cotton-like clouds that dotted the sky, the faint smell of pollen, and the gentle wind flowing through my hair. There was no mistake.

"Izzy, you know we've never been this far west," my mother said.

"I'm certain," I protested.

I had previously experienced unexplainable moments of clairvoyance, but never with such profound intensity.

"These things happen," my father said. "No one knows why."

My mother put her arm around my shoulder. Even if she was patronizing me, I knew she meant well. She was a well-educated woman who valued observation and investigation over difficult to describe feelings. Still, I couldn't help but feel there was something she wasn't telling me.

I took a few steps from the wagon and looked off into the distance. A rider was approaching. My father pulled me back.

"Careful, Izzy," he said as he took his rifle from the wagon.

If we dare to be authentic - to bare ourselves to the world -
we allow others to share in the full measure of the unique blessing
bestowed upon us.

I am privileged to know one who has the courage to do that, to light
the path for others by simply being the most unique expression of self
I have ever known.

And I dedicate this to you, Amy.
You dared to become the dragonfly.

"He means no harm," I muttered.

"How do you know that?" he asked, keeping his weapon ready.

A gust of wind blew, and with it, every single tiny hair on my arms stood at attention. A tingle washed over my whole body. As the handsome young man approached, I watched every moment in excruciating detail. He had dark, beaded long hair, and had determined, soulful eyes. I stood both enthralled and perplexed as he raced past me. Time slowed, allowing me to see each step in his beautiful black horse's graceful gait.

He knew me. Or I knew him. Or some impossible combination of the two. That was the impression I received the moment I stared into his eyes. I knew I had never seen that man before, and yet, I had. He was trying to tell me something in that perplexing gaze, not in words, but in thought.

As the surreal moment unfolded, there was no one present but me, that man, and his horse. Everything else was quiet and still, except for the thunder of the hoof beats. I had been transfixed by the moment, unable to perceive anything else around me. After he passed, I was shocked to find that my parents, the wagon, and oxen were gone. With what little breath I could summon, I screamed.

My heart raced and I thought I was going to faint. I scanned everything around me. I was completely alone except for the Indian who was riding off into the distance. That wasn't possible. How could everything vanish? I called out to him, but he continued as though he didn't hear me.

My body shook as a hand came to rest on my shoulder. "Izzy!"

I turned and noticed that my mother had a distraught expression. I was relieved to find my parents and our wagon exactly where they had been.

"What's wrong, Izzy?" my father asked.

"I don't know. You were gone, and now you're back."

"We've haven't budged an inch," he replied. "You probably didn't notice us for staring at that Indian boy."

I took a deep breath and looked away while I pondered what had happened. I was so flustered that I completely overlooked my father's casually-delivered sideways remark. "No, I know what I saw. You weren't there."

My parents exchanged confused glances. I noticed an odd reservation between them.

"We'd best be moving. Daylight is burning," my father announced.

As we drove away, with bewilderment and regret, the setting of that encounter faded into the distance. Though I can't say why, I had the strange sensation that if I left that spot, I wouldn't be able to understand what had happened. My mind associated it with that particular place on the Oregon Trail. That location was at least something tangible. I was grasping in vain for anything to make sense of that unusual experience.

As we resumed our travels that day, I couldn't stop thinking of the Indian that passed us by. Who was he? What was his name? Why was he staring at me? My previous focus on the event now seemed misguided. Surely he had something to do with it.

Discussion at evening camp was almost non-existent. I wasn't in a talkative mood, and I could tell my parents wished to avoid any mention of that day's events. Their avoidance of the subject didn't make sense. It seemed natural for them not to understand it. I didn't understand it. But shoving it aside was not in their character.

Right before I went to sleep, my mother approached and wished me a good night's sleep and pleasant dreams. I propped myself on my elbows and asked, "Do you know what happened today?"

My mother took a deep breath and sat next to me. "No, I don't. I wish I did."

She moved behind me and began brushing my hair. I leaned my head back a bit and smiled, appreciating the comforting gesture.

"You have such beautiful, thick brown hair, Izzy. I know you got it from your father."

"Thank you," I replied. "But you're trying to change the subject."

My mother scoffed. "Can't a proud mother admire her daughter's hair?"

"You know something."

My mother feigned confusion. She wasn't good at hiding things. "What do you mean?"

I turned and looked into her eyes. "What are you not telling me?"

"I really don't know what happened."

"That's not what I asked," I challenged.

My mother frowned. "I came here to wish you good night, not to be interrogated."

"I'm sorry. I didn't mean to —"

She put her hand on my arm. "It's alright, dear."

I had never seen my mother quite like that. She was clearly distraught, yet tightly restrained. "You have always been sensitive to things others ignore."

I didn't really understand what she was saying. My parents said that I was gifted with a strong sense of intuition, but I had no idea how that was connected to the incident with the Indian and their temporary disappearance.

"What are you trying to tell me?"

She looked at the ground. "I knew you were special from the moment you were born. Sometimes unexplainable things happen to special people."

I couldn't help but to grin with a hint of embarrassment. "Every mother thinks their children are special. You're hardly objective."

"Perhaps," she admitted. She took my hands firmly and looked directly into my eyes. "I want you to promise me something, Izzy."

My grin faded with her serious tone. "Of course."

"Always listen to that intuition. It will lead you down the right path. A gift like that will surely be a blessing on this journey."

I wanted to probe further. I opened my mouth to protest, but I thought better of it.

"I will," I replied.

Ironically, by giving up, I was ignoring her advice.

"Thank you," I said as I gave her a hug. "Sorry I scared you today."

"Sleep well, Izzy."

Sleep would not come easily that night. I stayed awake and stared at the stars, letting the focus of my vision drift as my mind danced from thought to thought. My muscles were tense and my body on edge. Despite persistent efforts, I could not shake the disturbing feeling that filled every corner of my mind. As the first hints of daylight broke, I succumbed to sheer exhaustion and fell into a light slumber.

I had scarcely little sleep before my mother woke me for breakfast. Heavy rain began to fall that morning and the deluge continued for the next several days. By the time we reached the Big Blue River crossing, we were soaked and miserable. We arrived in the early afternoon and surveyed the river. The murky, brown, rapidly flowing waters were intimidating, and the roar of the water was almost deafening. The trepidation in my father's eyes scared me more than the rapids.

"We'll have to wait for the river to settle," he surmised.

We camped near the river for the night and were relieved to find the next morning the rain had stopped. Before breakfast, my father and I went the bank to see the level of the water.

"It's risen!" I exclaimed. "It looks even more treacherous than yesterday."

My father sighed. "It may still be raining upstream. We'll have to wait another day."

"Do you think it will be better tomorrow?"

"I hope so," he answered with little enthusiasm.

Though the rain had gone, thick clouds persisted. They dampened our mood even more than the rain. We stayed another evening and were greeted the following morning by brilliant, warm sunshine. Fortunately, the Big Blue River's temper had settled a bit.

"It's still running awfully fast," my mother observed.

"It will be swollen for a while," my father replied. "We can't wait another day." And as soon as he finished his statement, I had a dreadful feeling. My logical mind began to argue with my intuition – the same intuition that my mother told me never to ignore. The water had receded but was still moving swiftly. My father knew what he was doing.

"Maybe we should wait until tomorrow," I blurted.

My father narrowed his vision. He seemed startled, and somewhat offended, at my suggestion. I looked at the river again, then back at him. Every second of his lingering silence increased my concern.

"One day won't make that much of a difference, will it?" I asked.

"Winter is deadly on the trail," he replied. "Every day of delay increases our chances of the cold settling in before we reach Oregon. The journey is hard enough in agreeable weather. Snow makes the mountain passes particularly dangerous." He paused. "But we could wait a few hours. Every inch the river retreats will make our job easier."

My mother smiled. "An acceptable compromise."

We certainly made good use of the time. I helped my mother rearrange our supplies and better distribute the weight of our belongings on the wagon so that it would be less likely to tip over in the river. Meanwhile, my father checked, in great detail, every part of the wagon, ensuring that every hole was caulked and everything was in proper order.

Shortly before midday, we took another look at the river and found no noticeable reduction in the water level. My father was becoming frustrated and restless. "It's time to go," he said, in a matter of fact tone.

The twenty-yard journey to the edge of the bank seemed more intimidating than the hundred miles we had already put behind us. As we rolled to the river, something strange began to happen. The ground picked up a tint of silver hue, and the blue sky became dull. I could find no clouds in sight, yet there was a faint but noticeable change in the light from the sun. All of my father's concentration was dedicated to leading the oxen into the water, so I doubt he noticed anything out of the ordinary.

As expected, the oxen were hesitant to enter the river. With some persuasion, they pulled the wagon into the water. The oxen's bodies were submerged with only a few inches to spare below their neck. Their powerful muscles fought against the surging water, and the wagon tilted in the direction of the current. The wagon groaned and creaked with the stress of the water on the tongue. My mother and I braced ourselves against the wagon bed to maintain our balance.

When we approached the midpoint, I knew something was wrong. The back wheels began to slip, giving way to the powerful current. The tongue and axles were making a deafening, frightful noise. My father eased up on the oxen and directed them to edge into the current, successfully reducing the stress on the yoke.

We continued a few more feet until the wagon swayed and tilted again. I heard a loud crack underneath us that shook me to my core. My mother and I screamed as we lunged forward, reeling from the shock of the wagon's sudden, intense vibration. A loud scraping sound followed, and the floorboards in the wagon began to moan. My father looked towards us briefly, then returned his attention to the oxen.

"The yoke cracked!" he yelled.

"We should stop!" my mother implored.

My father flicked the reigns again. "No, we're almost there."

The oxen pulled harder and we picked up speed. A multitude of forces were working against the smattering of wood and nails holding us afloat—the stress from the oxen's forceful tug, the relentless torrent of water, and the yoke dragging underneath us.

As we neared the bank, the ground beneath us forced the front wheel up first, increasing the pressure on the wagon bed. With the uneven tension, the floor boards snapped, sending water pouring in from below. My father yelled for us to get out, but we needed no encouragement. The cold water filled the wagon and we began to sink.

My mother grabbed hold of my arm and began to pull upstream, but I knew we wouldn't be able to fight the rapids. We managed to pull ourselves forward to the buckboard with my father, but we were all sinking. The oxen continued to move forward, making it harder for us to steady ourselves. The wagon fell apart, and within seconds we were in the water.

We desperately tried to cling to the remaining parts of the wagon with little success, then tried to swim to the shore. The current was strong, and my feet were being pulled faster than my body, preventing me from righting myself. We called out to each other and tried to join hands, but in the chaos, we were dragged apart by the raging waters.

I tried to stay afloat, but I was losing the fight against the surging cold water. Every second was a desperate, clawing struggle. My head dipped in and out of the water and I became dizzy from the constant gasping for air. The cold numbed my limbs and my muscles seized. I knew I couldn't remain conscious much longer, though I fought against my increasingly obvious fate with every ounce of my remaining strength.

It is strange the things your mind latches on to in life or death situations. In my struggles, I caught a glimpse of the sun. It couldn't have lasted longer than a second or two, but in that brief time I stared directly into its brilliance. I saw why everything looked strange when my eyes adjusted to the brightness. The moon had covered a portion of its disc, creating a partial eclipse.

While I fiercely struggled to remain on this earth, I couldn't help but to laugh at the irony of my situation. The strange tint to the sky puzzled me, and now I knew why. I had a surreal sense of satisfaction in obtaining that answer for a few seconds more, but then I suffered a tremendous blow to my head. Everything went black.

Chapter 2

"You don't look well."

"I don't feel well, Daniel," I reply.

"Maybe this will help," he says as he pours a hot cup of tea.

I shake my head. "It used to. I'm not so sure, anymore." I lean back and prop my head in my hands. "You're right of course. Writing all this down is the best thing I can do. My mind is filled with so many things, but I'm not really a writer."

"This memoir is for you, not others."

"I'd be afraid to see what others thought of what I had to tell. If they only knew what happened to me back in that fateful year of 1852, they'd think I was insane."

"Half the town thinks that anyway."

"Point made," I reply with a grin. "I'll get to writing."

Daniel sets a tray of cookies on my desk. "Good. I'll be back to check on you." He pauses at the door. "How far along are you?"

My breath catches in my throat. "I... I just wrote about the accident on the river," I say and place my hand across my chest. "You can't imagine how difficult that was."

Daniel's countenance softens. "You can't stop now. It's important you get the story on the page."

I nod. "I will. I owe it to... to him."

***

I awoke to a firm nudge on my shoulder. I bolted upright and immediately felt a huge pain in my head. My field of vision swirled in a sickening vertigo and I was forced to lie back down on the ground. It was dusk, and a campfire was keeping me warm.

We made it. I was filled with relief. I took a deep breath and turned my head to the side to greet my parents with a smile. As soon as I managed to focus my eyes, I noticed an unknown man sitting next to me.

"Who are you?"

I leaned up as best I could and refocused. It was an Indian. Best I could tell, he was the same Indian I had seen pass us by earlier on the trail.

"It's you!"

He narrowed his gaze and pointed at himself, then nodded. "Yes, me."

I would have normally been apprehensive about him, but I knew, at the deepest level, that this man was not a threat to me. His presence in my vision was surely no coincidence.

"Where are my parents?"

He didn't reply.

I tried to stand but the dizziness overcame me again. I might have made it except for a sharp pain in my leg. He rushed to my side and helped ease me back to the ground. When I stretched my legs, I noticed that my lower dress was in tatters. A strip of my undergarments had been torn and was wrapped around my shin. Blood stains were clearly visible through the cloth.

He pointed to my leg. "I bandaged it."

"Thank you," I replied. My pounding head kept my concerns of modesty to a minimum.

"I must find my parents."

"No," he replied.

"No, what?" I asked. "No I can't, or no they're not here?"

He was clearly confused by my question.

"Sorry. I know little English."

I realized I would have to take things slower. "I was with two other people."

He shook his head again. "You are one."

His answer was somewhat cryptic, but I knew he was trying to tell me my parents weren't here. I looked away from him and tried to recall what had happened. Everything had gone dark after something hit my head in the river. I noticed a goose egg to the right of my crown.

"It hurts?" he asked.

"Terribly." He didn't seem to understand what I said, so I added, "Yes." He remained silent, but I could see in his eyes he had a great deal of empathy for my situation.

He offered me some water from a skin and I took a few sips. He handed me a piece of bread, but I returned it, knowing I wouldn't be able to keep anything on my upset stomach. "Thank you, but I am sick."

He rubbed his stomach and frowned. "Hurt?"

"Yes," I replied, then I added, "Stomach" while pointing to mine.

"Stomach. I did not know word."

Catching a faint whiff of the bread increased my nausea. I laid back and tried to take my mind off food.

"You need rest," he said.

I knew he was right. I desperately wanted to find my parents, but I was in no shape to search for them, let alone stand. He put a blanket over my feet. "Rest."

I lost consciousness again and slept throughout the night, then awoke the next morning. He was missing. I looked around the campsite and noticed his horse was still there, so I reasoned he couldn't be far away. Within moments, he returned holding a dead rabbit in his hand.

He seemed happy I was awake. "Breakfast," he declared. He rubbed his stomach. "Still sick?"

"My head and leg still hurts," I replied. "But my stomach is OK."

He gave a quick, satisfied nod, then sat and began to clean and dress the rabbit. I told him thank you and he replied with a smile. "Have you seen any sign of my parents?"

He frowned and shook his head. "I am sorry. Nothing."

"Did you see our wagon?"

"No. But I saw wood in river, maybe your wagon?"

"Maybe," I replied. I pondered the situation more. "Probably. Yes, that's it – my parents must have made it to shore downstream."

He cooked the meat over our campfire, then handed me one of the portions. I took the piece and waited a moment for it to cool, then tried a bite.

"Good?" he asked.

"Good," I replied.

"What is your name?" he asked while we ate.

"Isabella. Some call me Isabelle. My parents have always called me Izzy."

"You have three names?"

"I've never really thought about it that way," I replied. "What's your name?"

"Kuruks."

I repeated the name slowly, sounding out both syllables, like kuh-rooks, to ensure I was saying it correctly. I have always been a stickler for calling people the precise name they wished. Kuruks nodded in approval.

"I like that name," I said.

"It means bear in our language," he added.

"A bear is strong," I noted.

"No, there are stronger men than me in my tribe."

"There are many ways to be strong," I replied. "Many strong men left our town to set up homesteads. When I was very young, I remember asking my mother why women weren't strong. She told me that women were often stronger than men - they just didn't feel the need to show it."

"A strong man can lift a heavy load, but a woman can bear new life," Kuruks said. "What man strong enough to do that?"

"Indeed," I replied.

"My father told me be strong in spirit and rest will follow."

"Your father is a wise man," I said. "Where is your home?"

He gave me a perplexed look, then extended his hands in a wide gesture. "Everywhere."

I realized the naiveté of the question and rephrased it. "I meant to ask, what tribe are you from?"

"Pawnee," he replied.

"Maybe my parents are at your village," I wondered out loud.

He paused for a moment, then replied, "My village is five days north," he said, motioning behind him. "They are not there."

I sighed and hung my head in resignation. "No, you're right. If anything, they'd be further down the river."

"I help you look," he said.

The small bit of hope I was clinging to was suddenly reinforced. "You would do that? You have already done so much for me."

"I am happy to help you."

"Are others with you? Maybe they saw my parents."

"I am alone," he replied. "Most of my people do not come here."

"Why not?"

His countenance shifted. It was clear he didn't want to answer, so I didn't push it. But after a brief pause, he volunteered. "Afraid of your people."

I pointed to myself. "Us? No, they have nothing to be afraid of. We are just trying to reach Oregon."

"Not you. But your kind do not want us here."

I heard many stories of clashes with the Indians – enough to be fearful of their motives. But as I studied them more in my schooling, I realized that they were just like any other people. They were not savages. My mother always said lack of education breeds ignorance.

"I am not like them," I said.

Kuruks chuckled. "You are. You do not act like them, but you are one of them."

"You don't know me."

"You do not know yourself. You are young."

"Only a year or two younger than you," I insisted. "You can't be older than twenty."

He smiled. "You have courage and fire. I like that. You are like my sister. She is your age."

I ate the last bite of my rabbit meat. "I would like to meet her. Why are you so far away from home?"

Kuruks looked away. "You ask a lot of questions."

"I am curious. I'm sorry."

"We should go now."

Kuruks helped me stand, paying careful attention to my leg. I was woozy at first, but managed. We broke camp and left together on his horse to search the banks of the Big Blue River.

Chapter 3

Kuruks and I spent all morning scouring the Big Blue River. He focused on the banks, while I looked for any peculiarities in the river. I examined each log that protruded from the water, and I frequently asked him to get closer for a more detailed look. He was patient, allowing me to methodically check the overgrown spots on the shores.

By noon, we had covered almost five miles to the south. Kuruks offered to find some game for lunch, but I told him that, unless he was hungry, I could certainly wait until dinner. He agreed and, after a short rest, we doubled back along our path at a faster pace to avoid rechecking already covered ground.

As we rode to our morning point of departure, I had more time to think – a most decidedly problematic proposition given my situation. In this idle time, I found my hopes draining of ever finding my parents. My mind quickly gave in to a whirlpool of depressing and morbid possibilities. My eyes began to water, so I wiped my tears and stiffened my resolve. That wasn't helping, and I knew I needed to focus. Energy wasted on my despair and anxiety could be better used on their rescue.

I was used to riding a horse with a saddle, so Kuruks's thick wool blanket was quite an adjustment. Since I was riding behind him, my view ahead of us was quite limited. I spent time staring at the back of his neck – an odd position to be in for sure. I admired the white beads that decorated a few strands of his long, black hair. A thin leather cord held a necklace adorned with bear claws, and another necklace held a shiny silver pendant that had previously caught my eye. I made a note to ask to see it in detail the next time we stopped.

After a couple of hours, we reached our initial campsite. We walked the horse to the river to drink, and I grabbed a few refreshing handfuls for myself. My torn dress made the heat bearable, and in more carefree times I would have dangled my exposed legs in the cool water. My wound ached and my dressing needed to be changed, but I didn't want to spare the time.

"The Big Blue runs into Kaw River. Unlikely they are north of us."

I had forgotten the simple fact that the river flowed south until he had mentioned it. I wasn't sure if it was blind hope or an oversight.

"You are assuming they are still in the river," I replied. "They are more likely on land, and I think they would head north."

Kuruks paused a moment and began to say something, but then he stopped.

"What is it?"

"Thinking."

"What?"

"Trying to think where they are," he replied.

I felt he was holding something back but decided there was no time to press the matter. "We still have plenty of daylight left. Let's go," I said.

Kuruks nodded. "We will not stop until we find them."

He said it with such confidence and surety that it helped lift my spirits. We departed as soon as possible, heading north, resuming our careful examination of the Big Blue River.

After a short ride, Kuruks abruptly stopped the horse. "Stay here," he said.

I started to get down, but he turned and held his hand out to stop me. "Please stay."

I took a deep, frustrated breath. "What is it? What do you see?"

He repeated his request, then walked off for some ways ahead of our position and knelt near the river. My curiosity and worry got the better of me, so I gently flicked the reins and walked the horse to him. When I got closer, I saw what caught his eye and quickly dismounted.

When I approached, my heart skipped several beats. My vision was tunneled with darkness and I was faint. My father's body laid awkwardly on the bank, his feet dangling in the water. Kuruks put his arm around my shoulder and helped me steady myself. I knelt and began to scream uncontrollably.

I put my arms around my father and hugged him, wishing desperately this was a nightmare. I loved him, missed him, and was upset that he left me. I was despondent and heartbroken. Anger added to the swirl of emotions surging through me as I recalled his eagerness to cross the swollen river. It was a needless tragedy.

"Why did I let him go ahead with the crossing?" I wailed.

"You could not know," Kuruks said.

"No, I had a feeling this would end in tragedy. I ignored it."

Kuruks tried his best to console me, allowing me to work through the torrent of doubts and emotions that seemed to come out all at once. Somehow, I managed to pull myself together enough to stand. There was no sign of my mother or the wagon.

"My mother has to be here somewhere. He wouldn't leave her."

"He walked here. Maybe trying to find you. I don't understand why upstream," Kuruks wondered out loud.

I grabbed his shoulder. "She has to be nearby. Maybe she walked here, too. Let's find her."

Kuruks looked back to the south, then stared at the river. I was anxious to know his thoughts. "It may take time to find your mother. We must bury your father before we go."

I looked at my father again through misty eyes. I knew he was right, but I wanted to find my mother as soon as possible. After a moment, I worked up enough courage to agree with him.

"My mother would want to be here for his burial," I said.

Kuruks allowed a bit of emotion to show on his face, and his strained English took on an even softer, compassionate tone. "Distance and death separate people, but family is always together in spirit. Your father now watches us, and his father before him. They will always be with you."

I started to cry again, and Kuruks put his arm on my shoulder. "I can take care of this for you."

"Thank you, but no. He is my father and I want to help. You have done so much for me."

"We cannot dig," he said. "You help gather rocks. There will be some that way." He pointed towards the shore, but I didn't see anything particularly different about that spot. "Go look, Izzy." With that, I understood he wanted me to leave, so I obliged.

After I walked away, I heard him dragging my father away from the river. I didn't want to look back. The thought of someone dragging my father's lifeless body anywhere struck a deep nerve. He had been so strong in life, and now, in death, his daughter was not strong enough to deal with the awful situation without help.

After walking a spell, I turned back to see that Kuruks had already begun searching for rocks. I approached the shore and did the same, finding several suitable stones. I could only carry three and thought how it would take forever to gather enough. I immediately threw one of the stones in anger. I was mortified I had even had such a thought about saving labor at my father's burial. I eased myself down on the bank and furiously gripped one of the remaining stones, then threw it into the water as hard as I could. Every ounce of my emotion was channeled into that throw. It hit with a tremendous splash, dousing me with water. It did little to cool my despair and self-loathing.

I cursed myself again for being so selfish and leaving Kuruks to do what should have been my job. I grabbed as many rocks as I could hold and returned to him. He had finished with the grave and was sitting on the ground.

I took the rocks I had brought and placed them on the pile, then knelt at the foot of his grave. "I should have been more help. I broke down —"

Kuruks shook his head. "No. You are doing all you can."

"I could have stopped this."

"Fate is persistent," Kuruks said. "You do not control it like you think."

Maybe he was right. I wanted him to be right. It would have certainly made it a bit easier to accept. But down deep, I knew I could have tried harder to delay our crossing another day.

"We need to find my mom," I said. "I don't want to leave his side, but she probably needs our help. She's alone." I looked up at Kuruks and smiled. "She isn't afraid. She is so strong, so fearless. But I don't want her to be alone anymore."

"We will go find her now."

I lingered at my father's grave for a moment while Kuruks readied the horse, and then we left. I took a few glances back at the unassuming rock pile, watching it grow smaller as we continued towards the south. When we reached our previous night's campsite, we returned to the river banks and began a meticulous search. Kuruks dismounted and began to walk along the shore.

"I track better this way," he said. "You stay on horse. No need for you to walk."

"I don't mind joining you. I need the distraction."

Kuruks seemed hesitant but didn't protest. I took the horse as close to the river as I could and walked along the banks with Kuruks. We searched on foot for well over half an hour when he spotted something. He indicated for me to stop, but I disregarded it.

"What is it?" I asked.

"Stay here," he insisted, then ran forward. His tone was terse and it was clear he didn't want to explain himself. I gave his order the same adherence and consideration I give to any other sternly delivered command - I dispensed with it and bolted to catch up to him. When I did, I saw my mother's body floating face down in the river, being held in place by a nest of logs and rocks near the shore.

I wish I had listened to Kuruks.

Chapter 4

The thin fabric of youthful inexperience that held my world together suddenly unraveled when I found my father. When I found my mother, the hope for any reunion that I was desperately clinging to had vanished. My entire family was gone in the blink of an eye - victims of a senseless tragedy that could have easily been prevented. They were all I had in this unfamiliar land. I was utterly alone.

The central core of my very being ached unmercifully. The pain was just as intense as though someone had stabbed me with a knife. Time moved at a snail's pace, and before I could even make it to my mother, I collapsed.

I'm not sure how long I was unconscious, but when I regained my wits, Kuruks was looking over me with deep concern.

"I'm alright," I said as I bolted to my feet.

"You are in shock," Kuruks noted.

My mind was so far removed from reality that his words sounded like a distant echo. I couldn't manage a reply, so I looked away. I didn't want to look back at my mother. I knew she was there, but if I could avoid laying eyes on her for a moment longer I could delay the inevitability of having to admit what had happened. Finally, I worked up the courage to turn around.

It's strange the things you notice in a time like that. I suppose it's a way of distancing yourself from the abject horror that is staring directly at you. My eyes went to the beautiful dragonfly hair comb in my mother's dark, wavy hair. Her body was completely devoid of life, and yet this trinket that had been in her family for generations brought me a modicum of comfort. The comb sparkled in the sun with astonishing radiance.

I knelt and began to pull her out of the water. Kuruks joined me and together we managed to bring her ashore. Her swollen body scraped against the rocks on the shore. The unnatural shade of death that colored her skin caused my stomach to roil. Her eyes were still open, staring into the sun with a dreadful, vacant gaze. Instead of sobbing uncontrollably, I was completely still. I had become accustomed to shock, and a wall of defense I didn't even realize I had erected itself so I could function.

"She would want to be near my father," I said.

"Of course," he said. "I carry her." He didn't wait for my approval. He fetched two sturdy branches from trees near the bank and began to fashion a litter with those, some rope, and his blanket.

I closed her eyes, turned her head, and removed the comb from her soaked hair. As I clenched it securely in my palm, I recalled her wearing it, dressed in her beautiful Sunday dress, giving a smile that could bring a bit of joy to anyone's day. She was strong, intelligent, and confident.

"Why did you have to leave?" I lingered a few moments and then kissed her forehead. "I love you," I whispered.

When Kuruks was done with the litter, he stood over her body with a respectful, patient stance. I was already learning that he could speak volumes without ever opening his mouth. He gently lifted her body in his arms and put her on the litter, then finished securing it to the horse.

My mind was still and calm for much of the half-hour walk back to my father's grave. I have never experienced such a feeling. I was collected and focused on the task ahead. Nothing else mattered except the dragonfly comb that I held in my hand. From time to time I glanced at it, staring at the most delicate details in its intricate design. I had been gripping it so tightly that it was leaving an imprint on my hand. I had always admired it and looked forward to the day when she would pass it down to me.

And then it hit me: I was now the owner of a family heirloom years before I had planned to receive it. I was all that was left of my family, and in my hand lay the solitary object I had with which to remember them. My focus on the comb was to protect me from the horror that I had, at least for a brief time, successfully repressed.

I felt as though I could collapse into the earth at my feet and drown in a pool of my own tears. But I knew I had to carry on. My grief could wait until she was buried. Each step I took behind Kuruks on our march back to the gravesite was agonizing, yet I knew it was an obligation I had to meet. I reinforced my grip on the comb and continued, barely holding myself together.

When we reached our destination, I helped Kuruks position my mother next to my father. I was determined I would not again get lost in my grief. There was a task to do and I dedicated myself to getting it done, both for my parents and for Kuruks, who had been so kind and generous. We eventually found enough rocks to complete the mound.

"I will make a cross from branch," Kuruks said in a tone indicating a question more than an announcement.

"My father was religious, but I don't know about my mother."

"She did not share her belief with you?" Kuruks asked.

"Our conversations were always about books, nature, science, or something like that. I don't think she was spiritual."

"We all have spirit, Izzy."

"I'm not so sure," I replied. "I can't believe God would allow this kind of tragedy."

"Nothing can protect you from trials of life," Kuruks said. "But the spirits of our ancestors make us strong."

"I know my father would like a cross. I will make it, though. It is not your religion."

Kuruks put his hand on my shoulder. "I will make it to honor him."

I wanted to be as light a burden on Kuruks as possible, so I helped him find the branches and fashion a cross to put at the top of my father's grave. As we worked, it began to increasingly bother me that I had never discussed faith with my mother. The more I thought about it, the more I realized that she was probably not religious. It was a topic scarcely discussed in our house. My father prayed at meals and my mother accompanied him to church the odd Sunday, but it was now clear to me she was simply supporting his belief.

When I put the cross in the ground, I recalled a picnic we enjoyed on the banks of the Little Blue River, not a mile from our house. I asked her why we didn't go to church as much as others in Independence. "We are in my church," she said and extended her hands to indicate the beauty of nature that surrounded us.

As the sun began to set, the previously menacing banks of the Big Blue River calmed. I looked around and noted that it wasn't too dissimilar from the beautiful Little Blue River campsite my mother had enjoyed.

Kuruks must have noticed me spending too much time in my head. I was so lost in thought I almost missed his question. "Tell me about your mother."

My mind was filled with fond memories of my mom. As a child, I had especially looked forward to our weekly nature walks. As I got older, my interest in them diminished, and I was instantly filled with regret for the recent times I had told her I wasn't interested. I realized how foolish I had been to give up that precious time with her.

My voice cracked a bit. "She loved spending time outdoors, reading, playing with me, collecting butterflies and all sorts of plants. She loved nature, and I know she would be happy that this is her final resting place."

"Her spirit is far away from here now," Kuruks replied. "But this is a nice place for bones to rest."

Kuruks lit a fire near the gravesite, and I sat on the ground facing my parents. He left shortly after dark and returned with game for dinner, but I wasn't hungry. I couldn't stomach the thought of food. After he ate, he came and sat by me, and we stared out into the darkness.

"Thank you for your help," I said.

"No need to thank me."

"Why did I live and they died?" I asked.

"It is fate."

"I don't believe in fate. We have free will."

"Fate does not need your belief. We make choices, but the big moments in life are set in stone."

"I chose to let my father go even though I knew it wasn't safe."

"It was not your choice. He made his own choice," Kuruks said. "It does not help to blame yourself."

"I could have. Maybe. I don't know." I put my head in my hands and exhaled deeply, lost in doubt. "What I'm going to do?"

"Answers will come," Kuruks said. "My ancestors and spirit guides speak to me at night. Maybe you can hear yours."

"I don't know what a spirit guide is," I admitted.

"You have at least one, only you haven't met them yet. Listen with your mind, not your ears."

I pondered his words, but they didn't make sense. My knowledge of Indian tradition and religion wouldn't have filled a teacup. I listened intensely and heard nothing but crickets, tree frogs, and the gentle flow of the river. I found my thoughts drifting back to my mother. I wished so desperately she was there.

"When the time is right, you will hear your ancestors," Kuruks said. "Keep your mind open."

We sat in silence for several hours. I began to worry that I was disturbing Kuruks's sleep. I looked at him and saw fatigue in his eyes in what little light the campfire offered. "I'm keeping you awake."

"No, I am fine. Do you wish to be alone?"

"No," I replied emphatically. "But you don't have to stay awake with me. I don't want to be a burden to you."

"You are not," he replied. "I will stay with you," he added with a subtle smile.

All the while, I nursed my simmering grief and clung to desperate hope for a glimpse of my spirit guide.

Chapter 5

The dream I had that night was among the most realistic I had ever had. Even now it gives me chills to think about it. I remember every detail with astonishing clarity.

I found myself in a rocking chair in the middle of a room. Faint moonlight flickered through the window, providing the only illumination. To my left, I could make out the scarce outline of an unlit fireplace. There was a mask in front of me. I thought it was attached to a person, but as my vision focused it was clear it was floating.

Dreams are filled with such strange images, so it's hard to tell if the mask was a metaphor or was simply a nonsensical artifact of my imagination. Either way, I was lucid enough to ponder the meaning of this symbol mid-dream. The mask was quite large - easily twice that of a dinner plate - and appeared to be made of polished bone. It had menacing eye-holes and strange green and red markings on it. Its mouth moved, but I didn't hear a thing. It seemed to be trying to communicate with me, and its frustration was evident. I may sound strange assigning emotion to an inanimate object, but nevertheless that is what I perceived.

The experience scared me, so I tried to move. I couldn't. I was bound to the chair, not by rope or chains, but rather some invisible and seemingly insurmountable force. After a frantic struggle, I began to relax, realizing there was nothing I could do. The mask hovered in front of me for a moment longer, and then I heard a voice.

"Why are you here, supposed Child of Darkness?"

I had no idea what was being asked. Who was the Child of Darkness? Why would it think I came here voluntarily? I tried to answer, but I could scarcely hear my own reply. "What do you mean?"

"The gift you hold was not meant for you."

"What gift? What are you talking about? Who are you?"

"You ignorant girl. You have no idea what you have done. You meddle in our affairs and have stolen what is rightfully mine!"

"What do you mean? I pose no threat to you. Who are you?"

There was nothing but silence in return. "Are you my guide? Kuruks said my guide would come to me when the time was right."

A wicked laugh emerged from the darkness, and the mask undulated in a strange manner. "He is wasting his time with you. Why would a spirit guide wear a mask? Why is the Child of Darkness so ignorant?"

"Why do you hide your appearance from me?"

"You have much to learn and such a short time to do it. Kuruks the traitor has his hands full. Leave! Go home, little girl."

I woke abruptly, my heart pounding and my skin dripping with sweat.

"You okay, Izzy?" Kuruks asked. I nearly jumped out of my skin when I heard his voice. I managed to catch my breath. "Yes." It was a lie, but I didn't want him to be concerned.

He moved over to me and put his hand on my shoulder. "No, you are not okay. What happened?"

"Just a bad dream."

"Want to tell me your dream?" Kuruks asked.

My first instinct was to decline, but since his name was mentioned in the dream, I figured he had a right to know.

"I don't know where I was. Some kind of building. It was dark, and I couldn't see. But there was a nearly full moon."

Kuruks pointed at the sky. "You are right," he said.

"I hadn't noticed, but it looked exactly like that," I replied. "There was a mask floating in front of me."

Kuruks frowned. "A mask? I do not know this word."

"A mask is something you can wear over your face to hide yourself. Like this," I demonstrated, putting my fingers in front of my eyes, imitating pictures of fancy masks I had seen in a drawing at school.

His eyes widened and I could tell he was concerned.

"I think it was made of bone. It had green and red paint."

"Tell me more."

"It spoke to me. I know that doesn't make sense, but I could hear it. It taunted me. It called me the Child of Darkness. Do you know what that is?"

The color drained from his face. "Paa."

"Paa? What is that?"

He took a deep breath and turned away. "We should sleep."

I wanted to know, but Kuruks seemed disturbed by what I said. He clearly knew more than he shared. I didn't want to press the issue tonight. "I'm sorry to disturb you," I said, then turned over and tried to go back to sleep. It was difficult to put the bizarre image of the dancing mask from my mind. I resolved myself to find out what it meant and drifted back into a fitful sleep.

The next morning, I discovered that Kuruks wasn't at the campsite. His horse was still tied to a tree, so I knew he hadn't gone far. I suspected he had gone to get food, but after his strange response the previous night to my dream I couldn't be sure. I went to the river to wash my face, then returned and became lost in thought as I gazed at my parents' graves in the early morning light.

After half an hour or so, Kuruks returned with another rabbit. He was even more quiet than usual as he cleaned and dressed the game. When it was ready to cook, I offered to help but he insisted on doing it himself. I stared into the campfire while he cooked the meat.

"Why will you not discuss Paa with me?" I asked.

"There is nothing to tell."

I took a deep breath to contain my frustration. "You know what it means."

"Dreams sometimes mean nothing," Kuruks said, and handed me a portion of the meat. His voice was stern, thinly hiding a sense of annoyance.

"The least I can do to repay your kindness is to drop the subject," I admitted. "I am sorry."

Kuruks glanced up at me with a perplexing expression and looked as though he were on the verge of speaking, then looked down and took a bite of rabbit. Our meal was strained and awkward. I resigned to keep my confusion about the dream to myself and not trouble him further on the matter.

"Where will you go now?" he asked after breakfast.

The question should have been obvious, but its answer completely eluded me. I hadn't given it much thought.

Normally I would have discussed that with my parents, asking for their sage advice in weighing my options. I had lost my two most confident and trusted advisors. His question, though entirely unintentional, deepened my sense of loss and abject bewilderment. Tears pooled in my eyes, but I didn't let them fall.

"I am sorry," he said.

"No, it's not your fault. Don't be sorry."

"You do not have to decide now," he replied.

I had to admit I had no idea. "I don't know what I'll do."

"You have other family at home?"

"My mother's parents are in New York. My father was born in Wisconsin. His folks visited one summer but I wouldn't know how to find them."

"I am headed north. I take you," Kuruks declared.

"Yes, but not that far. You said your village was only five days away. It would take us a month to reach Wisconsin. I would never burden you with such an arduous journey."

Kuruks thought a moment. "You going to Oregon, right? Is that not many months away?"

"There's no reason for me to go there anymore."

"I will not leave you alone without your people," Kuruks said.

"My people," I repeated with a sigh. "I have no people."

"White people will welcome you back."

I pointed toward Independence. "I know you better than I knew most of my people in my town. My friends never stuck around long. Their families couldn't wait to get to Oregon. My people died in that God-forsaken river. My people... "

It was all I could do to keep my composure. I made up a flimsy excuse to leave Kuruks and go to the river, then sat on the banks and pondered my situation. I needed time to think, and I was certain that he was tired of seeing my red, swollen eyes.

I had never had to make such a big decision like that before, and I didn't have the council of my parents to guide me through it. I took my hand and scooped up some water, washing my face and then drinking as much as I could to quench my parched throat.

I leaned my head back and closed my eyes while I considered my four choices. I could have followed Kuruks to his village, returned to Independence, gone to Wisconsin, or continued to Oregon. I eliminated the option of continuing the trail almost immediately. I had no supplies and very little money. I put my hand in my pocket to confirm that the only coin I had to my name, a shiny quarter, was still there.

Eliminating Wisconsin as a viable choice was easy as well. Even if Kuruks was willing to join me, there was no way I would ask him to do so. My father's parents would be strangers to me, and finding them would be next to impossible.

The option of returning to Independence held little desire for me. Yes, it was home, but it wouldn't be home without my parents. I would have to rely on the generosity of friends until I was able to earn enough money to sustain myself. I had the schooling necessary to teach, yet without my license I wouldn't be able to find employment.

The only remaining option was to join Kuruks on his journey home. I had no idea what I would do when I arrived, but at least I wouldn't be alone. I couldn't stay in the Kansas wilderness forever. I took a deep breath and committed to the decision, then stood to leave.

"I want to go with you to your village," I said. "If you don't mind."

"That is fine," Kuruks replied.

"I'm not sure what I'm going to do when I get there."

"You do not have to decide now," he said. "After something like this, you need time. Do not focus on big things. Focus on one day and then the next and the next."

"You're making a lot of sense," I replied. "Thank you for putting up with me."

Kuruks extended his hand. "Come on, let us go now."

We walked to his horse, and he offered for me to ride alone. "You don't have to walk," I said.

"The horse cannot bear us both for the entire journey," he replied.

"Then we'll take turns."

Kuruks smiled in acceptance.

I snapped the reins gently and turned the horse around to take one last, lingering look at my parents' graves. I studied the surroundings. "I don't want to ever forget this place. Someday I will return and visit them once more."

I looked at Kuruks and nodded. "I'm ready now."

Chapter 6

As strange as it sounds, a sense of peace and calm washed over me when we finally departed my parents' resting place. It was the first time since their death that I wasn't on the edge of falling apart. I felt horribly broken, but there was the small satisfaction that the long recovery process had now begun.

My slightly improved mood was due, at least in part, by simply moving past that cursed river. I know it doesn't make any sense to blame a body of water. It was my father's decision and a savage current that decided our fate. But all kinds of irrational judgements are made when faced with such all-consuming grief, and my anger towards the Big Blue River was certainly one of them.

As the day wore on, we saw signs of a settlement to the east on the other side of the river. Kuruks asked if I wanted to stop, but I saw little point in doing so. I could have sent a message to my mother's parents, but I wasn't sure if simply a name and city for the address would have sufficed. I didn't have much money to spare, and I had no idea what return address to use. Plenty of reasonable excuses filled my head, not one of them alone enough to justify not trying to make contact. I wanted to press on, and as selfish as it sounds, I felt no need, at that time, to look back to distant family.

As the sun began to set, we reached a small grove of trees near a brook that was perfect for a campsite. We tied the horse to a tree next to the water and began to make camp. Kuruks built a campfire and I took the small pot that he had in his saddle bag and boiled some water.

"What is that for?" Kuruks asked.

"Wishful thinking, I suppose."

"What do you mean?"

"I wish we had some coffee or tea."

Kuruks left our campsite without saying a word, clearly on a mission. Within a moment he returned with a handful of what looked like daisies.

"Tea," he said.

"Daisy tea? I don't know if you can—"

"Smell," he insisted, and handed them to me.

I took a whiff of the flowers and was pleasantly surprised. "Chamomile."

"Tea," he repeated.

I smiled and nodded. "Tea."

"I will go hunt," Kuruks announced.

I prepared the tea, poured it into our small tin cup, and then took a sip. I find myself at a loss to describe how wonderful it was. I was so enthralled with such a simple thing that I ignored the lack of honey and weak concentration of Chamomile. My mother told me the plant calmed the nerves, and I can certainly attest to that. But more than its relaxing effects, I benefited from the accomplishment of producing something. That feeling had been sorely lacking the past few days. It was good to do more than just watch in grief as Kuruks took care of me.

"You are an excellent hunter," I said to Kuruks as he returned with a rabbit. He had been gone no longer than fifteen minutes.

Kuruks gave a small but proud smile. "People tell me that."

"They are right," I added. "I don't think we are in any danger of starving."

"We need something else to eat," he said.

"Some berries would be nice," I replied. "Or some spinach. My mother…" I paused and took another sip of tea, then sighed as I continued my recollection, "she grew the best spinach. She was a wonderful gardener."

Kuruks motioned for a sip of tea, and I handed him the cup. "Remembering those lost keeps them closer to us." He pointed to his blanket. "My grandmother made that for me when I was young. She is no longer here."

"I'm sorry," I replied. I took out the dragonfly comb from my pocket and showed it to Kuruks. "This is the only thing I have of my mother's."

Kuruks examined it. "You have both your parents here," he said, pointing to his head.

"That, and her comb, will have to do," I replied.

We ate dinner and drank every last drop of our chamomile tea. I'm not sure if it was the long day of travel or the tea, but I was tired by the end of the meal. I leaned back and propped myself on my elbows and gazed into the campfire. Kuruks took some tobacco and placed it in a pipe and began to smoke. The odor immediately stirred a memory.

"My father used to smoke a pipe," I recalled fondly.

"I am almost out of tobacco," he said. "I only used a small pinch." He offered the pipe to me. "Want some?"

"No," I replied. "I once tried a puff of my father's pipe. I nearly choked to death."

Kuruks chuckled and took another drag.

"Everything I do throughout the day reminds me of my parents," I said. "My life revolved around them. I am not exaggerating when I say I simply don't know how to live without them."

Kuruks thought a moment. "You will learn. You may even be angry at yourself when you find way to move on. But you will."

I know his words were meant to be reassuring, but the idea of learning to do without my parents frightened me.

"Sleep is an easy escape for me," I said. "I don't have to think."

"Sleep is good," Kuruks replied. "Gives you time to heal."

He pointed to my leg. "I need to change your dressing." He moved to my feet and began to unlace my shoes. Previously, I had little time for modesty, but now that I had collected more of my wits, I felt vulnerable.

"I can do it myself," I replied curtly.

He looked up at me with confusion. "I am sorry."

I immediately regretted my tone. I leaned over and put my arms around my knees. "I know you are trying to help."

"It is easier for me to do it," he said.

I couldn't argue with his logic, but it still made me uncomfortable. I paused, searching for a way to explain my feelings to him. He took his hands off my feet.

"I would never hurt you."

"I know you wouldn't. It's not that. I trust you, Kuruks." I held the tattered end of my dress. "It embarrasses me that I am walking around showing this much of my legs."

Kuruks looked at them, then back at me. "I know you have legs. They are no secret."

"It's hard to explain," I said with an exasperated chuckle.

Kuruks shrugged. "Alright."

"Thank you. You are so kind and thoughtful."

I finished removing my shoes and took off the bandage. To my relief, the wound was healing nicely. Kuruks had done an excellent job dressing it. I boiled some more water and washed the cloth, cleaned the wound again, then reapplied the bandage.

I turned over and closed my eyes, pretending that the tobacco smell was from my father's pipe. It was a comforting and familiar distraction – one effective enough to allow me to calm my mind and drift off to sleep.

The next morning, I prepared another batch of chamomile tea with breakfast. After we left, I kept an eye out for more chamomile and any wild berry bushes that would offer more variety in our meat-heavy diet. My foraging skills proved useful, as I found a fair amount of chamomile and gathered two pocketsful of wild raspberries.

Well into the afternoon, we saw two men riding on horseback headed west. They were too far north to be part of the trail, and without a wagon it was unlikely they were pioneers. Shortly after we spotted them they turned to meet us. Kuruks stopped and dismounted, but I remained on the horse. It was clear he was uncomfortable with their quick approach.

Both men took off their hats, and one spoke. "Are you in any trouble, ma'am?"

"No," I replied. "Thank you for your concern."

The other persisted. "Are you sure?"

"Yes, of course."

"But you are with this Indian man—"

"He rescued me from drowning in the river," I replied. "I'm very grateful for his assistance."

Both men bowed at Kuruks. "Where's your husband?" the first one asked.

"I am unwed."

"Your father, then?"

"My parents were not as lucky as I. The river claimed them along with our wagon."

Both men lowered their heads. "Our deepest sympathies, ma'am. Do you want a ride back to Independence?"

"No, thank you," I replied. "Very kind of you to offer."

While I appreciated their concern, their tone revealed increasing frustration hidden behind a thin veil of polite discourse.

"I would hate for a woman of your obvious breeding and education to be left alone in the wilderness." He looked at Kuruks. "This place isn't safe for you."

"That is why I am so fortunate to have this man to accompany me on my way to Wisconsin," I replied.

"That's a long way from here, ma'am. It would be safer to—"

"It is a long journey, gentlemen, and that is why we have to make the most of each day's sunlight."

The men were clearly reluctant to let us go. After a moment of hesitation, the second one said, "We can follow you for a spell."

I shook my head firmly. "It's not necessary. Thank you both for your concern for my welfare. We'd best be going."

I gave the horse a gentle nudge, and Kuruks followed. "Don't look back," I whispered as soon as we were out of earshot.

Though I wanted to see if they were going about their business, I took my own advice and continued to look forward. Eventually, Kuruks confirmed they'd moved on.

"You looked?" I asked. "Did they see you?"

Kuruks smiled. "I was lucky. They already left. You handled them well," he said with surprise in his voice.

"They were suspicious of you. I wasn't sure about them or their motives. That's why I told them we were going to Wisconsin."

"You are smart, Izzy."

When the sun began to set, we looked for a suitable campsite. I had gathered enough berries for us to each have a decent portion. I wanted a break from the wild game that Kuruks had been so expertly preparing, and although it wasn't as fulfilling as rabbit meat, the sweet, tart berries provided a welcomed diversion in our diet.

I was disappointed that Kuruks decided not to use any more of his tobacco. I realized that I shouldn't have been so attached to a smell and tried to put it out of my mind as I went to sleep.

I rested peacefully until someone shook me. I tried to shrug it off but I couldn't ignore a more forceful jolt.

"Wake up, ma'am," a voice said sternly.

I opened my eyes to see a man standing over me. Once I could focus clearly, I noticed it was one of the men who had stopped us earlier that afternoon. I bolted upright and quickly looked around our campsite.

My heart skipped a beat when I saw the other man holding Kuruks at gunpoint.

Chapter 7

"Everyone just stay calm," one of the men said.

"What's going on?" I asked. "Why are you pointing a gun at him?"

"We're rescuing you from this savage!" the other said.

"Rescue? Are you two insane? He's my guide, not my captor."

"Your guide? You don't have to keep up the charade any longer."

"I told you we were going to Wisconsin."

"Yep, we heard you. But we watched you for a while and realized you weren't going in the right direction. Wisconsin is northeast of here," he said, motioning that direction with his gun. "You are headed to the Nebraska territory. Now either you're lying or you've hired the worst Indian guide possible."

"I don't have to explain myself to either of you."

"No ma'am, you don't. But it is our duty to rescue a woman in trouble."

"I'm not in trouble."

The two men gave both Kuruks and me an incredulous stare.

"Put the gun down," I commanded.

"Not until I know that we're safe from this heathen."

"You will not talk to a man in my employ with such disrespect! Now enough of this."

They looked at each other, and one asked, "What do you think?"

"Maybe she's telling the truth."

"But what if she isn't?"

"You should come with us. The sheriff can find your relatives."

"Come with you to where?" I asked.

"Marysville."

"I'm headed to Wisconsin."

"Something's not right, here, ma'am. For your safety, you are going to come with us."

I raised an eyebrow. "And how do you intend to make me comply?"

The man with the gun pointed at Kuruks gave me a sidelong glance. "There's no need for any of that kind of talk young lady. You're coming with us. I'm sure your father would be upset with us both if we left you out here with this wild man."

"My father is dead!"

"My condolences," he replied. "All the more reason to make sure this Indian isn't taking advantage of you."

"I'm not going anywhere," I stated.

The other man pointed his gun at me. "We'll have to insist."

Kuruks started to stand but the man with the gun pointed at him pulled the hammer back. "Don't," he commanded. "I have few qualms against shooting an Indian."

"I'll go with them, Kuruks," I said. "Once I convince these well-meaning idiots you are my guide and I am not a piece of property to be led around, I will return and we can resume our trip to Wisconsin."

I could tell by Kuruks' expression that he was not pleased with what I said, but I saw little choice. I didn't want him to get hurt trying to help me. I stood and dusted myself off and noticed the two men still standing like stones. One of them looked at my torn dress.

"If you are the gentleman you claim to be, you'll keep your eyes away from my legs."

They quickly averted their gazes. "Well, are we going?" I asked.

"Of course, ma'am."

As we walked away, one of the men kept his weapon pointed at Kuruks. "Don't be hanging around here, Indian."

"You will not harm him," I commanded.

I looked back at Kuruks. With one glance, we exchanged a non-vocal dialog that I still to this day cannot quite explain. I knew he understood that I had to do what I was doing, and I had every intention of returning to the campsite. It was an acceptance of the situation and a promise to rectify it as soon as possible. At that point in time, I was strangely confident that I would see him again.

As we rode to town, I considered staging an escape. It wouldn't have been hard to do. A sharp push of the man I was riding with could have caused the horse to throw him, or I could have reached for his gun. But either scenario would have been dangerous, and even if it had worked, more violence might have ensued. I realized the safest course of action was to accompany them willingly and explain my situation to the sheriff.

Though our path was only lit by a dim lamp carried by one of my captors, I did my best to remember the location and path we were following so that I could retrace my steps. I looked at the constellations in the sky and tried to remember their relation to the campsite. In my mind, I was able to form a reasonable approximation as to where we were in reference to Kuruks and the town's position.

After a short ride, we reached Marysville. We left the horses at the livery, and the men escorted me to the sheriff's office. They banged on the door, but he didn't answer.

"Is the sheriff usually in his office at this time of night?" I asked sarcastically. I received only a frustrated glare for a reply. They knocked once more to no avail.

"Well, if that's all, I'll be going. Thank you, gentleman, for your concern."

One of them grabbed my arm. "We have to tell the sheriff there's an Indian trying to run off with innocent young women."

I'm certain they both saw my eye roll. "You'll be lucky if I don't press charges for kidnapping."

"No ma'am, we saved you. It's not safe or natural for a woman to be alone with one of those savages."

"You can stay with me for the night, ma'am," one of them offered. "My wife will fix you up with a nice pallet."

"Are you going to hold me at gunpoint there, too?" I asked.

"Now listen—"

"No, you listen to me. Both of you. You have never once asked me what I wanted!"

My previously adamant captors seemed to soften. Their expressions reminded me of the reactions my mother received from some men when she expressed herself in her usual articulate and determined fashion. I am not a domineering person, but I was beginning to see that forcefulness was the only thing that they responded to. I figured that channeling some of my mom's strength and poise would be my best course of action.

"How are you going to explain to your wife that you forced a woman at gunpoint to follow you?"

"Well, now, it wasn't exactly like that."

"It was exactly like that!"

The two men looked at each other with a bewildered expression. "We just can't let you leave. It's late and it's a nasty, untamed wilderness."

"Then you plan to keep me captive?"

"You're making this very difficult."

"Good," I declared. "Will you two be satisfied if I speak with the sheriff in the morning?"

They reluctantly nodded in the affirmative. "If you can provide a bed for this evening and never show your weapons to me again, I will not breathe a word of your kidnapping to your wives or the sheriff. Do we have a deal?"

"Yes, ma'am," both replied, almost in unison.

One of them parted our company and the other, the taller, thinner man of the two with sandy blond hair, escorted me to his home just outside town towards our campsite. I glanced at the layout of their property as best I could in the dim lamplight so that I would have some bearings while making my escape. His wife greeted us at the door, and he briefly explained my plight, casting Kuruks in the worst possible light and making himself out to be a hero. I kept my word and remained silent.

"I'm Emma," she said, motioning for me to take a seat while she went to fetch a kettle for coffee. "And I'm Frank," her husband said. "Sorry for not telling you sooner."

"My name is Isabella," I replied. "Don't go to any trouble on my account."

"Nonsense," Emma replied. "If you have been out in the wilderness for days you surely want some coffee?"

I couldn't argue with her logic. "Chamomile tea is all I've had."

I savored the aroma as she poured my cup. "Thank you," I said, as I took a sip.

She wanted details about my current situation, but I was careful in my replies. I didn't want to contradict our stories. I chose my words well and avoided too much detail.

"I'm so sorry for your loss," Emma said, putting her hand on mine. "I cannot imagine how horrible and frightening all of this must be for you. What will you do now?"

"I have family in Wisconsin," I said, speaking the absolute truth.

"I told her she could stay the night," Frank said.

"Of course! You can stay with us as long as you need."

"Thank you, that's very generous," I replied. "But one night will suffice. I wouldn't dream of imposing longer than that. I must resume my trip to Wisconsin as soon as possible."

"Resume?" Emma asked. "I thought you said you were headed to Oregon?"

As careful as I had been, I realized I made a slight mistake. I replied quickly to cover my tracks. "My mistake. Yes, we were headed to Oregon, but now I'm going to Wisconsin."

"I was confused," Emma replied. "I don't think I'd have any of my wits about me if I had been through what you have." She looked around the main room. "We don't have an extra bed, but I have some extra blankets and a quilt that will keep you plenty warm in here." She was clearly distraught that she couldn't offer more.

"The floor is fine, Emma," I reassured her. "I have been sleeping on the ground, so adding a quilt is a vast improvement."

Emma helped me set up a nice pallet, and soon after, she and her husband retired for the evening. I lay there on the floor, reasonably comfortable, feeling sorry for Kuruks who was lying on the hard ground and worrying about me. I ran through the possibilities in my mind. I could have left during the night and returned to him, or I could have explained my situation to the sheriff in the morning.

After giving it some careful thought, I realized it would be best for Kuruks if I kept my word to Frank. If I didn't, they would very likely blame the entire situation on him. The wheels of justice spun considerably less predictably for Indians. I couldn't bear the thought of anything happening to Kuruks after all he had done for me. I did my best to reassure myself that everything would work out alright so that I could get some sleep.

Chapter 8

The smell of delicious maple syrup woke me from a peaceful slumber. I took another whiff of the air and was bolstered by the thought that I might be just yards away from the goodness that the maple trees so graciously allowed us to sample. Since I was sleeping in the main room of Frank and Emma's house, I didn't have to look far to see that breakfast was being served. I bade good morning to Emma and tidied up my pallet in attempt to make as little impact on their morning routine as possible.

I made no effort to hide the pleasure I took in that first bite of hot, buttered biscuit drenched in maple syrup. I hadn't had any syrup since we left Independence, and it was one of life's simple amenities that I had sorely missed. While I greatly appreciated the break from meat in my diet, I did eat one of the slices of thick-cut bacon that was on the table. I couldn't think of a way to take some breakfast to Kuruks without seeming greedy to Emma or alarming Frank.

Emma offered to help mend my dress, but I politely declined. I knew that would take a while and I was eager to get back to Kuruks. I did indulge her gracious offer to help change my bandage. The wound was healing nicely, and after a generous soaking with alcohol and a fresh, clean bandage, I felt better about it. Before I left, Emma handed me a basket of provisions. I accepted it with an eager smile and profusely thanked her. Frank escorted me to town, and the sheriff welcomed us inside his office. He was an older man with one of the longest beards I had ever seen.

"Howdy, Frank. How are ya?"

"Doing well, you?"

The sheriff coughed while he pounded his chest with his fist. "Still getting over this infernal cough." I hoped whatever he had wasn't contagious and kept my distance as best I could. As the wind from his cough reached me, I sensed a hint of whisky on his breath.

"Sheriff Tate, meet Isabella," Frank said.

"Pleased to meet you," the sheriff said.

I nodded respectfully. "Likewise."

"I rescued her from captivity," Frank eagerly declared. "An Indian heathen had her."

The sheriff's eyes widened. "Oh dear. Are you alright, ma'am?"

"I'm fine. Frank was mistaken. He thought I was being held captive, but the Indian he references is merely my guide."

Tate broke out into a smile. Frank's gaze narrowed, seemingly unable to determine the sheriff's reaction. Eventually, Tate chuckled. "A damsel in distress, eh Frank? What does Emma have to say about that?"

"No, Tate, you don't understand, I—"

The sheriff shook his head. "Was there something you needed, Isabella?"

"No, sir. I was doing fine until yesterday when Frank insisted on rescuing me. I will say, Emma is an excellent cook."

"Indeed," the sheriff replied. "That reminds me, Frank, when are you going to invite me over for dinner again?"

"I will let you two gentlemen catch up. In the meantime, I am eager to resume my journey. Emma was kind enough to give me some provisions, so I best be on my way."

The sheriff looked at me incredulously. "Just you and your Indian guide, eh?"

"That's right," I nodded.

"A young woman shouldn't be traveling alone out in the wilderness with just an Indian guide for protection," Tate said.

"Exactly," Frank added.

The sheriff walked over to his desk. His gait seemed a bit disturbed. I wasn't sure if it was from his ailment or the spirits he drank to help drive it away. He picked up a pistol and handed it to me. "I would give you a rifle, but I think a pistol is more appropriate for a lady. Have you ever used one before?"

Frank had a stunned expression on his face.

"I have fired my father's rifle before. I've never used a pistol."

"That's a Colt Walker. A mighty fine revolver. Five of the six chambers are loaded. The current chamber is empty. That's so you don't accidentally blow a hole in your foot or something."

I held the pistol in my hand, appreciating its weight. "I appreciate your generosity. But I can't accept it. This must be quite expensive, and I have no way to repay you now."

The sheriff refused. "No, I insist. I have several extras – I won't miss that one at all. Besides, the trails around here are full of unsavory characters."

"I've been fortunate so far," I replied, giving Frank a sidelong glance. "As soon as I can, I will send your office a donation to compensate you for your kind assistance."

"But Sheriff," Frank protested."

"Well good, Isabella," Tate replied, pausing to release a strange sound – an unexplainable mix of a burp, cough, and hiccup. "If you need anything else, you come and see me, you hear?"

"Thank you again, Sheriff Tate. Frank, please thank your wife again for her hospitality and the provisions."

Frank nodded, still stunned in silence by the sheriff's dismissal of his concerns.

"Good day to you both," I said as I gave a polite curtsy to both men. I left his office and walked directly out of town without looking back once. I had considered myself lucky to escape without a serious inquiry into Kuruks' activities.

I immediately decided to return to the campsite, hoping Kuruks was still there. As I walked in a hurried pace, my mind grappled with the distinct possibility that he had decided that I was simply too much to deal with. I wouldn't have blamed him one bit if he had left me with my insane, yet possibly good-intentioned captors. I would have been lost, or possibly dead, without his help.

After I crossed the wooden bridge over the Big Blue River at the edge of town, I stopped and scanned the horizon, hoping to see a sign of him. I'm not sure what I was expecting. I asked myself why he would be there waiting for me when he could be so easily captured. I shook my head at my own naive hope and continued onward, recalling my steps as best I could to reach our campsite.

Well before I reached the spot, I saw a man walking through the field with his horse in tow. I suspected it was Kuruks, so I walked as fast as my wounded leg would allow to meet him.

"Izzy!"

I don't think I could have possibly beamed a wider smile. "Kuruks!" I quickly closed the gap and gave him a hug. I savored the faint smell of tobacco on him as I held him tightly, thankful to be reunited. He seemed a bit taken aback by my forwardness.

"Oh, I'm sorry, I didn't mean to—"

"It is alright," he chuckled. "Glad to see you."

"It's not safe for you around here," I said. "We need to head north."

"We will," Kuruks replied. "Are you ok?"

"Yes, I'm fine. And I even have some food!" I proudly exclaimed, holding out the basket that Emma had given me. "I'm so glad you waited for me."

"I did not sleep all night. I worried about you. But I had feeling you would return."

"I'm glad you stayed," I said. "Although, to be precise, you didn't stay at our campsite. Were you coming to get me?" I studied his face carefully. "You were!"

"I had faith you would return," Kuruks replied. He looked away to avoid my incredulous grin. "Maybe I was coming to get you," he finally admitted.

"I thought you had faith in me?" I asked.

"In your return," he replied. "I was not sure if I had to get you or not. But I should have known you would escape."

I hugged him again. "Thank you, Kuruks."

"Do they know you escaped?"

"Yes," I declared proudly. "The sheriff understood me. At least, I think he did. He even gave me this," I said, holding out the pistol.

Kuruks took a step back. "To protect you from Indians?"

"To protect us," I corrected.

The weapon's presence instantly changed his mood. "We should not stay here any longer."

"I agree, but — "

"Come, Izzy," he said. "Ride with me, at least until we get further away."

He was genuinely worried, and the joyful expression he wore upon my return was now replaced with consternation.

"He just gave me this to protect myself," I added, trying to reassure him.

"He thinks I am threat to you. They will not stop."

I climbed on the horse and he quickly flicked the reins. As we rode away at a thunderous pace, I feared that Kuruks either thought I was naive or that I secretly held some fear of him. Neither of which was true, but I understood why he felt that way. He and his people had been treated poorly at the hands of the white man. The more I thought about it, the more I grew sick to my stomach.

After we had cleared sight of the town, he slowed, and I motioned for him to stop. I climbed down from the horse so that I could look directly into his eyes.

"I want you to know, Kuruks, that you have been nothing but kind and caring to me. You saved my life, and you saved my sanity. I don't care what anyone else says, I am not afraid of you."

I couldn't read his expression. If he had an emotional response to what I said, he hid it quite well. "We have much sun left today."

"Yes, but the horse is tired. Why don't we walk?"

He nodded in agreement, then climbed off the horse. We walked through the prairie in a hurried pace with barely a word. I had feared the incident had changed our relationship. I had made it clear that I trusted him, but it was obvious that his faith in me had changed. After stewing on this for quite some time, I stopped.

"They may be scared of you, but I'm not. You are judging me by my race and not by who I am."

"I do not think any different about you," Kuruks insisted in a frustrated tone. He hesitated a moment, then added, "But your people have done that to my kind ever since you came here."

He took the horse and began to walk away, then added, "We go to my people. They will not harm you. If one of them threatens you, I will deal with it."

Chapter 9

Kuruks's words cut through me like a knife. In a rush of sudden realization, I understood the incident with my captors from his perspective. My cheerful return with a weapon given to me by my kidnappers' people must have seemed suspicious and dismissive of the threat they posed to him. I cursed myself for being so foolish.

"I have been terribly shortsighted," I said.

Kuruks turned and gave me a strange look. "Your eyes OK?"

"Yes, I'm sorry, I should have better explained myself. I meant that I did not look at what happened back there from your point of view."

Kuruks took a deep breath, and with his exhalation, his demeanor changed. His eyes softened, and he instantly looked more relaxed. "Don't worry, Izzy. We all get," he paused, then pointed at his eyes, "shortsighted sometimes. I learned new word," he added with a grin.

"How do you do that?" I asked in astonishment. "In one breath you go from being upset to smiling at me."

"Anger not good for us," he replied. "It will sit in belly and stew. Create much upset. You hold it in or let it go."

"You had every right to be angry at me," I admitted.

"Anger is not right word. I don't know — "

"Frustrated?"

"That means tired?"

I chuckled a bit. "Yes, tired of me and my problems."

"Maybe a little frustrated. But no more," he said with a somehow reassuring shrug.

I held up the provisions that Emma had given me. "We could eat lunch."

Kuruks nodded in approval. We walked the horse to a tree and tied it to one of the lower branches. We ate a biscuit and halved an apple and both remarked how glad we were to be eating bread and fruit again. The fresh, juicy apple instantly bolstered my spirits. I delighted in our light conversation, a pleasant break from the emotional turmoil of the past few days.

We took a moment after lunch to just sit and be. He confidently scanned the horizon. I envied how comfortable he was with our rugged traveling. Before my parents and I left for Oregon, we had stockpiles of provisions and a map of the route we planned to take. Kuruks had neither, and yet he seemed perfectly within his element. The thought of trying to make it to Wisconsin, Oregon, or even back to Independence without the meager comforts of trail provisions was frightening, and yet his certainty and resolve quelled my fears.

The afternoon was fortunately uneventful save for an afternoon thundershower. Most of the wind and heavy rain went around us, though we still got wet. We found a good place to camp next to a small pond with a protective circle of trees. I enjoyed watching Kuruks make the campfire - his delicate skill in teasing a small ember out of the kindling was an art.

"I have a hard time with a flint," I said as the fire began to roar. "You make it look so easy."

"It is easy now but not when I was young," he said. "My father taught me. My hands would blister from rubbing stick together. Now I know how and my hands do not blister."

My amazement in his abilities wasn't diminished by his modesty. We talked a while more, ate some more of our provisions, then laid down to sleep. A gentle rain fell. The trees protected us from most of it, but a few bigger drops made it through. Kuruks insisted I take the blanket and then leaned up against a trunk.

"I am no more entitled to stay dry than you. And this is your blanket."

"The tree will keep me dry."

"Nonsense!" I exclaimed. "By morning you'll be soaked." I walked over to the tree and sat next to him, then extended the blanket to cover both of us.

The tree bark made a terrible pillow, but it was better than getting wet. As I drifted off to sleep, a rumble of thunder echoed across the plains, startling me. In my slumber, I had leaned my head against Kuruks's shoulder. I noticed he was already asleep, seemingly unaware. I wasn't sure if he would approve, but I didn't want to move. His presence comforted me. Between that and the gentle sound of rain, I could hold my eyes open no longer.

Suddenly I was in the middle of a field. There was no tall grass - only well-trampled dirt beneath my feet. Heat radiated from a brilliant bonfire no more than ten yards from where I stood. Almost a dozen people danced in two circles around it, one in front of me and one behind me. A strange, low chanting, punctuated by a rhythmic, primal drumming permeated the night air. The drumbeat was low in volume yet I could distinctly feel each percussion inside my chest.

There was no sign of Kuruks. The air was dry and filled with wood smoke, yet the brightest stars pierced the haze. Somehow, I was in a completely different location than our campsite. I was bewildered. Where was I? What was happening to me?

"The Child of Darkness now joins our ritual!" a woman shouted. She did not speak in English, yet I could understand her perfectly.

There was a strange cheering and wailing from the crowd. I felt a presence staring at me.

"Move!" The command startled me to my core, yet it wasn't clear who delivered it.

"Move where?" I asked.

"To the center."

"Into the fire? No!"

"You will not burn."

I ignored the nonsensical order and looked closer at the woman. She wore a simple skirt and had a completely bear chest. Much of her body was painted, but I could tell she was an Indian. I looked away, not wanting to stare at their half-naked state of dress.

She touched my shoulder. "Isabella," she said, then reached for my hands. "Dance with us. Go into the fire. This ritual is for you."

"Why?" I asked. "No, I can't. I'll be burned."

"The fire will touch you but you will not burn."

"Who are you? What I am I doing here?"

"I am Sakuru. You are the Child of Darkness. Claim your rightful place."

"What are you talking about?" I demanded.

Sakuru began to unbutton my dress. I shooed her hand away. "Stop!"

"Your clothes will burn."

I shook my head. "Not if I stay away from the fire. This is insanity!"

"It is your destiny. There are those who wish to take it from you."

"You have me confused with someone else."

"There is no confusion. I know who you are, Isabella."

"How can I understand you?" I asked. "I don't speak your language."

Sakuru smiled. "You have a destiny to fulfill. There is no time to waste."

"I'm not walking into a fire."

She looked deeply into my eyes for a moment, then sighed. She was clearly disappointed. "I thought you were ready. But you are not."

"Ready for what?" I was more confused than ever.

Sakuru again studied my face with an empathetic smile. She put her hand on my cheek and replied, "Soon, Isabella. Soon. Go back to sleep. But not for too long. Paa is close."

I bolted awake. Sweat dripped from my skin and my heart pounded. The word Paa was on my lips. I knew that name.

Kuruks had mentioned it after my dream with the dancing mask. His warm body stirred beside me as he awoke.

"Tell me everything you know about Paa," I demanded. "I have to know."

Kuruks paused a moment. "Paa is my sister."

Chapter 10

Kuruks broke the awkward silence. "What is wrong?"

I had so many things to tell him and they all tried to come out of my mouth at once. I wasn't making any sense. He put his arm around my shoulder. "Take a breath."

"I had an awful dream. At least I think it was a dream." I put my head in my hands in frustration. "Why does this keep happening?"

After pausing a moment to regain my composure, I recanted the dream to Kuruks. "Sakuru said that Paa is close."

"Paa in my village. We are only a few days away."

"If Paa is your sister, then who is Sakuru?"

"She is our tribe's healer. I know her well."

"So how do I know these people's names?"

Kuruks looked at me with concern. It was clear he was trying to make sense of it all. I had become used to his experience and wisdom, yet this was puzzling to him. After some consternation, he replied, "I don't know."

"My mother always said I was clairvoyant," I said. I realized Kuruks didn't know the word so I explained. "She said I could see into the future or know what was going to happen before it did. My father told her she shouldn't fill my head with superstitious nonsense. He said I was simply a good, intelligent observer."

"You are smart, but this is something else," Kuruks replied.

"These dreams are too vivid. And there's no way I could have known the name of your sister or your tribe's healer." What is happening to me? None of this is making sense!"

"They called you the Child of Darkness," he said. "An ancient prophecy. I not sure I believe it. Sakuru can explain it better."

"Just tell me what you know."

"When a child is born at the same time the moon passes in front of the sun—"

"An eclipse?"

"Yes. When this happens, they are called the Child of Darkness. Paa was born the last time this happened."

"How old is your sister?"

"She is eighteen."

"I'm eighteen. I was born during a solar eclipse as well. November 30th, 1834, right?"

"Late fall of 1834. I don't know your dates."

"That's an amazing coincidence," I said. "But I don't understand why being born during an eclipse has anything to do with these dreams or your sister."

"I do not know much about prophecy. Sakuru is wise. When we get to my village she can help you with these dreams."

"You are wise, too" I replied.

Kuruks deflected my compliment with silence. "There is something else about this that you aren't telling me, is there?"

Kuruks sighed. "The Child of Darkness has great potential for evil. This used to bother my sister greatly."

"Used to?"

"She different, now."

"A prophecy about yourself must be difficult to live with," I said. "Especially if it's bad."

"She believes it. But I think it is just a story from long ago. She no child of darkness. She only my sister." He paused a moment then smiled. "You are feeling better now."

I hadn't noticed it but Kuruks's patience and reassuring presence had calmed me. I breathed normally and the sweat from my dream turned cold on my skin. "Thank you," I said.

"No reason to thank me. You calmed down on your own."

The dream, or whatever it was, had left me completely drained, so I soon returned to sleep. When I opened my eyes, the sun had risen and I was still leaned up against Kuruks, his arm around me.

"I'm sorry, I must have overslept," I said.

"You needed sleep."

"I kept you up late with my dream and kept you pinned against this tree all morning by being my prop."

"Prop?"

"A support to hold me up. You've been doing a lot of that lately."

"Being a prop not so bad. You worry about me too much."

Kuruks reached into the bag of food and pulled out some biscuits. "Maybe we can make these last till we get to my village. Then we eat smoked fish and corn cakes."

"That sounds delicious."

We had already lost enough daylight to oversleeping so we hurried through breakfast and resumed our journey. The rain had cleared but the skies were still gloomy. We pressed on, trying to make up the time we had lost dealing with my zealously overcautious captors.

The next two days were mostly uneventful. The weather remained decent enough for travel and between small stops to gather berries and rationing the rest of our provisions we did well. The monotonous travel through the prairieland offered no distraction from the vivid images from my dream. I felt the heat of the bonfire, heard the crackling of the wood, and smelled the smoke from the flames no matter what I was doing. The drumbeat echoed through my head in a maddening rhythmic pulse.

Eventually, late in the afternoon, a small village came into view. Kuruks stopped and turned to me.

"My people do not trust outsiders," he stated.

"With good reason," I admitted.

"Let me talk. Just be patient."

I nodded and we slowly continued with Kuruks in the lead. When we approached there was a tall, middle-aged Indian woman staring at me. Before Kuruks could speak a word, she rushed toward me.

"You have returned to us, Isabella."

Chapter 11

"Returned? You must be mistaken."

Kuruks gave me a stern look. "Sakuru is rarely mistaken."

Sakuru raised an eyebrow. "Rarely, Kuruks?" He remained silent. I couldn't help but to smile.

"I am not mistaken, Isabella," she added. "And I'll do almost anything to make Kuruks grin."

She spoke much better English than Kuruks did. I was surprised by her accent.

"Ah yes, my accent. My father was a French trader. I learned English from him."

"How did you know I was wondering about that?" I asked, amazed that she seemed to know what I was thinking.

"I am often asked about it. I know three languages. It is sometimes difficult to keep them all straight in my head." Sakuru walked up to me and took my hands in hers. "But nevertheless, I am not mistaken. This is not your first time here."

"That can't be. Before we left for Oregon, I had never been any further west than Independence."

As we talked I couldn't help but to notice the gathering crowd of Indians around us. They were giving me strange and unsettling looks.

"I will explain everything," Sakuru said. "In private," she added with a not so subtle hint of sternness. Everyone around us backed away as she led Kuruks and I through the village.

Most of the structures were earthen mounds covered with mud and straw, but there were smaller tipis scattered amongst the larger buildings. Sakuru led us into one of the bigger mounds. The entrance was reinforced with tree trunks and was low enough that we all had to duck when entering. In the middle of her home was a small fire surrounded by stones. The stones served as a griddle, where fish sizzled. To the side sat several baskets filled with maize.

"You both must be starving," Sakuru said. "Please sit down and eat."

We were both hungry so we promptly thanked her and accepted the invitation. The fish was delicious.

"We didn't have any salt to season our food while Kuruks and I were traveling. I missed it."

"We are fortunate that the streams have provided plenty of fish for us this season," Sakuru said. "And salt is plentiful for our western neighbors who trade with us from time to time."

"Where is Paa?" Kuruks asked.

"She left on a hunt early this morning. She is not back yet."

"Paa does not usually go on hunt," Kuruks observed.

"I told her it would be a good idea," Sakuru replied.

"I surprised she listened to you," he said.

"I told her I had a vision. And it was the truth. I dreamed last night that Isabella would arrive in our village this evening."

"You told her Isabella was coming?"

"No, I told her I had a vision. That was all she needed to know."

Kuruks gave me a sidelong grin. "I told you Sakuru was wise."

After I finished my meal I thanked Sakuru. "I appreciate your hospitality and kindness. I hope you will indulge me a bit further by answering a few questions."

"Tonight, Isabella, I will tell you the story of your life. The first phase of your life is over. Now it is time to fulfill your destiny."

A chill ran through me. It was shocking for her to say that I didn't know my own life. How could someone I barely knew know me better than I knew myself?

"I am sorry that this troubles you."

I became defensive. "With all due respect, Sakuru, I do not believe in destiny."

"This is not about belief. This is about what has been and what you will become. Are you ready to hear it?"

"Yes," I replied. My answer surprised me as it was immediate and seemingly unintentional. I was skeptical of Sakuru, but I intuitively knew she had much wisdom to offer me. My defiance faded and I listened intently, ready to soak in her words.

"You no doubt believe you were born in the American town of Independence. It is this lie we must dispel before I explain your current situation and what is to come."

"Lie?"

"Yes. I wish I could put it another way, but I cannot. Your parents lied about the place of your birth."

"Why would they do that?"

"I know this must upset you given your recent loss, but it is true."

"I'm not so sure they lied to me," I said. "I don't think they ever told me where I was born." I didn't think how strange that was until I said it. "I can't believe it. I never asked them. And they never volunteered it. I just assumed I was from Independence."

"You were born about one hundred miles to the west of Independence in a small village on the banks of the Saline River in Kansa territory. I recall your birth quite vividly. My mother and I helped with your delivery. I was just about your age then." A playful smile crossed her lips. "Alright, perhaps a few years older."

"You were present at my birth? Astounding. Why were my parents out that far, though? They never mentioned interacting with Indians."

"They were headed west."

"That doesn't make any sense," I replied. "Why would they never tell me about this? And why would they leave when my mom was pregnant, only to return home after I was born?"

"It is not uncommon for there to be a birth along the pioneer's trail. But your birth was not easy. You were breach and we had a difficult time turning you. Your mother took a long time to recover and that could have been why they decided to return home.

"I never knew any of this," I said, shaking my head in bewilderment.

"I believe I know why they never told you. They were protecting you."

"Protecting me from what?"

"Well, as you know, there was an eclipse on the day of your birth."

"Yes, my mother did tell me that. My father said it was a good omen. From what Kuruks tells me Paa was born on the same day. That is an amazing coincidence."

"It is not a coincidence," Sakuru insisted. "It is a grave problem for all of us."

"Kuruks told me what he knew of the Child of Darkness prophecy. It may have caused Paa great trouble as she believes in it but it meant nothing to me."

"It should mean a great deal to you, Isabella. You see, an eclipse of the sun is a very precise thing. The shadows cast are narrow and only last for a few moments. Timing is everything. Paa was born that day and at roughly the same time as you."

"Then Paa has nothing to worry about. The time of her birth was not unique. I mean no disrespect to your beliefs, Sakuru, but the prophecy was created before we understood how an eclipse worked."

"No offense taken, and it is clear you are quite intelligent. This will be helpful in the struggle you will soon endure. But there is something you are missing. Time is not the only element of an eclipse. Location is important. You see, Paa was born in this village. The eclipse blocked the sun here too, but for a shorter time. Your birth was precisely at the right time in the right location when the moon cast the longest possible shadow. Paa was in the wrong place at the right time."

"So what are you saying?" I asked.

Sakuru took a deep breath and looked into the fire. "Isabella, you are the Child of Darkness."

Chapter 12

I shook my head in disapproval. I was shocked by Sakuru's suggestion I was the Child of Darkness.

"That cannot be."

"It is the truth," she said plainly.

I began to rationalize away her bizarre assertion. "Even if it is true, it means nothing. There is no significance of being born during an eclipse. It is simply a scientific phenomenon."

"There are many factors that exist before we are born that influence our life. And the moment of our birth - the very second air first enters our lungs, is important. That is when our souls finalize possession of our bodies for this incarnation."

"This incarnation?"

"Oh yes, Isabella - you, and I, and every living thing, has lived many times before."

I began to stand but Sakuru put her arm on my knee. "This is a lot to take in, but — "

"It is. And I respect your beliefs, but I am not Pawnee. I do not follow your ways. This prophecy has nothing to do with me."

I left Sakuru's home and walked into the village. The previous crowd had dissipated but I still received glares from many of the villagers. I walked to the perimeter and stared out into the twilight. Sakuru's words echoed through my mind. I was prepared to dismiss them as superstitious nonsense, but the strange occurrences I had experienced were undeniable and unexplainable.

After a short while, Kuruks approached.

"You cannot hide from fate," he said.

"Who's fate? You told me yourself you aren't so sure of the prophecy."

"I do not know what to think," Kuruks replied. "But Sakuru is wise. She would not lead you astray."

"Just because Sakuru, your sister, or even your entire tribe believe something does not make it so."

"It doesn't matter," Kuruks insisted. "My sister will be upset when she learns she is not the Child of Darkness." She is... not stable."

"What do you mean?"

Kuruks looked to the sky for answers. "To her, the curse is also a blessing. Darkness surrounds her. She makes it who she is. Take that away, and she will be lost."

"I don't want to take anything away from her!"

"It will not matter to her."

I didn't know how to respond. I just stood there, contemplating his words and the overall situation. He remained quiet for some time. "She is my family. I cannot abandon her."

"I would never ask you to do that," I replied. "I don't want to come between you two."

"But I will not allow her to mistreat you. I love her, not all of her actions."

"That's very nice of you, Kuruks, but there is no way for you to remain impartial if she begins to cause trouble. I will not place you in that situation. I refuse."

"It's not your choice."

I made up my mind then and there to leave the village and leave Kuruks's kind and generous company. The very thought pained me, but I had to do it. I had grown to rely on him way too much, and it was time for me to repay the generosity. It was not fair for me to drive a wedge between him and his family. I decided not to tell him as he would surely try to talk me out of it and, failing that, accompany me.

I took his hand in mine and smiled. "You have been very kind to me. In just this short time you have grown to be my best friend. I treasure that, Kuruks. I want you to know that."

"You are welcome," he replied. I could tell he was confused by my sudden outpouring of affection, but he took it in his usual calm, collected manner. "Let's go back to Sakuru. She will know what to do."

I nodded and complied. I kept my head down, ignoring the strange looks I got from the villagers. When we returned, Sakuru smiled. "I am sorry for scaring you off."

"I was just… overwhelmed," I replied. "It's been a long day. Could I trouble you for a bedroll for the evening?"

"It would be no trouble at all," Sakuru said. "But it is early. Are you sure you want to retire so soon?"

"It's been a long day. And I haven't been sleeping well."

"The dreams," Sakuru said. "I know they are intense."

"Yes. I need my rest."

"I will go home," Kuruks said. "I will be not far away if you need me."

"Thank you, again," I told him. I gave him a hug. At first he was stiff and hesitated to return my gesture. I think it took him by surprise. He eventually put his arm around me, then left.

"Kuruks does not hug just anyone," Sakuru said. "I can tell he cares a great deal for you, but he is not in touch with his emotions as perhaps he should be. I'm sure it is a lesson for him in this life."

I returned to my bedroll and pulled the blanket over me. Sakuru worked on some beads as the fire crackled. I closed my eyes and pretended to sleep, but I found it hard to stay awake because I was so exhausted. My entire body ached and it was impossible to resist the temptation to fully relax. Despite my best efforts, I'm certain that I drifted off a few times, but I managed to catch myself.

Once I heard her snoring, I carefully watched her while I stood slowly and quietly. I crept to the door.

"At least take some food with you, Isabella. Oregon is a long way from here."

I stretched, hoping to feign insomnia. "Just having a hard time sleeping. I thought some fresh air would help."

"I will join you, then," Sakuru replied. Her voice was clear and her eyes didn't have the least bit of sleep in them.

"You haven't been asleep yet, have you?" I asked.

Sakuru grinned. "I was snoring, wasn't I?"

"You had me convinced."

Sakuru laughed. "I was just waiting on you to leave. I knew when you returned that something wasn't right. What is wrong, Isabella?"

"I don't want to come between Kuruks and Paa. I've already inconvenienced him."

"You don't understand. This isn't a simple family dispute. Paa knows you're a threat."

"I am no threat to her. I don't even know her."

"She will try to stop you from completing the ritual. I tried to help you complete it in the dream world but you were not ready. We don't have much time."

"What ritual? Please, stop. I don't want anything to do with this."

"If you don't stop Paa you will not only be putting yourself in danger but Kuruks, me, and all Pawnee." Her gaze held intensity that scared me.

"No, Sakuru!" I yelled, then turned to leave. Before I could take another step she firmly grabbed my arm. "If you turn away from your destiny you will most certainly die."

Chapter 13

I didn't really know Sakuru, so I wasn't sure if she was prone to hyperbole. But the look in her eyes was deadly serious.

"Did you hear me?" she asked with a hint of annoyance.

"I don't believe—"

"It does not matter what you believe. Paa will kill you because she covets your abilities."

I took a step away from Sakuru. "I am not filled with darkness. I may not be religious like my father but I do believe in being a good person."

"There is darkness within us all. If will only grow and fester if you deny it."

I wrung my hands against the folds of my skirt. "If Paa is as big a threat as you think she is, what can I do?"

"The ritual will stop her from gaining your power. That is what I tried to do with you in your dream but you were not ready."

"I don't want it. She can have it!"

"No!" Sakuru grabbed her necklace so hard I feared it would break. She took a deep breath, then paced as she continued. "Like you said - you are a good person. The darkness within you is powerful but you stand a chance at channeling that power - harnessing it for good instead of evil. Paa has no such concern. She cares only for her desires. And she desires power. She will do anything she can to ensure she gets it, including killing you." She paused a moment. Her face paled and she stumbled back. "She would kill her own brother if she had to."

"That's why I am leaving. I don't want to put Kuruks in danger."

"He is already in danger," Sakuru replied sternly. "You can protect him and prevent the tragedy that Paa will soon cause. But you can't do that if you leave."

"What kind of tragedy?" I asked.

Sakuru started to answer, then turned away. "No one can tell the future with certainty. But if my visions come true, and I am very afraid they will, Paa could be the end of you, Kuruks, me, and perhaps our entire village."

I stood silent a moment, taking in the gravity of Sakuru's words. "I can see how you thought my plans were impetuous."

"You didn't ask for any of this. I understand you were trying to protect Kuruks."

"What do you suggest I do?"

"We must perform the ritual as soon as possible. That is the first step. That will block Paa from taking your power."

"What ritual?"

"There is no direct translation of its name, but the closest approximation would be the Twilight Burning. You must confront and embrace the darkness, claiming the powers that the prophecy bestows upon you. It will not be easy, but you are far more equipped to deal with the challenge than Paa."

"What will it do to me?"

"The evil that is inherent within the Child of Darkness will surface. Your powers of clairvoyance will be dramatically enhanced, your strength will increase, and you will turn on your closest friends."

"That sounds horrible! How can that possibly help?"

"I will be there to help you through it. You will adjust and adapt, and eventually contain the darkness. Paa will make no such effort. She will seize the strength and use it to do great evil. You can do this, Isabella."

I wasn't sure of that. But I realized the alternative was far worse.

"There is something else you should know," Sakuru continued. "The recent eclipse we had awakened your powers. They are stirring with you. It will take several months, perhaps a year, for them to fully manifest. We don't have that long."

"The last eclipse happened the day our wagon broke apart in the river," I recalled solemnly. "Oh no," I whispered, struggling with the realization I just had. Sakuru put her arm on my shoulder. "That means I killed my parents!"

Sakuru held me as I began to shake with overwhelming guilt. The more I thought about it the more I realized it must be true: the dark magic must have caused the accident. "It's all my fault!"

Sakuru tried to console me. Her words blurred in my ears and made no sense through the throb of painful truth in my head. Her fingers curled around my arms as she squeezed until I had no choice but to meet her gaze. "Isabella. What are you talking about?"

"Our wagon broke apart in the river because of this power. The accident was at the exact same time as the eclipse."

"No, dear, that is not your fault."

"It can't be a coincidence!" I wailed through tears. "They had nothing to do with this. This is my problem, not theirs. Oh God, what have I done?"

Sakuru continued to hold me as I cried. The crushing responsibility of what I'd done caused fresh torrents of grief to crash against my body and jar me to my bones. She made me sit while she dried my tears and pushed my hair back from my face.

"Please understand this has nothing to do with you. Do not burden yourself with this."

I shook her words from my brain as wishful thinking. I knew what I had done. "Then why did it happen at that exact moment?"

"It was their time to leave this world. We don't always know why things happen the way they do."

I withdrew into silence, trying to come to terms with everything Sakuru had told me. I had barely begun to make sense of my world after my parents had died. I was reluctant to accept the prophecy that Kuruks had referred to and she believed in so strongly. And now it was clear to me it was no superstitious dark magic. This was real and it had already hurt ones I loved. The weight of the task I didn't seek out rested squarely on my shoulders. I sat straight and lifted my face to the only woman who could help. "Sakuru. When do we do the ritual?"

"Tomorrow night. I was foolish for trying to complete it your dreams. You were not ready. For now, we will rest, and prepare tomorrow morning."

"What about Paa?"

"She will return in a few days. We'll perform the ritual in a spot far from the village. She will not find us, even if she comes home sooner than expected."

Sakuru's confidence in her plans brought me a modicum of relief. She wiped my face again and gave me a hug. In her compassionate, caring arms I felt less alone.

"You should sleep, Isabella. We have a big day ahead of us tomorrow."

"Thank you," I said, and returned to my bedroll. Despite my mental state, I quickly fell asleep from utter exhaustion.

I awoke to the unmistakable smell of fish frying. Sakuru offered a plate of fish and cornbread with a smile. I thanked her for preparing breakfast and began to eat.

"The sun has been up for several hours," she said, taking a bite. "I thought about waking you earlier but you were sleeping so soundly."

"I appreciate that, I was tired."

"You were snoring, too," she added with a grin.

A wave of embarrassment passed over me. "No one has ever told me I snored."

"It's nothing to worry about. You needed the rest, anyway. We have a long day of preparation ahead of us. After we eat I will find some appropriate Pawnee clothing for you. Please don't take offense to this, I simply believe it will help you draw less attention. It is also a matter of tradition for our ceremonies.

"I wasn't offended. I'll be relieved to wear some new clothes," I said, pointing to my tattered dress. But in the dream, you and the others were nude."

"I know that being naked may offend your American sensibilities, but it is not given as much thought in our culture. But don't worry, that is only for the ritual itself. You will be fully clothed the rest of the time."

I was relieved. I didn't relish the thought of parading nude around the village. After breakfast, Sakuru rooted through her trunk. She held up a nice, long, light-brown dress with simple but elegant beaded fringe, and big, flowing shoulders, and a cloth shawl.

"That's beautiful," I said.

"When I was your age I wore this quite well. But it is the dress for a young, unmarried girl like yourself, not an old woman."

"I would hardly call you old, Sakuru."

"You may call me whatever you like, but I call myself old."

"The shawl is gorgeous, but may be too warm for this time of year."

She removed the shawl and then held the dress up again for me. It had a lower neckline than I was used to wearing. "My father wanted me to wear the shawl. Which I did, of course, at least in his presence."

I grinned. "It is beautiful. I'll wear the dress without it."

Sakuru took my old dress and stored it neatly in her trunk, then handed me the Pawnee garments. As I put it on, I had the same feeling of destiny that I had experienced the first time I met Kuruks. The clean material felt wonderful against my skin. The new dress fit me perfectly, and I felt free and natural wearing it. I looked up at her and smiled.

"You are a gorgeous young woman, Isabella."

"Thank you. This feels–"

"Right?" Sakuru offered.

"Yes. It feels right."

I couldn't really explain what I meant, because I didn't fully understand it myself. However, I could tell that she knew, and our brief exchange on the subject spoke volumes. The tumultuous events of late seemed so distant in this moment. I saw a glimpse at my mother's smile in Sakuru. I knew they weren't related, and I must fully admit it have been simply a wishful longing for my mother to still be in my life.

"Good morning," Kuruks said as he entered Sakuru's home. He nodded at her then stopped and gave me a prolonged glance. "Izzy."

"Sakuru suggested I wear traditional Pawnee clothing. What do you think?"

Kuruks smiled. "It is beautiful."

"Thanks," I replied. I am certain I blushed.

"We will do the ritual tonight, Kuruks. Oh, and Isabella, you will need this," Sakuru said, handing me my pistol.

"Wait, I had it on me. How did you –"

"I removed it before we ate dinner last night," Sakuru admitted. "I wasn't sure how you'd react to what I had to tell you. I hope you understand my precaution."

"I didn't notice," I replied. I cursed myself for missing such an important detail.

"You will have to be more aware of your surroundings," Sakuru said.

"I feel foolish."

"Don't worry. You are not a warrior, yet."

"Yet?"

"Your trials have just begun," Sakuru said. "You have enemies. You will need to know how to defend yourself."

"Why do you trust me with this?" I asked. "You said I may betray you with the power of darkness." I handed the pistol back to Sakuru. "Maybe you should keep this."

Sakuru refused. "I considered it. But after some pondering, I decided that the need to protect you outweighs my concern for personal safety."

"I would never hurt you."

"Do not make promises you may not be able to keep," Sakuru scolded. "You have yet to taste the power. That pistol may very well be the least of our concerns. Kuruks, is there any word yet of Paa's return?"

"No," he replied.

"I must help Isabella prepare a medicine bundle. Please meet us back here before sundown."

Kuruks nodded in approval. "Send word if you need me sooner." I smiled and thanked him, and he left.

"He has been so kind to me," I said. "I don't know how I can ever repay him."

"You can marry him," Sakuru replied. "He is strong, good natured, and his lineage is quite virile. He would make a good husband."

Chapter 14

My mouth hung open at Sakuru's blunt suggestion.

"Why does that surprise you?" she said. She put her hand on my chest. "Yes, I feel a heartbeat, so you are alive. You have certainly noticed Kuruks is a handsome man."

"I hadn't thought of him like that," I replied.

Sakuru raised her eyebrows in disbelief. "Oh, Isabella. I've seen how you two look at each other. He would make a fine husband. And unless you choose to go back to your people, you will have to take an Indian mate."

"I don't have to marry anyone," I protested.

Sakuru chuckled. "Yes, it is easy to say that, but we are drawn toward each other. It is difficult to escape the call to procreate. My husband died five years ago and I often long for his touch. I have even entertained the thought of taking another man."

"Did you have any children?"

"Yes, two. A daughter and a son. Both have married off to neighboring villages. I do not see them as much as I'd like."

"I'm sorry."

"They are happy. But travel is more dangerous for Indians with the trail. Settlers are taking over more and more of our land, and the disputes are not always peaceful. Someday we will likely have to leave this village."

"Why was Kuruks traveling so far south?"

"He didn't tell you? I asked him to go. I knew your destinies were intertwined, and that the eclipse would be a major catalyst in your life."

"His timing couldn't have been better."

"The map of our lives has certain fixed points. We may wander, change roads, and even take detours, but we always find our way to the important events that shape our destiny. I had confidence in Kuruks's safety, nevertheless I was relieved to see you both return."

"I wish it was possible for our people to live peacefully together."

"Your country is intent on bending everything, and everyone, to its will. You can make people do what you want, and you can pretend that the land does as you wish. But this is an illusion. Eventually people will rise to assert their freedom, and the earth will reclaim its true nature. This cannot be changed."

I could not dispute her logic. "I've heard of many tragedies on both sides of this senseless conflict. It doesn't have to be this way."

"In time, a balance will be found. It may take centuries. Now, as much as I would love to discuss politics and men, we have much work to do. First, you must assemble a medicine bundle."

"What's that?" I asked.

"A collection of objects that are special to you."

"Like what?"

"It doesn't matter what they are, as long as they hold spiritual significance for you."

"Most of my possessions are in the Big Blue River."

"You must have something."

I walked over to Sakuru's trunk. "May I?"

Sakuru nodded her approval so I opened it and removed my dress. I gathered my mother's dragonfly hair comb and my quarter and showed it to her.

"This is all I have of my mother's."

"It's beautiful," she observed. "Then it certainly is valuable to you. And the coin?"

"Twenty-five cents," I replied. "The great fortune I am supposed to start my life over with, I suppose."

"The coin does not belong to you," Sakuru said. "It belongs to a bank. It is only valuable to them."

"I can buy things I need with this," I replied.

"With that coin, you can only buy other's time. But you can fulfill your needs yourself. The earth provides you what you need."

"Maybe in this village, but not in Oregon."

"I was not aware that the laws of the universe worked differently in Oregon," Sakuru remarked.

Of course, in the larger sense, she was right. But in America you needed money, and that quarter was the only thing I had to rebuild my life. Her acute philosophical observations gave me pause to consider her intriguing suggestion to stay with the Pawnee and settle down with an Indian man. I caught myself daydreaming of possibilities.

"I do not mean to argue," Sakuru added. "I know you come from a different culture. But you have stepped into the Pawnee world and the task at hand requires a new line of thought. I challenge you only to expand your mindset, not to quarrel."

"I understand," I replied in earnest. "You have given me much to think about."

"Your mother's comb is a good start to your bundle. Now you must gather some additional items. We will head out into the fields and find what speaks to you."

We left Sakuru's hut and walked out of the village. Her prediction was correct that my Pawnee clothing would reduce the glares from others in the village. Instead of long, puzzled stares I received lingering passing glances. The sky was overcast and the air sticky and warm. I was glad to be in more comfortable clothing as I would have been miserable in my dress. After a brief walk we came upon a collection of river birch trees that surrounded a small pond.

"This is my favorite spot," Sakuru observed. "It is even more beautiful when the sun is shining and the wind rustles through the tall grass. But there is beauty in nature in even the worst of weather. Take a seat, Isabella."

I found a suitable spot next to the pond. She joined me. "Now, close your eyes and clear your mind."

It was easier said than done. Thoughts of Paa, my parents, and Kuruks crossed my mind. I did my best to ignore them and focus, but I was having considerable difficulty. Sakuru sensed my problem.

"I should not have said clear your mind. It is difficult to think of nothing when you are not used to it. This can take much practice, and I forget that you have just been thrown into this world. Close your eyes and listen. Absorb the nature around you. Tell me the first thing that comes to mind."

At that precise moment, a dragonfly buzzed past me. I smiled as I recalled watching them dance across the water with my mother. "A dragonfly."

"An important messenger," Sakuru said. "And no coincidence that it matches the insect on your comb. They live an interesting life, you know. They spend quite a while preparing for the moment when their beautiful wings will emerge, allowing them to take flight. You are not unlike the dragonfly, Isabella."

As I considered her insightful interpretation, I heard a bird chirping in the distance. "That bird sounds happy." I laughed. "And blades of grass are tickling my arm."

"Then you have the first new item in your bundle," Sakuru said. She directed me to open my eyes and pluck some of the grass that was touching my arm. She handed me a small cloth bag and told me to put the grass inside it.

"Now for the bird," she said. "We would not put a bird in the bag, obviously. But what might be around that would represent that bird?"

"A feather?"

"Precisely. Look along the bank. There will be one."

I started to survey the ground and then paused. "How do you know we'll find one?"

"It was the first animal that spoke to you."

I was dubious but I continued to search the ground. In just a few minutes, I was astounded to find a beautiful brown and black striped feather. I wasn't sure what kind of bird it was so I showed it to Sakuru.

"That is a hawk feather."

"I don't believe it was a hawk that I heard when I closed my eyes."

"Perhaps not, but it led you to this feather," she replied. "A hawk is a very powerful, majestic creature. It is an honor to you to have one of its feathers in your bundle."

I added it to my collection with a newfound sense of respect. "What's next?"

Sakuru opened a pouch removed an even smaller bag then handed it to me. "I recommend adding this."

"What is it?" I asked.

"Tobacco."

"Is that your medicine bundle?"

"Yes. But this is an extra pouch of tobacco. It is not part of my bundle."

"What do you keep in yours?"

"It is not appropriate for me to share that with you. I realize that I know some of your items, but there is no other choice. You do not know our ways, so I must teach you."

"I meant no offense by asking."

"I know. And because its contents are meant to be private, from here on you are to decide what goes inside of it. I will now return to the village and let spirit speak to you and guide you in completing your bundle."

"How much more do I need?" I asked.

"You will know, Isabella."

You might think I would have felt completely alone and confused as to what to do next, but I didn't. In such a short time, I went from not believing in anything other than what I saw to letting an Indian woman and my intuition guide me as to what to put into a medicine bag. My paradigm had completely shifted. I paused to reflect on this a peculiar moment as Sakuru disappeared.

I took a deep breath and returned my attention to the matter at hand. I looked around for a while, giving careful consideration to any subtle or stray observance that caught my eye. Eventually I turned my attention to the water. I looked along the bank of the pond and noticed a few pebbles in the water. I picked up one of them and admired the rich red hues in the small, shiny rock. I dried it off and added it to the bag.

I spent the better part of an hour searching with great scrutiny for things to add to my bundle. I collected several more pebbles from the pond, an unusual vibrantly green variegated leaf, and a broken fragment of a pine cone. Again, Sakuru was right – I knew when the bundle was complete. I took the leather strings of the bag and cinched them tight, then held my new possession with pride.

The walk back to the Pawnee village wasn't far. While I had become accustomed to walking through the plains with Kuruks, I actually enjoyed this brief time alone. When I reached the village, I saw Kuruks talking with a woman near Sakuru's home. I wasn't sure what they were saying and I didn't want to seem rude, so I kept a polite distance until I could introduce myself into the conversation.

"Kuruks," I said with a smile.

"Izzy, you are back," he replied. "This is Tuhre."

"Pleased to meet you," I said with a polite bow. "My name is Isabella."

"She does not speak any English," Kuruks replied. He turned to Tuhre and seemed to translate what I said. I heard my name mentioned, and then she looked at me. "Izzy," she managed. She turned back to Kuruks and spoke some more, and the two shared a laugh. It bothered me that I didn't know what they were saying.

"I have known Tuhre for many years," he said.

I wasn't sure how to reply. I couldn't think of any common reference we had to start even the smallest of conversations. I looked to Kuruks to provide some assistance but he turned and spoke to her more in their language.

"I must return to Sakuru."

"Yes, she is waiting for you," Kuruks replied.

"Right, well, that's where I'll be," I said, then walked away to Sakuru's home. Before I proceeded inside I took a second look at Kuruks and Tuhre.

As soon as I entered, Sakuru eagerly greeted me. "Did you complete the bundle?"

"Yes," I replied, showing the bag to her.

"What's wrong?" she asked.

"Nothing," I replied. "Who is Tuhre?"

"She is a friend to Kuruks. A nice young woman. You met her?"

"Yes."

Sakuru's eyes lit and her lips formed a peculiar grin. "Kuruks introduced you to her."

"Yes, briefly. I didn't stay. She doesn't speak English."

"And this surprises you?"

The two Indians I had come to know spoke my language. I immediately realized it was short-sighted of me to assume that Tuhre would be bilingual as well.

"So what did you think of her?" Sakuru asked.

"I really know nothing about her."

Sakuru gave up all attempts to hide her smirk. "The human spirit astounds me, Isabella. In the midst of all of this chaos, danger, grief, and loss, it still can be distracted by the heart."

Chapter 15

"You must focus on the task ahead of you. And I can see Kuruks is becoming a distraction."

I had to admit to myself, and her, that she was right. "I sound like a jealous schoolgirl."

"A little," Sakuru replied with a grin. "But no matter. We will plan your marriage to Kuruks later. For now, we have much bigger issues. You have your medicine bundle. Now you need to meet your animal guide."

I ignored her comment about marriage. "How do I do that?"

"There are many ways. Sometimes it takes years to learn commune with our guides. But we don't have that long. We will spend the day in what your culture would call prayer. But instead of praying to Tirawa, our creator god, or Atira, his wife, we will be asking your ancestors for guidance."

Sakuru sat on the floor and asked me to join her. She took some tobacco and stuffed it into a pipe, then lit it. She took a drag on it to produce some smoke, then handed it to me.

"Exhale completely, then take in as much of the smoke as you can, then hold it until you can hold it no more."

I did so, nearly choking as I inhaled. With considerable struggle I held my breath, then exhaled. I began to feel dizzy.

"Close your eyes," she said.

I did, but the lightheadedness continued. The room start to sway, but I managed to hold onto my senses. I instinctively gripped my medicine bundle as though it were my lifeline to reality.

"What is your favorite time of year, Isabella?"

I thought the question odd, but answered anyway. "Winter. I love winter. Christmas especially."

"The birth of your culture's savior?"

"No, the warmth of family. In the frigid cold we enjoyed a hot meal together, sat by the fire, told stories. It was wonderful. It was a refuge from the horrible conditions outside. And after our feast I'd always feed the birds outside our scraps of bread."

"It is no coincidence you have a feather. It sounds like the birds call to you."

Sakuru's words sparked a memory I had long forgotten. "I remember one time I was feeding the birds in the snow and a beautiful red bird came up to me after he had his fill and tilted his head to get a good look at me. He stared at me for quite a while. This sounds strange, but, I believe he was thanking me."

"That is not strange," Sakuru reassured me. "You had communion with that animal. A sacred moment, indeed. Take several more puffs."

I did so, and with each breath the lightheadedness that was beginning to fade progressively returned.

"Bring yourself back to that moment. Picture the animal clearly in your mind. Listen to it, not with your ears, but with your spirit. What does it say?"

If someone had asked me before this day what an animal said to me I would have thought they were joking. But in this exact moment I not only considered Sakuru's question perfectly reasonable, I immediately had the answer. I could hear the bird calling to me in my mind.

"It said I am with you."

"That is profound," Sakuru said. "Birds are powerful yet graceful. Much like you, Isabella."

I smiled at the compliment. "Thank you."

"You will commune with the red bird throughout your life. You will find it present at important moments in your journey, and you will find strength in its companionship. Our guides and our ancestors are with us always. Remember that. Spend some time contemplating this."

Sakuru and I sat quietly. I don't know exactly how long because I lost track of time. Thoughts of my parents, the bundle I had created, Kuruks, and even Paa flowed through my mind until I eventually reached an almost perfect calm. The sensations I had during this time are difficult to describe. I'm certain a more seasoned, eloquent writer could craft some majestic phrase to relate the sheer peaceful calm I experienced. As long as I live I will never forget it.

Eventually, my bliss was gently interrupted by a familiar hand on my shoulder. "Izzy, we must go. Paa is coming."

I opened my eyes. Sakuru's gaze was already wide with anticipation and urgency. "Now," she said.

I turned to see Kuruks standing over me. "Do not worry. I will protect you."

Sakuru gathered some items then escorted us outside. I was startled to see it was almost twilight. I had let hours pass by with scarce sensation that they had elapsed.

"Follow me," Sakuru said, motioning for us to follow. Sakuru and Kuruks both grabbed a torch to light our path.

We walked in a general eastward direction. The sun had set by the time we reached our destination – a large empty field with only one large ash tree in sight. A fair distance from the tree was a large pyre.

"I don't think Paa will find us here," Sakuru said. "Kuruks, our time is short. I will need your assistance to paint Isabella before we light the fire."

"Paint?" I asked.

"Black and red paint from charcoal and berries. And we will apply white to your face from ashes. It will help the spirits recognize you and to increase your stamina and strength for the trials to come."

Sakuru rooted through her belongings and took out small containers of the paint, then asked me to remove my clothes. I immediately rejected the request and motioned to Kuruks. "We are not alone, Sakuru."

"I know. We must hurry. He will help me apply your paint."

"But I…"

Sakuru sighed. "I forgot about your culture's fear of your own bodies." She took off her clothes and laid them neatly by the trunk of the tree. It was a strange sight to see a woman standing before me completely nude in the presence of a man.

"Do you now feel more at ease?"

I wanted to say yes, but I would have been lying. However, I realized I had trusted Sakuru and her instruction so far, and I was eager to prevent Paa from causing more harm. I removed my dress and turned away from Kuruks. Sakuru began applying paint to my back, making intricate circles along my shoulder blades.

Kuruks walked toward me. I clenched my hands over my chest and shied away from him. "Please be still," Sakuru said.

"I will apply it," I insisted. "Hand it to me."

"You do not know how," he replied.

"Just tell me. I'm embarrassed."

"There is no need," Kuruks said. He repositioned the torch he had previously placed in the ground so that there was less light in front of me. "I will not see much of you. Only what is necessary."

I was trembling from fear. I felt so exposed. I knew I had little choice, so I reluctantly nodded. He intricately painted my arms and the front of my shoulders, then gently nudged on my wrist. I took a deep breath and shoved all of my anxiety and embarrassment aside and let my hands fall to my side.

I watched his eyes as he painted my stomach. His gaze never faltered from his task. As he proceeded, some of my panic eased. He knew what he was doing and it was extremely evident he treated my concerns with the utmost compassion. My skin anticipated a tickling sensation from the gentle movements, but I didn't experience that. I was somehow used to his touch. It felt perfectly natural.

Sakuru and Kuruks moved down to my lower legs, meticulously applying the paint and swirling symbols on the tops of my feet. He stopped at my knee and said, "I will let Sakuru finish."

To this day I cannot tell you exactly what changed in me that precise moment. I don't know if it was a strange sort of sexual curiosity, the confident nature of Kuruks, or the relaxation he instilled in me through his respect and care. He had been my stalwart friend and protector. And now I am certain that is the moment I finally admitted to myself I loved him. Of course, it wasn't this action that caused me to feel this way, rather it was his kind and gentle nature, his compassion, and his confidence that brought out the best in me and gave me strength. I was filled with warmth and comfort as this realization washed over me.

I placed his hand above my breast. "I want you to finish the paint on my front."

"Are you sure?" Kuruks asked.

"Yes."

Kuruks continued the paint to my upper thighs. I had never had a man touch me so intimately, yet the fear that I had previously felt had vanished. The remaining tension in my body melted away as he finished his work, covering the rest of my legs, stomach, and breasts in ceremonial paint. When they finished, Sakuru instructed Kuruks to take one of the torches and start the pyre, then completed the paint on my face. The texture of the ash was slightly uncomfortable, but I stood as still as I could to not disrupt her efforts.

I turned and saw that the pyre was now engulfed in flames. Kuruks was standing a fair distance away from it with his bow at the ready. Sakuru picked up a small drum from her belongings, took my hand, then escorted me to the fire. We stopped a bit closer than I would have liked. The heat warmed my skin, and the flames almost filled my entire field of vision. The fire crackled and popped and the smoke filled my nose with the aroma of birch and sycamore.

Sakuru beat on her drum, its skin echoed a penetrating rhythm. "Move as you feel compelled to do by your own spirit. We dance to commune with our ancestors and guides, and to allow spirit to flow through us. Isabella, you must call to your ancestors for the acceleration of your destiny, and the strength to deal with the trials to come."

Sakuru body moved gracefully as she danced around the fire. Her gaze became transfixed as though the fire had a captive hold on her imagination. I was compelled to dance as well. The rhythm of the drum seemed to draw movement out of me. I had very little experience with dance, other than an awkward square dance at a church social with clammy-handed boys. Despite that, I managed to find a pattern and began to sway.

The fire was hypnotic. As I moved around it and swayed with the drum I couldn't look away. I fell into a rhythm that was captivating and all-consuming. My mind was filled only with the two objectives that Sakuru had mentioned: accelerating the power of darkness within me and to strengthen my will to make it through the process. Despite the intense heat from the fire I wanted to move even closer. Beads of sweat formed on my skin.

There was a moment where I thought I might lose consciousness. My entire body felt like it was vibrating, as though a church bell had been placed over me and struck. It was both disturbing and fascinating. The muscles in my stomach tightened and my shoulders clenched as this sensation reverberated through me. Something changed inside me in that moment. I was calm yet powerful, strong yet graceful. I knew, beyond any doubt, that the prophecy had come true. I was now the Child of Darkness.

In the distant corner of my mind I heard someone yell. It seemed so distant, yet I now know it was only yards away. I looked up to see Kuruks with an arrow nocked in his bow, pointing it at someone in the distance. I strained my eyes, but the light from the fire made it difficult to see who it was. I stepped away, closer to him, then noticed a woman with a bow on her back and a dead rabbit in her hands.

I walked towards her.

"Be careful, Izzy," Kuruks warmed.

The woman laughed. "So, the imposter Child of Darkness. We now meet in person."

She drew her bow and nocked an arrow, then pointed it squarely at my chest.

I was not the slightest bit afraid.

Chapter 16

Paa's hand was steady, and I should have been shaking like a leaf. I wasn't.

"Put it down!" Kuruks yelled, but Paa ignored her brother's request.

"I see you've made my brother your lapdog," Paa remarked.

Despite the mortal danger I was in, I simply made a passive note of her Pawnee-French English accent.

Paa looked at my body, then returned her angered gaze towards me. "I see that you don't need magic to control a man. I'm disappointed in you, Kuruks. So easily swayed by the supple flesh of a white whore."

"Stop it," Kuruks insisted as he took a step closer. "I will shoot."

Paa laughed and casually dismissed him with a wave of her hand. "You're not going to kill your sister. So, tell me, Child of Darkness, why do you meddle in our affairs? Why don't you return to your home and be a good English wife?"

"I harbor no ill will toward you," I replied.

Paa's top lip curled into an angry sneer. "I want you gone. Wipe our sacred paint off your pale body, go get your clothes, and leave. Don't *ever* come back."

I normally would have been intimidated by such words, but something had changed in me during that ceremony.

"I will come and go as I please, Paa."

I don't think she knew how to respond. Her face made several small contortions as she processed my indifference to her commands.

"Leave, now. I'm warning you for the last time," she replied, pulling back even further on her bow.

I responded by holding my ground.

"Isabella is not your enemy," Sakuru said, approaching me from behind.

"The prophecy is what you groomed me for," Paa replied. "Why are you now fawning over this pathetic girl?"

"I tried to help you deal with the powers I thought you had," Sakuru said. "But you weren't ready. You never accepted them. You felt entitled to them. I realized you were not the one."

"And she is?" Paa replied with a snide laugh.

"Yes," Sakuru answered succinctly. "Now leave us, Paa. Do not interfere with the prophecy."

"I will not trust the future of our tribe to this," Paa said.

"Go," Sakuru commanded.

Paa hesitated for a moment, then lowered her bow. "To think I used to respect you, Sakuru. You have changed."

"No, Paa, it was you that changed. You let the idea of power consume you. You have become a spoiled brat. Go."

Paa released her arrow. The instant the feather left her hand, time for me slowed to a crawl. I could see every detail of its graceful movement as it left her bow. I thought the strangest thing as her arrow raced toward me: *her skill in archery is impeccable*. Her draw was perfect and her release was smooth and well-practiced. I knew that it wouldn't kill me despite its perfect trajectory.

Kuruks slammed into my body with such force I lost my breath. The arrow missed its mark but grazed my shoulder, drawing blood before it skittered across the ground. We continued backwards and fell flat on our backs. I leaned up to see Paa's face fill with an intense, burning anger. Her fierce scowl did little to cover the sense of frustration and resignation that began to wash over her. She screamed something to him in their native tongue, spun on her heels, then left.

Sakuru rushed to my side and examined the wound on my arm. I wasn't concerned about it in the least. I stared into Kuruks's eyes as he hovered above me, still holding me tight as though my life still depended on it. His grasp was firm and protective. I could clearly see the caring and concern for me in his eyes. I knew my deep feelings for him were reciprocated. Neither of us could speak, but words would have been in the way of the emotions that flowed between us.

"Move your hand, Kuruks. I need to see her arm."

Kuruks released his grip and blood trickled down my arm. It was warm, but there was very little pain. I was in a strange daze, and the events that had just occurred had not yet caught up to me. I turned to notice Sakuru smelling the blood from my wound.

"Poison," she said. "We must get her back to the village!"

"What? No, I'm fine."

"The arrow was poisoned," Sakuru said. "We need to clean the wound and purge the toxins from your system."

"I feel fine," I insisted.

"Why didn't you move when she fired?" Kuruks asked.

"I knew I would be alright. I don't know how I knew, but I did."

"You could have been killed!"

"I knew that wasn't going to happen," I said.

"She is an expert hunter," Kuruks replied.

"She'll still die if we don't get the poison out of her," Sakuru said. "We can debate this later."

Sakuru fetched my clothes and I pulled them on as we walked towards the village. Kuruks kept a sharp lookout for Paa while Sakuru paid close attention to my mental status. She continuously asked me questions and looked carefully at my eyes, hoping that there was no change in my condition.

When we got back to her home she rushed me inside and instructed me to sit. She pulled my sleeve up, fetched a wet cloth, then cleaned the wound and applied a poultice to it.

"I'm sorry my sister attacked you," Kuruks said.

"It is not your fault," I replied. "You saved my life. You keep coming to my rescue."

He answered with a smile.

"If the arrow were poison, would I not be feeling its effects by now?"

"I have cleaned most of it from your wound, but I am certain some has seeped into your blood," Sakuru replied.

"Paa will not give up so easily," Kuruks said.

Sakuru sighed. "No, she won't. I think she will have little support from the village, but she has a persuasive, sharp tongue."

"So do you," Kuruks said. "Don't worry, Izzy, I will protect you."

I put my hand on his face. "I know. Thank you." When I turned my head I felt a bit dizzy. I had hoped the sensation would go away but it didn't. I grabbed his shoulder to steady myself.

"What's wrong?" he asked.

"I'm… feeling…"

The rest of the words wouldn't come. I could barely keep my head upright. Kuruks and Sakuru helped me lie back and relax. I was flushed and I broke into a sweat. He fetched some blankets and put one over me, then bundled up another and placed it under my head.

"You are strong to hold off the poison's effects for that long," Sakuru said. "But you must rest now and let your body fight it. We will be by your side and help to drive it from you."

Kuruks took my hand and gave it a reassuring squeeze, then continued to hold it while Sakuru gathered some herbs. She ground them into a small bowl, put the bowl next to my head, then lit them. The herbs smoldered and filled the area with smoke. I am certain sage was among them. I tried to stay awake, but my vision blurred and I fell into a deep sleep.

Vivid dreams crept into my consciousness. Many were brief fragments of events I had experienced, but occasionally I saw a flash of a face of someone I knew. They would often appear to speak, but I heard nothing. I was trapped and afraid in the non-stop bombardment of seemingly nonsensical and disconnected imagery.

Eventually, through the torrent of visuals, the flashes of people turned into longer vignettes of meaningful thought. I saw my mother, my father, a few people I knew from Independence, and even Sakuru and Kuruks. They spoke to me with varying voices but they all said they same basic thing. *You are changing, Isabella*. I challenged them with *Changing into what*? but my question was ignored.

They were right – I was changing. In such a short while I had moved from a mindset of logical rigidity to complete acceptance of the now quite evident spiritual world that had surrounded me. But they were speaking in the present, immediate tense.

Soon, the images of my family and friends faded away and I saw a large, sweeping open plain. I stood on the top of a hill and watched a fierce battle unfold below me. I couldn't identify the combatants individually, but most were Pawnee. I somehow knew I was connected to the event. I was at a loss to explain the powerful surge of emotion and energy that flowed through me in this vision. I felt responsible for the violence, and was sorrowful for the bloodshed and death before me. The battle faded, and only darkness remained.

My mother approached and spoke softly and deliberately. "I am proud of you."

My heart sang with joy at hearing her words. I wasn't sure how it was possible, but I didn't dwell on my disbelief too long. I wanted it to be real. I reached out to touch her, but I couldn't reach her. She was both solid and ethereal, here, and yet so far away.

"Mom!" I yelled. "I love you. I miss you."

"I am always with you. Worry not, as this trial will not last long. You have an important destiny to fulfill. You will meet these challenges with strength and grace."

And then she faded away. I raced toward her but my feet stuck to the ground. I extended my arm to reach for her, and she completely vanished. I cried out in agony as the darkness returned.

Chapter 17

The first thing I did after emerging from my fevered sleep was drink a full cup of water.

"No wonder you are thirsty," Sakuru said. "I've never seen anyone sweat out a fever like that."

She refilled the cup and I finished another serving.

"Take it easy, Isabella. If you drink much more, you'll be sick."

I heeded her advice. I was wet and sticky from the sweat, and I ached all over, but my head was much clearer. "I feel better, I think."

"Good," Sakuru replied. "You gave us quite a scare."

Kuruks returned and brushed the hair from my face, then gently took my hand. "I am glad you are awake."

"I remember you by my side," I said. "Thank you. Thank you both. I don't know what I'd do without either of you." I took another sip. "Where is Paa?"

"She left the village," Kuruks replied. "I do not know where she went."

"Why would she leave?"

"Sulking, maybe," Sakuru wondered out loud. "No matter. She will return. We must be better prepared."

"I saw my mother," I said.

"You had visions?" Sakuru asked.

"I guess. I don't know. I saw her. She said I had a destiny to fulfill. I don't know what she meant."

"It may take time to understand what you saw," Sakuru said. "You are still undergoing the transformation." She inspected a bowl and handed it to Kuruks. "Will you fetch us some more water? Isabella has consumed all I had."

He took the bowl and backed toward the door, his gaze never leaving mine. "I will be back," he said as if reluctant to leave me again.

After he left, Sakuru turned to me and smiled. "He stayed by your side the whole time. The moment he decided to leave, you woke. He cares for you a great deal."

"And I him," I replied. "How long was I asleep?"

"It's almost noon."

"That's not too bad."

"You were poisoned two nights ago."

"Oh," I said. "Two days? That would explain why I am so thirsty. And hungry."

"I was worried about your appetite. It is good that you want to eat. The poison must have fully left your body."

"Did he really stay here the whole time?"

"With only short breaks. He slept next to you. He stayed turned to you and would periodically check on you then go back to sleep."

"Oh my," I replied.

"You need to tell him how you feel before your transformation becomes more difficult. You will lash out at those around you, and the experience can be quite dark. If he

117

knows your love for him beforehand, he may be able to deal with it."

"You're right," I said. "But first, I really am starving."

"I have some pumpkin and maize for you. Perfect to build back your strength."

Kuruks returned, and I watched with wide, eager eyes as Sakuru prepared a bowl of food for us. The pumpkin strips were sweet and nourishing, and the maize was delicious. I wanted to hurriedly finish the meal, but I remembered Sakuru's advice about the water and paced myself. When we were finished, I stood, but then kneeled back down as a wave of dizziness passed over me.

"Be careful," Kuruks said, reaching out to help.

"I'm fine," I replied. I stood again, this time more slowly. "I think I just got up too soon. I need some fresh air. Would you come with me, Kuruks?"

He looked at Sakuru as though he needed permission. "She is not our prisoner," she said with a laugh.

"I'm sorry," he replied.

"You're just watching out for me. And I love it. Now come, Kuruks, I want to see the sun."

Kuruks took my hand and we walked outside. The warmth of the midday sun felt good on my face. My vision took a while to adjust, so my view of the village was through squinted eyes. He led me to a secluded spot near the edge of the village, then checked to make sure no one else was around before lowering his guard.

"What's wrong?" I asked.

"I do not want to be caught by surprise again. I worry what my sister is planning."

"We will face it together," I said. "Try not to worry."

I could see, though, that he was still on alert. "I have something important to tell you."

My announcement garnered a bit more of his attention. "Kuruks, you have been so kind to me, so helpful. You have saved my life on numerous occasions, and given me the hope and courage I needed to carry on after losing my parents. My whole life was washed away in that river and you helped me rebuild it. Without you, I would have fallen apart. I want to thank you, again, for all that you've done."

"There is no need to thank me," he said. "You have told me this before."

I struggled to find words to express my feelings, but I knew that the direct approach would be best. I took Kuruks's strong yet gentle hands, gazed into his eyes, and savored our newfound connection. "I've fallen in love with you, but it's much more than that. I don't even know how to put it into words—"

"And I am in love with you. We said this at the ritual, but not with words."

"Precisely," I said. "And I think it is wonderful we don't need words to convey these kinds of emotions between us. But it is important to me I tell you. I want you to know, both in your heart, and in your mind, how I feel about you."

"I love you," Kuruks replied, then drew me closer and put his arms on my shoulders.

"I wanted you to know my appreciation for what you have done and my love for you are not connected. I have not fallen for you because you saved me. I have fallen in love with you because of who you are. You are an amazing man, Kuruks."

"I understand," he replied. "And I think you are a good woman."

I wanted to kiss him. My mother had always encouraged me to be plain with what I want and not be coy. During this train of thought, he gave me a hug. I savored his embrace, but wanted more. I dispensed with my trepidation and reached up and gave him a kiss. It was a quick peck. It was my first romantic kiss, so I wasn't entirely sure what I was doing. It didn't seem like that big of a deal.

Kuruks smiled, drew me in, and then gave me what I can now say was the first real kiss of my life. Our lips lingered in a very passionate, soft touch, and then afterwards, he grasped the back of my head and pulled me closer against his chest. Until that point, it was the best I had ever felt in my entire life.

I was so comfortable in our embrace. It knew that it was where I belonged.

"I don't know what is going to happen with the change that Sakuru has mentioned. She says I will lash out at those I love the most, and that is most certainly you."

"I will stand by you no matter what," Kuruks said.

"I cannot bear the thought of even saying a cross word to you. I don't know how we're going to get through this."

"But we will," he replied.

I don't know how long I stayed in his arms. I lost all track of time. I couldn't get close enough to him. Eventually, he pulled me back and smiled. "You should return to Sakuru. You are still weak."

"I am not weak. I feel strong."

"You are a strong woman. But you were sick from the poison. You need rest."

"I spent two days resting," I replied. "Isn't that enough?"

He knew I was right, but he couldn't admit it. There was care and concern in his eyes, and I loved it. "I know you're just looking out for me. Like you always have."

I was startled when Tuhre approached us. I apologized for jumping out of my skin, but then I remembered she didn't understand what I was saying. Kuruks greeted her and repeated their words in both their tongue and English.

"I heard about what happened with Paa," Tuhre said via Kuruks.

I wasn't sure how to respond, and Kuruks seemed to know this. "My sister is confused and angry," he said.

"Paa has a temper," Tuhre replied. "She has been angry with me, too."

As Tuhre continued, Kuruks smiled broadly and reinforced his tender embrace around me. It took him a while to translate, but he eventually relayed, "She is very happy for us."

"Thank you, Tuhre. Your acceptance means a lot to me."

Although I couldn't understand what she was saying, and I was certain that Kuruks wasn't translating everything precisely, I could tell that her expression was genuine. I was surprised at how accepting she was. It was in stark contrast to

121

the reaction I knew that my parents would have had. Even though my mother was open-minded, she would have her reservations, and my father would have certainly objected. That life was now behind me.

"I'm going to have to learn your language," I said.

"Sakuru taught me English," Kuruks replied. "She can teach you ours. I would teach you, but I am not good."

"You do just fine," I said reassuringly.

"If any of the women in our village treat you unfairly, tell me," Tuhre said. "I will help. I trust you because I trust Kuruks."

"I am honored," I replied. "I fear I may have to take advantage of your offer."

Tuhre left us, and we continued our embrace. I reached up to give Kuruks another kiss. "I can't possibly describe how much I love you."

"You did already," Kuruks replied.

I am certain the meaning of my words was lost in translation. I smiled, knowing our unspoken bond made up for my inability to express the depth of my emotions.

After a while, we walked back to Sakuru's home. Because of our cultural differences and my place as an outsider, I was unsure how to display my affection for Kuruks as we strolled through the village. I must have seemed a bit distant to him, and despite this, he didn't assume the worst. Instead, he proudly took my hand. Many of the villagers seemed concerned. The men ignored us, but most of the women had expressions of disapproval. I was immediately reminded of Tuhre's offer of assistance.

When we returned, we were greeted warmly by Sakuru. She looked at me strangely. "You told him, didn't you?"

I was embarrassed she discussed this in front of Kuruks. I nodded in agreement.

"I think you two make a wonderful couple."

"Tuhre was excited for us," I said.

"She is a good woman. I believe she will become a good friend of yours."

"Sakuru, I want to learn the Pawnee language. Will you teach me?"

"Of course. I was worried that you would not be interested."

I looked up at Kuruks. "I want to speak my love's native tongue. And, of course, communicate more effectively with you and the rest of the village."

"It will be my pleasure," Sakuru replied.

I was delighted that she agreed. I looked forward to learning something new and to have more in-depth conversations with Kuruks. I knew he often struggled to understand some of my words and to find the right phrases to express himself to me.

My time in the village had been very stressful. I had been dealing with one crisis or another since the moment I had arrived. I had completed the ritual and had a dangerous run in with Paa. Not only was I certain she would return but I had a supernatural transformation looming over me. This was no time to relax or to celebrate, and yet I felt comfortable and secure. I knew that times ahead would be difficult, but with Kuruks's love, I was confident in my ability to face them.

Sakuru, Kuruks, and I conversed throughout the evening, and we enjoyed a wonderful dinner. After a second large meal, my appetite was finally sated from my two-day fast. Afterwards, Sakuru taught me several Pawnee words. They chuckled a bit at my clumsy pronunciation, but after repeating a few of the phrases several times I became proficient. Before long, though, I could tell something was wrong.

"I feel strange," I observed, clutching my stomach.

Kuruks put his hand around my shoulder. The pain was intense. My perception tunneled and my thoughts became a blur.

"Poison still in her system?" Kuruks asked Sakuru.

"No, I don't think so," she replied. "Tell me what you are feeling?"

I couldn't reply. I ran outside and promptly vomited the entire contents of my dinner. I fell to my knees as I wiped my mouth, then turned and saw a concerned Kuruks and Sakuru behind me. I was shocked at the first thought that entered my mind: I wanted them to go away. I wanted nothing to do with them. I didn't say anything as I still barely had my wits about me, but that is what I was thinking. It was clear that they noticed my distressed state.

"Come sit down," Kuruks said.

I returned to my bedroll, my stomach still rumbling.

"What's wrong?" he asked insistently.

I shook my head and gritted my teeth, trying to suppress the strange and uncomfortable thoughts pouring through my head. Sakuru put a finger under my chin and lifted my gaze. She stared into my eyes a moment then gasped. "It has started."

"What?" Kuruks asked.

"The transformation."

"But I thought the poison—"

"No, that only delayed it."

It was infuriating to hear them talk about me as though I wasn't there. The grasp on my temper rapidly slipped.

"What can we do?" Kuruks asked.

I couldn't contain myself any longer. "You can stop asking her idiotic questions and give me some space!"

Chapter 18

"What?" Kuruks asked, clearly taken aback.

"Ignore her," Sakuru said.

I turned from them. My stomach eased, but the thoughts in my head grew darker.

"I can't," Kuruks admitted.

"Yes, you can," I replied under my breath. It was the most civil warning I could formulate.

"I warned you about this," Sakuru told him.

Kuruks ignored her and reached for me.

I know now his touch was meant as a loving, thoughtful gesture, but that's not how I took it. I spun around and flung his hands off of me. "Don't touch me!" I snarled.

He reached out again. "I want to help."

I pushed him away. He stood firm, and in my twisted frame of mind I took that as patronization. I shoved at him again, and he simply stood there. His lack of response angered me further. I yelled at him and shoved him as hard as I could, nearly knocking him over. He managed to steady himself and grab me by my shoulders.

"Let me go!" I screamed.

"Izzy, you need to—"

I broke free of his grasp, balled up my fist, and hit him as hard as I could. He fell to the ground and looked up at me in shock. His expression nearly killed the small fragment of sanity within me. That part wanted to help him up, to comfort him, apologize, and spend every moment I could making it up to him. But that part of me couldn't move. I fled the hut.

As I left, I heard Kuruks start to follow, but Sakuru must have held him back. I marched out into the fields until I was out of earshot of the village, then screamed as loud as I could. It was completely primal and unrestrained. Even though I was far away from the village I was sure everyone heard it.

My throat ached from my intense outpouring of emotion. Other than my guttural cry, there seemed no way to release the excruciating anguish inside me. I had never felt anything like that. I was mad at everything, including myself. I had no idea what to do.

I cannot explain what happened after that. What I do know is that a loud noise violently permeated every corner of my mind. It was a dull hum, but so high in volume it felt like it would shake me apart. Something peeled away from me, and then suddenly was above my body. I saw myself collapse, but I still hovered and watched it from a position a few feet above where my head used to be.

Was I dead? That was what I asked myself. But then I reasoned if I could ask a question of myself I probably wasn't. Somehow, I was detached from my body. I tried to move my arms to feel if I had any kind of form, but they didn't seem to be there. I tried to scream but I couldn't. I was pure energy and thought without form. It is the only halfway plausible explanation for my state of being.

Once I settled a bit from the initial shock of what just happened, I wondered how to get back into my body. To my surprise, I could slowly change my position with considerable effort, so I moved down to my body and tried to jump back into my head. I know the word *jump* sounds completely nonsensical, but I don't know how else to describe it. I reached out but nothing was happening. I panicked. Could I ever get back into my body again?

My next thoughts turned to Kuruks and Sakuru. I hoped they could help me figure out how to reunite with my physical being. As soon as I thought of them, I heard them talking. It was faint, but I managed to make out a few words. When Sakuru spoke it was louder, but I could hear them both. The horrible humming noise returned when I began to concentrate on what Sakuru was saying. I tried not to think of her to reduce the sound. It didn't work.

Suddenly, I moved at tremendous speed. Then, after an inexplicable jolt, I was looking at Kuruks. I tried to cry out to him for help, but I couldn't. I could only hear Sakuru speaking to him. I realized I was somehow in her head, listening to her speak. I tried to speak again, then resigned myself that a passive view may be the only connection I was able to maintain. The more I relaxed, the more clearly I could perceive what was around her. Despite the anguish, panic, and frustration, my only possible hope to escape this nightmare was to observe. I had no other options.

Chapter 19

"We cannot go after her, Kuruks."

Sakuru spoke those words, but it felt as though it came from me. I was inside Sakuru's head, listening to her speak.

"She may get hurt."

I noticed Kuruks was already developing a mark on his face from my strike. On top of that, the desperation and concern in his voice broke me. I wanted to hug him and apologize. Despite what I had done to him, there he was, nursing a wound that I had so savagely inflicted on him. All he cared about was my welfare.

"It will not go well. We need to give her time," Sakuru said.

"Time for what? She needs us. She needs me."

"She does not know what she needs right now. But it is not us."

Sakuru fetched a cool cloth and handed it to Kuruks. "It will help the swelling."

Kuruks didn't seem concerned, but at Sakuru's insistence, he used the cloth.

"You must listen to me, Kuruks. We have to give her some space."

"But what if she doesn't return?"

"She may not return on her own," Sakuru said. "But if we go after her now, we may lose her forever. This transformation can take time."

"How long?"

"Days, perhaps weeks."

"I will not wait weeks!" Kuruks yelled.

I certainly didn't want to wait weeks, either. The thought of being stuck outside my body for that long was not much better than the prospect of staying trapped in my own mind, a mind ravaged by some dark medicine.

Sakuru put her hand on Kuruks's shoulder. "I know you love her. I have grown quite fond of her myself. But we have to be patient."

"I cannot explain how much I love her," Kuruks said. "Our connection is deep. I have never felt like this about anyone."

I was touched my Kuruks's words. I felt our connection even though we were far apart.

"I love you too," I replied.

Kuruks gave Sakuru a strange look. "I... love you, Sakuru, too, of course," he awkwardly said.

"I didn't say that," Sakuru insisted.

"You did. I heard it."

"No, it wasn't me. Kuruks, I love you like a son. But that was not what I meant to say. I don't even know what I was going to say next. Maybe—"

"What?"

"I... I think someone is with us. Don't you feel a presence?"

Kuruks paused. "I am not sure. There is something."

"I feel love around us," Sakuru said. "It is a very strong love for you. It is not from me. It is romantic."

"Izzy!"

"Yes, perhaps." Sakuru paced while she pondered the situation. It was exciting to see them notice that I was around. Since Sakuru picked up on my love for Kuruks, I decided to intensify the feelings by concentrating on our connection even further.

"It is stronger," Kuruks said. "Why did I not know her spirit was here?"

"I have had more experience with spirits, Kuruks. Do not feel bad about it."

Kuruks jumped up with great urgency and put his hands on Sakuru's shoulders. "If we can feel her spirit, then, is she —"

"Dead?" Sakuru asked. "No. She is alive."

"Are you sure?"

"Yes. This is a different sensation from when the spirits of recently departed loved ones come to visit us. She is projecting herself. That means she has progressed much further than I would have thought."

"Can we talk to her?" Kuruks asked.

"I believe she can hear us now," Sakuru replied. "But she may not be able to speak."

Sakuru was correct, but it was clear that my direct thoughts could influence her. If I tried even harder, perhaps I could repeat my brief insertion of speech into their conversation. I concentrated on letting them know that I was alright but needed help getting back into my body. I thought of both Sakuru and Kuruks when I sent the message, and hoped that if they weren't able to realize the full intent of what I was saying they would be able to mutually agree on the general idea. After a few moments, it appeared to work.

"What if she cannot return to her body?" Kuruks asked.

I was surprised with how quickly he picked up on my thought.

"It's possible," Sakuru admitted.

Kuruks fetched a torch and lit it, then motioned to Sakuru. "Then she needs our help. Come on, let's go!"

I stayed with Sakuru as they left out into the night. Kuruks held the torch low to the ground and tried to locate my tracks, but was having difficulty. I concentrated on my path and within moments Sakuru gestured for Kuruks's attention.

"Isabella went that way," Sakuru said, pointing in the correct direction.

Kuruks smiled. "She is helping us."

The two walked through the fields until they found my body lying motionless on the ground. Kuruks rushed to my side and held my hand.

"She is cold!" Kuruks yelled.

Sakuru examined me then put her hand on Kuruks's shoulder. "She is not dead. Her heart beats and she draws breath."

Kuruks shook me. "Izzy, wake up!"

"That won't work," Sakuru said. "Let's get her home so that we can help her."

Sakuru had every intention of helping to carry me, but Kuruks picked me up in one swoop and walked back to the village. It was odd seeing myself being picked up by the man I loved so dearly through the eyes of another. This sight made me wish I was in my body even more – to feel his loving arms carry me to safety.

As they returned to the village, I took note of the fact I was completely devoid of the anger I had previously experienced. Even the anxiety I had when I had first separated had disappeared. The more time I spent away from my body the more I felt grateful. My understanding of my mind and the nature of spirit had considerably increased. I still wanted to reunite with my carnal form, but I couldn't deny the wonderful feeling that surrounded me.

I was sorry for what I had done to Kuruks, and bothered by the imposition I placed on both of them, but despite that, I wasn't in despair. I began to see it as a necessary step to complete my transformation. I wondered if I could complete my work outside my body. It was an appealing prospect, albeit at the terrible cost of not being able to physically interact with Kuruks. For that reason alone, I shoved that thought aside. Whatever I had to do to be with him again I would do. I hoped Sakuru could help.

As they took me inside Sakuru's home and laid me down on some blankets, I made the observation that I could adjust my point of view to be independent of Sakuru's. I found this less jarring and disorienting because I could dictate the direction of my vision. Kuruks took extra care to bundle me up as though it were frigid outside, and then lovingly ran his fingers through my hair to straighten out the tangles from lying in the field. Though I couldn't feel what he was doing, my soul was soothed by his compassionate gesture.

"You can help her, Sakuru, right?" Kuruks asked.

"I will try my best."

While I wanted to return to Kuruks, I also was becoming more enamored with my spirit form. The calm and reflective experience was intoxicating. I could analyze issues with clarity and without the distraction of conflicting emotions. I had never experienced such insight into my own life and the actions of others. I didn't want to leave.

"I will attempt to guide her," Sakuru announced, then took some tobacco and inhaled deeply from her pipe several times, filling the room with smoke. She then closed her eyes and began to meditate.

I soon felt her presence more acutely. I heard faint whispers from her stray thoughts. The more deeply she relaxed, the closer she approached my realm.

"Isabella. Please talk to me," Sakuru called to me telepathically. Her mouth didn't move, yet I heard her with unmistakable clarity.

"I am here, Sakuru," I said. "I am sorry for the trouble I have caused."

"Think nothing of it," she replied.

"Thank you."

"You are needed here, Isabella."

"I know. But it is peaceful and calm where I am. There is no suffering or pain. Things are so clear to me, now."

"We can interact with the spirit world whenever we want," she replied.

"I'm not as good at that as you."

"Your transformation has begun. You will have an even deeper connection to spirit."

"I have that connection now, Sakuru. Why leave it?"

"Your destiny cannot be fulfilled in the spirit realm. And your love, Kuruks, is lost without you. I know you can feel his pain."

She was right, of course, I could. I looked at Kuruks. It was heartbreaking to see him desperately scanning Sakuru's face for any sign of contact with me, yet the pull to remain in my current state was strong.

"Use the clarity of mind you have in the spirit realm to examine this carefully, without emotion. You came to this life to accomplish many things, Isabella."

I did as she asked. My thought process was different. Instead of using an inner dialog, I thought more in overall concepts, pictures, and sounds. I wasn't debating my own ego or sense of self, rather I examined the issue. It was a rich and deep experience. To adequately describe this process of mind would require words and concepts that are not found in our language.

After a moment of quiet contemplation, I replied with certainty, "You are right. I must return."

Sakuru broke her solemn, meditative demeanor and smiled. Her spirit reached out to me with a guiding embrace. "I can help you back into your body, Isabella. Imagine yourself lying on the ground, looking up as you would if you were awake."

I wasn't sure how to imagine anything in that state of mind. Normally when I thought of something I could see a scene in my head as though I were looking at a painting in motion. Instead, my entire current existence felt as though it were a figment of my imagination.

"How do I do that?" I asked.

"I will show you."

After she said that, I began to receive concepts from her that, at the time, I could not put into words. Rather than receiving images, sounds, or words, I began to gain knowledge from her. I can't exactly identify the mechanism she used to transmit it to me, but nevertheless I received it as though it originated within me.

Rather than attempt to imagine, I formed a connection with my body and began to let my consciousness flow into it, not unlike a river flows into a lake. I had been thinking in terms of physically moving to my body, but that was the incorrect approach. I had to establish a link with it and channel my very soul back into my physical form. From what I learned from Sakuru, this is the method our souls use to incarnate into this life. Our spirits link with, rather than completely fill, our physical bodies.

Within moments my perception went blank and everything went dark. The positively annoying vibration returned and I shook with a tremendous fury. I heaved upward, and then my vision returned. I saw the top of Sakuru's hut, and then two very concerned sets of eyes gazing at me.

"Welcome back, Isabella," Sakuru said to me in Pawnee.

I understood her perfectly.

Chapter 20

Kuruks's handsome face was the first sight I took in upon returning to my body. I wanted to tell him I was alright, but I couldn't move my mouth. After a moment, the shock of my return faded, and I found myself in full command of my faculties.

"I now speak Pawnee," I proudly declared. "You will both have an easier time understanding me."

"I understand you perfectly! Do you know what I'm saying?"

"Every word," I replied with confidence.

"She has no trace of an American accent," Kuruks observed to Sakuru.

"Can you still speak English?" Sakuru asked.

"I can," I replied in English.

"Fascinating," Sakuru said. "You have a native accent in both languages. I am impressed." She paused a moment. "Parlez-vous françois?"

"Non," I replied.

"And you speak French, too!"

I shrugged. "Sorry, I only know how to say yes and no in French."

Sakuru laughed. "It was worth a try."

"Everything is… different," I said.

Kuruks hugged me. "I'm so glad you're back."

I was jarred by his touch. He sensed it and backed away from me. "I'm sorry."

"No, no," I replied as I hugged him. "It's not you. I'm still getting used to being back in my body. And I assure you, my love, you have no reason to apologize."

I delicately touched the bruise on his face, hoping it wasn't sore. He tried to hide a wince. I gave it the gentlest kiss I could and held him.

"I cannot begin to express how sorry I am," I said.

"You don't have to—"

I put my finger over his lips. "No, I do. And I will apologize it until I'm convinced that you don't harbor a sliver of animosity towards me. I did and said horrible things to you."

"I don't. I promise."

"I still have to forgive myself, and I haven't. So, until then, please, do not tell me I don't have to apologize."

"I understand," Kuruks said. I'm not sure that he did, but it was clear he was giving me the space I needed to atone for what I had done.

"You are not responsible for what you did," Sakuru said.

"That's a nice sentiment, but if I am not, who is?" I asked.

"It is the transformation. It can be a dark medicine."

I sat fully upright and took a drink of water that Sakuru had offered me. "Before my parents died, I didn't believe in anything. I shared my mother's assertion that religion was just superstition. I see now that the spirit world is beyond what any book or legend can describe."

"I am envious of you," Sakuru admitted. "We can peek into the spirit world through meditation, but our soul does not separate from our body so drastically as what you experienced."

"You mean I can go back?"

"That's not exactly what I mean," Sakuru replied. "Do you want to go back?"

I almost answered yes, but then stopped myself. I put my arm back around Kuruks. "I am happy where I am."

He smiled at my reply.

"I see," Sakuru said. "Now that your transformation has begun, it will soon be time to share the full prophecy with you."

"I am ready now," I eagerly replied.

Sakuru shook her head. "No, you are not, Isabella. You need time to take in this experience."

"But we don't have time. Paa—"

"I doubt she will return anytime soon," Sakuru replied. "And even if she did, it's too late. Once the transformation has begun, it cannot be stopped. You need to rest and prepare for the next stage of your journey."

I started to protest, but the look on her face told me there would be little use. Kuruks extended his hand, "Come, Izzy. Let's go home."

I held Sakuru's hands. "Thank you."

"You are most welcome, Isabella. We will speak tomorrow."

"Good night."

Kuruks escorted me to a small home in the village. It was shaped just like Sakuru's – a large round room. In the middle were faintly glowing embers in a fire pit. He knelt and added wood to the fire, and within minutes the room was brightly lit. I could see that it was only sparsely decorated and had only a few pots and assorted items wrapped in blankets next to the outer wall.

"This is my home," he said. He took my hand and smiled. "Your home."

"It is lovely," I replied, though I wasn't being completely honest. It was functional, but certainly could use a woman's touch. Though Sakuru's home was modest compared to a typical American house, it had a wide assortment of beautiful blankets on the floor and an array of interesting knickknacks. Kuruks's home seemed bare and cold.

"I know it is not much," he admitted. "But you can make it nice."

Kuruks's suggestion took me by surprise. "You want me to decorate your home?"

"It will be our home."

"But we have not—"

"Chief will approve," he said confidently.

"Approve of–"

"Marriage," he replied. "You will make a great wife and we will have many healthy children."

I raised my finger in the air. "Now wait - don't you think you're getting a bit ahead of yourself?"

Kuruks seemed bewildered. I had heard rumors of Indians giving little regard to marriage ceremonies and even engaging in polyandrous arrangements, but I had lent them little credence.

"In my culture, we get married. Then we live together."

"Pawnee get married, too," Kuruks replied. "We love each other. I thought you approve."

I didn't know how to respond. I loved him dearly, but I hadn't thought much about marriage.

I sat on the ground. "Everything is happening so fast."

Kuruks sat next to me and put his arms around me. "I am sorry. I offended you."

"No, I love you very much. I just… we are different."

"I will do anything you want," he said. "I love you. I want you to marry me."

I had gone from my first kiss, separation of my spirit from my body, then to proposal for marriage. It took me a moment to let that fact settle. The more I thought about it, the more I realized the Pawnee didn't have the same concept of marriage. A ceremony or formal declaration beyond a passing reference seemed outside of his experience.

"This misunderstanding is not your fault," I said. "Our cultures look at marriage in a completely different way. It will take me some time to adjust."

"I understand," he said. "Marriage means to live together."

I kissed him and looked directly into his eyes. "You already have my heart, Kuruks. I will adapt. It will just take some time."

"I can adapt, too," he said. "You do not have to make all the changes."

"I appreciate that. But I'm in your home and in your village. It would be wrong of me to expect you to conform to my ways."

"We will do what you want. We will have," he paused, and hesitated as he said, "Christmas."

"You would love Christmas!"

"What is Christmas?"

I was too lost in thought to give him a simple answer to his question. "My mother didn't believe in Jesus. She said it was simply a time for family. I certainly know now that there is more to life than what you can see. I guess she has discovered this, too."

If I had listened to the fire and brimstone preacher in our town I would have feared my mother's soul was being tormented by all sorts of unspeakable demons in hell. But I knew such hate and fear didn't exist in the spirit world. I was calm, warm, and accepted as I was. The only horror I felt was briefly after separation from my carnal form. My fear came from the unknown, not from what existed beyond the veil.

"She is in a better place," I said. "That's what people say when someone dies, you know. I always thought they were just trying to be kind. But they are right. There is more."

"Our ancestors are always with us in spirit," Kuruks said.

"Yes. I remember you telling me that after my parents died. I didn't believe you. Oh, I wanted so desperately to believe you."

"We all will eventually rejoin our friends and family in spirit," Kuruks said. "That is why I think our people's religions are mostly the same. Just different rituals and traditions."

"We have some wonderful traditions. My mother and I baked the most delicious Christmas foods. I can't wait to share them with you."

"We will eat this Christmas, then, and it will be good."

"It is a holiday, not a food," I replied with a giggle. "We have much to learn about each other's worlds."

After our chuckle, the conversation slowly wound down and the pauses were increasingly filled with yawns. I was completely exhausted, and I knew Kuruks had to be tired from rescuing me from my insanity-filled evening. Even though we had both spent the night under the stars, it was somehow different for me since we had declared our love and we were alone in his home.

"I am not ready to sleep with you," I said, hoping to clear the air.

"We have already slept together," Kuruks replied with confusion.

"Yes, but… I am not ready for more. Not yet"

"That isn't what I meant," he replied.

"No, it wasn't," I realized. "I am being presumptive."

"I only want to be close to you."

"I do want to be with you in that way, Kuruks. Just not now. I… our cultures are quite different in this regard. I was raised to believe that sex is part of marriage."

"I understand," he said. "I want to sleep next to you. I will know you are safe. Someday, when you are ready, we will do more."

143

"Thank you. I would very much love to sleep next to you, Kuruks."

Back in Independence, it would have been scandalous for me to spend the night in an unmarried man's house. But I was beginning to shed those ways. My heart yearned to be near my love, and I simply couldn't pass up the opportunity. I took some of his extra blankets and spread them as neatly as I could around the bedroll, then we laid near the fire. I adored the feeling of his arms around me, holding me tight and protecting me. I could feel the intimacy we shared in my very core.

"I love you, Kuruks."

"It sounds better to hear you say that in Pawnee," he replied. "I love you, Izzy."

We spent quite a long time in silence, gazing into the fire. Eventually, I nestled my head in the bend of his arm. The beating of his heart lulled me to sleep.

Chapter 21

I woke before Kuruks, which was unusual. He was often the one to wake me. I wanted to prepare breakfast for him, so I looked at the food he had stored in his home. Most of the pots were empty, but I did find one with some dried meat. I took a tiny sample and found it to be sweet. I wasn't sure what it was, but I figured it would be suitable for breakfast.

I sorely missed coffee. Since I was twelve I had a cup every morning with breakfast. My mother made me wait until I was twelve because she said coffee wasn't good for little girls, but I sincerely doubted that statement even then. Perhaps she was referring to its addictive quality. If so, I can understand why she wanted to keep me from becoming addicted to the pleasant burst of energy it provided me in the morning.

I had seen ample amounts of wild berries near the village, so I took one of the empty pots and collected some water from the brook, then gathered some berries and returned. I boiled them in the water and poured two cups. I took a sip and noted that the water had a pleasant tartness to it. Back in Independence I would have declared it an acquired taste, but it was nice drinking something other than water for a change.

Kuruks began to stir, so I laid next to him and gave him a gentle kiss on the cheek.

"Good morning, love."

He returned the greeting with a smile before he opened his eyes.

"I have breakfast ready for us," I proudly declared.

Kuruks sat up and I handed him a cup of my simplistic but pleasing berry concoction. He took a large sip and nodded. "Very good."

I believe he was trying to make me feel better. "It's not that good. It needs more sweetness."

He looked at the cup, then took another drink. "It is not as good as your chamomile tea," he replied. "But I like it."

"That's not a good drink for the morning, it makes me tired." I took the meat out of the pot and handed him a piece. "I don't know what this is, but it tasted good, so I thought we might enjoy some."

He took a hearty bite. "Pemmican. Dried meat, fat, and berries. It keeps well."

"I wanted to prepare more food for you, but I'm not familiar with Pawnee cooking."

"You will learn. And maybe we can find ingredients for you to cook the foods you like."

"I am beginning to like your foods," I replied. "But I've considered sneaking into an American town to buy some coffee."

"We do not have their money," he said.

"I have a quarter."

I briefly paused to think about how much importance I had placed on that shortly after my accident. Now it seemed almost trivial.

"How much coffee will that buy?" he asked.

I sighed. "Just enough to make me wish I had more." I put my arms around him. "But I will gladly give up coffee for you, Kuruks."

After we finished our breakfast, he stood. "You need to learn how to use a bow to defend yourself."

"That's a good idea, but I don't have one," I replied. "I have the pistol — "

"Your pistol is useless once it runs out of bullets. I can show you how to make your own arrows." He carefully unwrapped a bow from a blanket and gave it to me. "For now, you can use mine."

I handed it back to him. "I don't want to be around anything sharp right now. I don't trust myself."

"What do you mean?"

I pointed to the mark on his face, but he shrugged off my concern. "I will tackle you if you become unruly."

His comment interrupted my self-deprecating train of thought. I laughed. "It's a deal."

"It takes years for someone to become an expert archer," Kuruks said. "Now, take it."

I accepted the bow and examined it. "Very nice," I said, admiring the handcrafting and delicate curvature of the wood. "Did you make this?"

"Yes, my father taught me."

"I would love to meet your parents. Though, I will admit, the thought makes me nervous. I can understand why they might be concerned about me."

"Both of my parents are dead," he replied.

I put my arms around him. "I'm sorry, I didn't know."

"It is a grief we share."

I thought of all of the times I expressed to him how much I missed my parents and immediately was filled with regret. "I'm sorry that I went on and on about my family."

"Do not be sorry," he said. "You did not know. But I know how you feel."

"How did they —"

"We need to train while it is still light," he said and clutched the bow.

I put my hand on his arm to get his attention. "Kuruks, tell me."

He looked away from me while he spoke. "Something happened with a group of settlers. I do not know what."

"Oh no," I replied. "Were these settlers brought to justice?"

"White men do not pay for crimes against Indians," Kuruks said.

"How long ago?"

"A few years."

"When you said Paa was your family, I didn't realize you meant that she was your only family. I feel terrible. I have come between you two and —"

"No," he interjected. "Paa already had anger in her heart. Our parent's death made it worse. It is not your fault."

I could see now that Paa had two reasons to be angry with me – denying her the prophecy she believed was hers, and being a reminder of the people responsible for her parent's death. I now understood the look in her eyes. It was more than jealousy. It was revenge.

"Paa has been through so much — "

"It's no excuse. She never thinks before she acts. My parents were wise and were sometimes able to help her. But I have failed."

I took his hand. He didn't immediately accept by touch. I could tell that he wasn't paying much attention to me or anything around him. He was lost in thought of his departed parents. I understood the look all too well.

"If she cannot use the unfortunate events in her life as an excuse, then neither should you bear the burden of her sanity. She is responsible for her own actions."

"Sakuru tried to help her. She has been like a mother to us. But Paa is stubborn."

"She is a kind woman and a great teacher," I replied.

Kuruks motioned for me to join him. "Now we practice with the bow."

"You don't like talking about yourself, do you?" I asked.

"No," he replied. He paused a moment as he looked at me. "But I will try. For you."

Kuruks and I held hands as we proceeded to a spot just outside the village that he said was his favorite area to train in archery. He showed me how to nock an arrow, draw the string, and aim at my target. He then handed the bow to me and guided me through the steps.

When I had full control of the bow, I feared that those horrible thoughts would return, but they didn't. Instead, I was gifted with an incredible sense of calm and clarity. The bow seemed to be a natural fit in my hands, and none of the motions that Kuruks had instructed me to make felt forced. It was as though my muscles remembered how to perform the actions. I pulled back on the string and released the arrow. It gracefully left my charge and flew well over a hundred yards.

Kuruks was surprised. He looked at me, then at the arrow, then returned his gaze to me. "You have done this before!"

"No, I haven't," I replied.

He studied my face for a moment.

"I promise."

"I suspected you would learn quickly. But I never imagined this."

"It was as though I have done it before," I replied.

"The spirits favor you."

I wasn't sure exactly what was guiding my hand, but my newfound expert skill in archery was undeniable.

"I will make you a bow," Kuruks said.

"Thank you. Hopefully I will only have to use it for hunting."

Kuruks spent the remainder of the day crafting my bow. He helped me pick out the wood and I watched with amazement as he created a true work of art. He smoothed the wood so that I wouldn't encounter splinters and strung it with deer sinew with considerable expertise. He worked right up until dusk, then proudly handed me the finished weapon.

"I will make a better one for you soon," he said. "But this will serve you for now."

"I am honored. Thank you."

"Sakuru will have food for us," Kuruks said.

After admiring his skill in woodworking, I wasn't hungry. I made a mischievous suggestion. "Let's go back home, first."

"Why?" he asked.

I couldn't think of any valid reason for my request. "I could tell you that I want to put away my new bow, but that wouldn't be telling the full truth."

There was no need to question my admission. Our deep connection telegraphed my desire for him without the need to exchange a word. I grabbed his hand and led him back to his house. As soon as we entered, I pulled him close and gave him a passionate kiss. He pulled away, his hands still holding my head, and stared at me with an intense longing that I had never seen in his eyes. I let my eyes lose focus, allowing my softened field of view to absorb every detail of his adoring gaze.

From the intensity of the next kiss, it was evident that he too yearned for more. His hands moved to my shoulders, pulling me even closer to him. The masculine scent from the thin layer of sweat he had accumulated while making my bow was no longer just endearing, it became something I desperately craved. I instinctively tilted my head back, encouraging him to kiss my neck. He obliged.

I caressed his hair as his warm lips slowly worked their way to my shoulders. His pace slowed as though he was awaiting my permission to proceed further. I was grateful he respected my limits, but my body cared not for the increasing signs of his compassionate restraint. I leaned back to encourage his gentle caress with his mouth to continue. To my dismay, he stopped.

Before I could tell him he didn't have to stop on my account, his hands moved to my waist. His head moved back a bit, making no attempt to hide the fact that he was giving my figure a complete appraisal. He then slowly slid his hands to my breasts and gently held them through my dress. I inhaled sharply as the muscles throughout my body tensed in anticipation. I saw the admiration in his gaze, and I felt wanted. His gentle caress of my breasts excited me so much that I noticed myself panting.

In one smooth motion, as if it were choreographed, we moved to the floor. I worried that my nervous anticipation would cause me fall, but he easily handled my weight as he guided me on my back. Seeing him over me stirred powerful feelings within me. After unfastening the buttons on my dress, his lips moved to embrace the exposed skin. I instinctively arched my back as he took a nipple into his mouth, urgently wanting to draw myself closer to him.

His lips left my breasts and began to move down to my stomach. The sensation was intensely erotic and yet exquisitely tickling. My abdominal muscles tightened as his tongue worked its way to my navel. I desperately wanted him to go further, but the voice of doubt and inhibition in my head that I had so easily blocked out began to rear its ugly head.

As its judgmental drumbeat grew louder, I bargained with it, pleading that I could just let his lips linger no further than my breasts, but the intoxicating motions of his tongue on my torso made it nearly impossible to stop. The imaginary lines I was drawing were being crossed with no resistance. Despite all odds, I somehow regained my sanity. I grabbed his head and urged him back up to my face.

"We can't do this. Not yet."

I knew he was disappointed, but he didn't show it. He pulled away. "I am sorry. I did not mean to—"

I put my finger over his lips. "It's not your fault. I got carried away. You were just doing what I wanted."

"Then why stop?"

I hated his question. My body saw his perfectly reasonable logic as carte blanche to give into the desires that were raging inside me. In a protest against my inhibitions, I reached up and grabbed him, then pushed him back onto the ground and straddled him. I finished unbuttoning the last few buttons on my dress and arched my back as he ran his hands all over my chest.

The wetness from his kisses covered my chest, and it cooled my skin. My body responded with the prickling sensation of goosebumps. To quell the chill, and to rebelliously fight the urge to behave, I leaned over and kissed him, then moved up further and let the very tips of my breasts hover just out of reach of his lips. He reached up to take them into his mouth, and I pulled them out of the way, taking pleasure in teasing him.

Despite the sense of erotic empowerment I had gained, I suffered for my coyness. I desperately yearned for the warmth of his lips, and I figured he had waited long enough. I gave in and let him freely caress every inch of my breasts with his tongue until we were startled by a noise. I turned to see Sakuru rushing out of the room. I raced to button my dress as Kuruks prepared to leave, but I stopped him.

"I'll handle this," I said as I adjusted my clothes. "Stay here."

Chapter 22

I rushed outside to catch up with Sakuru.

"I'm sorry," she said. "I didn't mean to interrupt. I should've asked before entering."

"It's alright," I replied. "Look, I am—"

Sakuru shook her head. "No, don't apologize. You did nothing wrong."

"I'm not so sure about that," I replied. "I was enjoying myself just a bit too much. If you hadn't interrupted us, I likely would have—"

"Done something completely natural with the man you love, right?"

The only reply I could offer was an awkward stammer. Sakuru pulled a twig from my hair as I tried to find my words.

"You are a beautiful young woman in love with a handsome man. There is nothing wrong with enjoying each other's bodies."

I wondered if Sakuru wasn't regarding my growing embarrassment as a challenge. "You have not been with a man before, have you?"

"Of course not," I replied.

"Then your shyness is completely understandable. It will fade."

"I am impressed with the confidence you approach the subject."

"Well, Isabella, I have had a lot of sex," Sakuru plainly declared. "I quite enjoy it. Well, used to. I have not taken a lover in quite some time."

"Why not?" I immediately realized how personal my question was and tried to retract it. "I'm sorry, I shouldn't have asked."

"If I don't want to answer your question, I won't."

I expected her to continue, but she didn't. I didn't think I could possibly feel more awkward. I rushed to fill the void of uncomfortable silence. "Oh, I didn't mean—"

"Do not worry, Isabella. I don't have an answer for you because I don't know. Something has been holding me back. I am not sure what."

"You could have just told me that. I thought you were offended."

Sakuru laughed. "You're right - I should have. But I am having too much fun at your expense. You so clearly want to be with him and are ashamed to admit it. I know it is the way of your people, but I find it humorous."

I was too tense to share her humor. "I was taught differently."

Sakuru put her hand on my shoulder. "I know. And you have shown remarkable patience with our ways. I should do the same."

"I would have asked my mother how to handle this kind of situation."

"What do you think she would say?"

"I think she would encourage me to get married."

"And you will. But that is what your culture has taught you. Think of her, then look into your heart for the answer."

I gave her question careful contemplation. "She would tell me that life is short."

"The path of the Child of Darkness is not easy," Sakuru replied. "It is filled with peril and uncertainty. We are not guaranteed any length of time with our loved ones."

"Can you marry us?" I asked.

"You do not need anyone to marry you. The two of you simply need to make solemn vows with each other. It is not a commitment to be taken lightly."

"Will he ever take another wife?" I asked, hoping for the answer I wanted. "I heard that Pawnee marriages are sometimes shared with multiple partners."

"I do not know," she replied. "Will you take another husband? These matters are entirely up to the two of you. I am sure that Kuruks will honor your wishes if you do not wish to share him."

"I don't," I replied adamantly. "I don't want to break your customs, but I believe marriage is for two people, not a crowd."

"I can respect that. And since he loves you, I am certain he will, too. Do not fret over such things, Isabella. He loves you dearly."

"I have a lot to think about."

"Yes, but not tonight. Now you must eat. Go tell Kuruks that I have dinner ready."

When I arrived back in his home I found him fully dressed and patiently waiting for my return.

"Thank you for letting me handle that," I said. I sat and put my arm around him. "I was horribly embarrassed. In my culture, I would have endured quite a negative label for what she saw. But instead she was merely sorry that she intruded."

"We do not worry about sex as much as white people do."

"At first I thought that was bad. But I am beginning to see things differently."

Kuruks pulled away. "Still, you were not ready, and I let things get too far out of hand."

I reached over and gave him a kiss. "It was both of us. And, right before she walked in, it was mostly me. Kuruks, I want to be with you. I'm just... scared."

"There is nothing to be scared of," he said, putting his hand on my face. "As long as I can hold you close to me at night and hold your hand by day, I will be fine."

"Of course. The rest will come soon, I promise."

I gave him another kiss and then we walked to Sakuru's house.

"We will eat well tonight," she announced with pride as we entered her house.

I looked at the meat she had prepared but couldn't identify it.

"It is elk."

"I've never had it before," I replied. "I've been too dependent upon your gracious hospitality. I hope you can show me some Pawnee recipes. I want to earn my boarding."

Sakuru chuckled. "I've enjoyed cooking for you. And I'll show you some of our meals if you will teach me how to make American bread."

I initially thought it was strange that she didn't know how to bake bread, but then I remembered that wheat was not a typical part of their diet.

"I'd be glad to," I said. "But we'll have to find some wheat flour."

"I will see what I can do. In the meantime, enjoy some of this fine elk."

I was expecting a gamey taste, but I was pleasantly surprised. The meat had a faint, pleasant sweetness. I complimented Sakuru on her cooking. After dinner, I showed her the bow that Kuruks had made for me.

"Your father would be proud," she said. "You are a fine craftsman, Kuruks."

He accepted her compliment with a simple smile. "She is an expert with the bow."

"I told you that you would learn quickly."

"It was more than that, Sakuru. I can't explain it. I picked up the bow and fired an arrow as if I had done so a thousand times before."

"The skills of our ancestors are sometimes inherited. Pair that with your powers and this is easily explained."

Sakuru's simplistic appraisal of my newfound proficiency with archery didn't quite satisfy me, but I had little else to go on.

"When you first arrived at our village, I was worried about how you would handle your destiny. But after seeing how far you've progressed, I believe it is time to teach you the full prophecy of the Child of Darkness."

"I am eager to learn," I replied.

"I will teach you the sacred song tomorrow evening."

"I appreciate your trust in me," I replied. "Not too long ago I thought all of this was complete nonsense. And then when I did finally admit there were things I didn't understand, I tried to shrug my own responsibility."

"We are never the person we were yesterday," Sakuru said. "With each sunrise we are born anew, learning from our previous mistakes and making new ones before sunset. Remember that it is a privilege to be a part of this cycle of learning - of living."

"You are wise, Sakuru."

"Only because I have had many sunsets to ponder my mistakes. You are well on your path to wisdom, despite your young age. Kuruks, you have picked an excellent wife."

"Fiancée," I corrected in English. I didn't know the Pawnee word.

Kuruks looked at Sakuru with a puzzled expression. "It means soon to be wife," she translated for him.

"You two should get some sleep," Sakuru said. "I want your mind well rested for tomorrow, Isabella."

I nodded. "Thank you for dinner."

"That reminds me," she said as she handed a basket to me. "Here is more meat for your breakfast, and some other ingredients you will need. You can cook the root vegetables near the fire."

Kuruks chuckled. "She is getting tired of feeding us."

"He's right," I replied. "If I am to be his wife, I should be feeding him."

"It was not a criticism," he insisted.

"These old bones don't move well in the morning. You'll be on your own for breakfast."

"You are not old," Kuruks said.

"I'm older than you know," she replied. "Although the art of Pawnee cooking is quite low on the list of your priorities at the moment, I will show you a few things tomorrow."

"Thank you," I replied.

We bade Sakuru goodnight and returned to our home. While I was putting away the food that she had given us, I noticed that Kuruks was rubbing his shoulder. I asked him to sit near the fire, then proceeded to rub his back and neck. I did my best to repress my thoughts as my hands ran over his muscles.

"I do not know why I am so sore," he said. "I only made a bow. I have done more strenuous work without discomfort."

"You're getting old," I explained.

"I am not old."

"I'm just joking, Kuruks. Though, you're older than me. How much younger is Paa?"

"Best I recall, five winters passed between our births."

"So, you're in your early twenties, then," I said. "As I said, and old man. Is that better?"

He rotated his shoulder blade. "That feels much better. Thank you, Izzy."

"No need to thank me."

"Are you sore?" he asked. "I will be glad to rub your shoulders."

"No," I replied. "But I would like you to do something for me if you don't mind. It has been ages since I've been able to properly brush my hair. I love the feeling of having my hair brushed, but since I don't have one, I would gladly settle for you running your fingers through it."

"I would be glad to. But I do have a hairbrush," he said as he went over to search his possessions. He produced a strange looking bristled brush with a short, stocky handle. "This was my mother's. You can have it."

"Thank you," I replied as I examined it. The bristles stuck straight out of the wood like a paintbrush. Despite its odd design, I ran it through my hair and found it to be very suitable. He sat behind me and used it to brush my hair.

"Your hair is very different from Pawnee women. It is lighter and… swirling."

"Curly?" I asked in English, running my finger through a curl at the tip of my hair.

"Is that the word? Alright, curly. It is beautiful."

"My hair isn't that curly," I replied. "But it does tend to curl at the ends."

"I like it," he said.

"Your friend Tuhre has very nice hair," I remarked. "I love how dark it is."

At the risk of interrupting the wonderfully soothing feeling I enjoyed, I felt the need to ask him more about her. I didn't want to sound jealous, but I was curious about their relationship.

"You said you have been friends with Tuhre for a long time. Was there ever anything more between you two?"

"I never felt for her like I do you," he replied. "She is a friend."

While I was relieved to hear that, his reply didn't answer what I wanted to know. I decided to be direct with my request. "Please don't take offense to me asking, but was she ever more than a friend?"

"It is your right to know," Kuruks replied. "I take no offense. I have never loved her. But we have been close."

"How close?"

I could feel his body before he answered. "We have been intimate with each other, if that is what you mean. It was quite some time ago."

I wasn't completely surprised by his answer, but nevertheless it sent a cold chill through me. His words hurt, yet I had no reason to feel hurt. I regretted having asked, but my curiosity had gotten the better of me.

"Does this bother you?" he asked.

"A little, yes."

"We care for each other," he said. "But we were learning. There is no reason to worry."

"You have an advantage over me," I replied. "You do know what you're doing."

"You will not do anything wrong," he reassured me. "Please do not worry."

"You won't grow tired of waiting on me?"

"No. I will happily wait as long as you need me to."

"I want to be closer to you, Kuruks. You have been very patient."

"I understand."

I wasn't sure he did, but I deeply admired his restraint. "I want to give more of myself to you, but I'm not fully ready to go further. I don't want to tease you unmercifully, either."

"Go at your own pace," he said. "But I will not turn down anything you offer."

I laughed. "I wouldn't expect you to. In fact, I think I'd be offended."

I decided then and there that he had been patient enough, and I wanted to show him my appreciation for his kindness and compassion. I stood and completely removed my clothes, then sat back down and kissed him very passionately. He was a bit hesitant at first, but my advances were rather insistent.

"We should be careful," he warned.

"I'll be careful," I said. "You should throw caution to the wind."

I took off his shirt and pushed him gently onto his back, then finished removing his garments. I was simultaneously flattered and intimidated by how excited he was. I examined him in detail, getting to know every inch of the man I would soon marry.

"I want to make you feel good," I said. "But I am ashamed to admit I don't know how."

"There is no shame in that," he replied, then took his hand and guided me.

At first, I was anxious about touching him so intimately, but he was kind and gentle.

"You've put up with all of my merciless teasing. You're an amazing man."

I surrounded him firmly with my hand and began to stroke him. I wasn't sure what I was doing, as evident by his need to take my hand and guide me, with loving reassurance, through his preferred motion. But his groans of appreciation and warm smile helped me feel as though I wasn't a complete novice. Even in a moment completely about him, he made a deliberate effort to ensure I was comfortable with what I was doing.

I grew more confident in my efforts and began to experiment with different speeds and grips. His sensual moans and the feel of his hands running through my hair excited me. His breathing quickened, his muscles tightened, and he began to rock his hips in the steady rhythm that I had established. Soon after, he suddenly set free the strain of the torture my sexual rigidity had caused. I was startled by his substantial release.

Kuruks stared into my eyes with the deepest, most sincere expression I had ever seen from him. He was vulnerable and exposed at his most intimate moment, and I was privileged to share such a special time with him.

"It is not fair that I get to have all the fun."

"I had fun," I replied.

He sat up and kissed me. "I can make you feel just as good."

165

"I'm not ready for sex," I admitted.

He shook his head. "That is not what I mean. I can touch you the same way you touched me."

"Why?"

"You will just have to trust me. Lie down and I will show you."

I trusted him, so I did as he asked. He noticed me shaking from nerves. "There is nothing to be afraid of."

Kuruks held me and slowly brushed his open mouth along my neck. The warmth of his breath and the anticipation of his touch sent shivers over my body. After returning a moment of teasing that I had so mercilessly given to him, his lips found mine. He gracefully followed the contours of my body from my throat down between my breasts and caressed my stomach.

My anxiety gave way to a fiercely burning desire within me. He placed his hand between my legs and held it there a moment. My hips involuntarily moved to meet him. It was an interesting sensation, but I was puzzled as to what he intended to do.

"It feels good," I said.

"I haven't started yet," he replied with a chuckle.

When he first moved his fingers, it felt like he was tickling me. I laughed and squirmed a bit until I realized that it wasn't his aim. After a few seconds, the tickling sensation settled and I started to understand what he was doing. A pleasurable sensation built with each stroke of his fingers. He continued this for some time, and eventually my nervous hesitation completely melted away and my hips began to move with him. Something began to feel strange, so I put my hand on his arm and asked him to stop.

"What's wrong?" he asked.

"I don't know. It feels different."

"I am not hurting you, am I?"

"No," I replied.

"Be patient. It will feel better."

I nodded and he resumed. Within moments the strange sensation returned. I decided this time I wouldn't fight it. He leaned his head down and began to gently suckle my breast. Soon, the sensations began to move throughout my entire body. My breathing turned into a pant and beads of sweat formed on my skin. I was completely consumed by the wonderful feelings emanating from his delicate efforts. I arched my back, then began to spasm. I cried out with surprisingly intense pleasure. He held me with his other arm as I rode the waves of ecstasy.

His loving grip on me helped return me to reality as the exquisite sensations diminished. When I regained my senses, I looked to see him staring at me with an enamored gaze. My skin was wet with sweat.

"That felt more than better," I said.

"How did it feel?" he asked.

I struggled to find words to describe the experience. "I… It was, well… amazing." I had to pause a moment to catch my breath. "Amazing is an understatement. It was so intense. And completely overwhelming."

"You made me feel just as good."

"I want to do that a lot more of that," I eagerly replied. "But tomorrow. Definitely tomorrow. I am so tired."

"Me too," he said as he laid his head on my breast.

I was completely drained of energy. I didn't want to move, but summoned the energy to pull the blanket over us. It was usually me who fell asleep on his chest, but this time it was the reverse. His lips pursed when he exhaled, and he was softly snoring. I closed my eyes and fell asleep within seconds.

Chapter 23

I woke in the middle of the night. Something was wrong.

A female whispered near me. "Such beautiful hair. Light, brown, silken strands."

Paa sat on the floor next to me with a lock of my hair in her fingers. I was too terrified to move.

"I sense fear in you. That's good. You should fear me. But I did not come to fight."

I reached to wake Kuruks, but she grabbed my hand. "Don't." I opened my mouth to yell but she put her other hand over it. "I said, no."

I flung her hand from my face and jerked my wrist free. "What do you want?"

Paa put her finger over her lips. "Be quiet. We don't want to wake my brother. Let's talk in private."

"I'm not going anywhere."

"Like I told you, I did not come to fight. Let's peacefully discuss this situation."

"But, I—"

"The Child of Darkness needs no escort." She motioned to the door. "Come, now."

I was hesitant, but I relented to her demand. I slipped on my dress and followed her outside. She took a torch that she had staked in the ground and we walked a few hundred paces from Kuruks's house.

"What do you want, Paa?"

"To talk," she replied.

"Make it quick."

"You now speak our language," Paa observed. "I'm impressed. You come to our village, ingratiate yourself with our customs and traditions, whore yourself out to my brother, and—"

My fist connected with her mouth as a fit of rage flew over me. Dark, violent thoughts surged within me as I knocked her to the ground. It took a moment for her to regain her footing. I picked up the torch that had flung out of her hand and held it between us. I could see her lip bled. She laughed as she wiped away the blood.

"Alright, maybe whore was a strong word."

"I find you far too obsessed with your brother's intimate affairs for my taste. Get to the point or I'll shove this down your throat."

Paa stood and smiled. "I like this new you. You're so… tough. You've got a little temper on you."

I pushed the torch dangerously close to her face.

"I have come to propose a compromise," she said.

I pulled the torch away. "I'm listening."

"You leave and forget all of this happened. And I'll spare your life."

She grabbed my arm as I walked away from her threat. Anger flared at her touch. "Let go of me," I seethed.

She relinquished her grip.

"You must think I'm an idiot, Paa. That's no compromise. I am the Child of Darkness."

"I am the Child of Darkness," she repeated in a mocking tone. "How disgusting. You've actually convinced yourself of that."

"You have one more chance to tell me what you want before I leave and wake your brother."

"I have discovered a way to remove the curse from you and return it to its rightful owner. I say curse, because the medicine that flows within you is not a blessing, Isabella."

There was a hint of truth to what she was saying. Despite its benefits, the rage, violent thoughts, and confusion were not something I enjoyed.

"You're probably lying, but I'll briefly entertain this fiction. How would you do it?"

"Just as a ritual hastened the medicine, another can free it from you."

"Sakuru never mentioned that."

"Of course she didn't. She'd much rather have you fulfill her precious prophecy. I refused to allow her to control me."

I laughed. "You pretend like you had a choice in the matter."

Paa flashed a livid expression. She caught herself and took a deep breath, presumably trying to remain calm to bolster my interest in her plan.

"I can't trust you, Paa."

"You're right," she admitted. "But that's not my problem. You'll be the one who pays dearly, not me."

"What do you mean?"

"Do you honestly think that all of that power comes without a price?"

171

"Sakuru never —"

"Sakuru is not the benevolent woman you think she is. She has her own interests, and you are simply being used as a tool to achieve them. You are so naïve."

"We all have our own interests," I replied. "But yours are so painfully obvious. You want to be the Child of Darkness because you have allowed darkness to consume you long ago. It fits you well."

Paa laughed. "I see you've been listening to my brother. He doesn't understand me."

"I think he knows you better than you realize. And I can relate to you more than you might think. Most of your family is gone and you're mad at the world. Instead of battling the darkness, you embraced it."

"Darkness gives me strength," she replied and wiped her lip again. She held her blood-stained finger towards me. "You channeled that darkness for revenge. You are no different than me."

"I didn't try to kill you!"

"You could have. You could now, too. You just don't realize it. The medicine flowing within you is the strongest there is."

Her pointed brought a resurgence of that rage I was trying to control. The fact that there was some truth in her words angered me more than anything else. I clenched my fist.

"Go ahead, Isabella. You've already stolen my identity - might as well steal my life!"

I resisted the fury within me with all of the strength I could muster. I wanted to pound her snide, petty, jealous, and admittedly insightful face into the ground.

"The more you give into the anger the easier it will become to channel it. You will become used to it. Use it on me. Finish me off."

I threw down the torch and put my hands around her neck. My fingers ached with tension as I resisted the urge to silence her. Paa lifted her chin, presenting the most vulnerable part of her body to me to do with as I pleased. I wanted her to die. I began to press hard. I felt her blood rushing through her veins and the tough cartilage of her throat. My problems would be over with so little effort.

"Izzy!"

I was livid. I knew Kuruks was approaching and my window of opportunity was closing. I couldn't kill his sister in front of him. I relaxed my grip but kept hold of her neck.

"What are you doing?"

I released Paa and flung her to the ground. Kuruks picked up the torch and hovered it near me. "Are you alright?"

"Why are you asking her, brother?" Paa demanded in a raspy voice.

"What have you done to her?"

"I came to make peace," Paa insisted.

Kuruks looked confused as he appraised the situation. "Did she attack you?"

"No," I replied, realizing that it would make me look horrible in his eyes.

"You're angry about the poison arrow," Kuruks said. "Paa, go! You're not welcome."

I couldn't bear to listen to Kuruks's equivocations for my behavior. I looked away.

"We are family!" Paa yelled.

"So is Izzy! I have asked her to marry me. She will be your sister."

"No," Paa replied, backing up. "This is not right, Kuruks. She is using you."

Kuruks stood firm. "If you cannot be civil, go!"

"You will regret this!" Paa yelled. "I will give you two days to consider my offer, Isabella. After that—"

"Now!" Kuruks yelled. I jumped at the intensity in his voice.

He rushed to me and put his arms around me. "I am sorry."

Tears fell as regret washed over me for the way I treated his sister. I nearly killed her. I certainly wanted to. He tried to turn me to look at him, but I refused. I was so ashamed. He moved in front of me and held me as I sobbed.

"She will never hurt you again," he consoled.

His soothing words made my heart ache that much more. He led me back to his house and we laid down. He silently held me securely in his arms. I desperately wanted to ask what he was thinking, but was even more afraid of the answer. Worse yet, I suspected he thought the best of my intentions. That pained me even more.

"I love you, Izzy," he said, pulling me closer.

I dried my face and looked at him. "I love you. You are too kind and patient with me."

"You are going through a difficult time," he replied.

"I've been going through a difficult time since I met you. And you've put up with it. Have you once stopped to consider that your sister may be telling you the truth?"

"Not once. I trust you."

"She's filled with darkness," I said. "But so am I. Are you sure there is a difference?"

"I love Paa because she is my sister. I love you because of who you are. You did not seek the darkness, but she did."

"Are you not going to ask why I was trying to choke her?"

"She tried to kill you."

"That doesn't justify what I did, Kuruks."

"You defended yourself. You are a good person."

"I'm not so sure," I admitted.

"Good people are not good all of the time."

His wisdom was simple and undeniable. "You are such a kind soul to be so forgiving. I wish I saw myself as you see me."

"Maybe you will in time," he replied. "What offer did she make to you?"

"She offered to remove the medicine from me and become the Child of Darkness."

"I am not surprised. She is always scheming."

The conversation slowed and I became lost in the thought of my conversation with Paa and the offer she made. While I had no intention of accepting her self-serving bargain, I was bothered by her insistence that there would be a hidden price and that Sakuru was keeping something from me.

"What are you thinking?"

"Oh, sorry. Just something Paa said."

"You cannot believe everything she says."

"Paa may have been right about one thing: Sakuru may be hiding something from me."

"I have never known Sakuru to lie," Kuruks insisted. "I would believe her over Paa."

"I am not saying she's lying. I don't know. I will ask her tomorrow."

"We should get to sleep."

I closed my eyes and tried to relax. I found it difficult to settle down after what had happened. Violence was not in my nature and yet I hit two people in as many days. I was a stranger in my own body. After a long bout of persistent worrying, I succumbed to sheer exhaustion.

Chapter 24

I closed my eyes and grunted when Kuruks stirred. I pulled him closer as he ran his hand through my hair. We shared a gentle, loving kiss, then fell back asleep. He woke me again shortly before noon.

"We should eat outside," Kuruks suggested. "It's a beautiful day."

"That sounds wonderful."

I packed a light meal, then we headed out into the plains. We took our bows for protection, hoping we wouldn't need them. We walked westward until we ran upon a small brook nestled by a grove of trees. Our conversation in the Pawnee language flowed smoothly and was enriched with nuance that wasn't possible without using Kuruks's native tongue.

"I never thought I'd say this, but I miss wandering about with you. I know it was difficult, and we faced a lot of challenges, but there was something wonderful about us being the only ones around for miles."

"We are alone now."

"The village is an hour away, and that's not far enough. I want you all to myself."

"We do not have to live in the village. We could build a home anywhere you want."

"My family was headed to Oregon," I said. "I thought I'd end up there."

"White people will not welcome me," he replied. "Especially since I am with you."

"In Independence, I would agree with you. But I am not sure about Oregon. I heard there are lots of Indians there. Perhaps they would welcome us."

"At some point, all Pawnee will have to move west."

"Probably," I replied. "But our home is wherever we make it. As long as we're together."

Kuruks pulled me closer. "I agree. We will go anywhere you want to go."

"I feel the same way. Someone has to make a decision."

"We will end up where we are meant to be," Kuruks said.

I think he had more trust in fate than I, but I could offer no better suggestion at the time. Perhaps, I thought, with Kuruks', Sakuru's, and Tuhre's help, I could manage to make a decent living in the village. Any domestic planning would have to be put on hold until the situation with Paa and the prophecy was settled. I had so many questions unanswered, and my mind began to drift into an anxious loop.

"I will find out tonight," I said.

"I don't understand."

"Sorry. I was thinking out loud. Sakuru will tell me the full prophecy this evening. Our life together can't begin until we know what we're dealing with."

"We are living it now, Izzy."

I couldn't argue with that. After lunch, we held each other as the sound of the brook and the warm breeze lulled me into deep relaxation. I drifted off to sleep on his chest.

Kuruks nudged me awake and put his finger over his mouth, instructing me to keep quiet. I looked but didn't see anything. He continued surveying the fields around us.

I put my arm on his shoulder. "What do you see?" I whispered.

The western skies were darkening, but he wasn't interested in the weather. He pointed to a covered wagon far into the distance. We spoke in the faintest of whispers.

"Settlers. They're quite far off the trail," I observed. "They aren't going to hurt us."

"They may not hurt you, but they won't like me here."

"We have every right to be where we want."

They were crossing from east to west, perpendicular to our location. There was no indication they saw us. I noticed Kuruks was watching me as much as he was them. He had a firm grip on his bow.

"I don't trust them."

"I was one of them not long ago," I replied.

Just as they faded into the distance, they stopped. Fear began to overtake me. My heartbeat raced as my mind created a slew of improbable scenarios. What if they were turning to attack us? Kuruks would surely fight them and he might be hurt. Or worse. I cursed myself for leaving the pistol with Sakuru. A crack of thunder rumbled in the distance, startling me half to death.

"Maybe they're worried about the storm."

He reassuringly put his hand on my shoulder. I couldn't believe I feared my own countrymen.

"I'm worried about the storm, too," I replied.

I managed to distract myself by focusing on the weather. The clouds were dark and ominously low to the ground. A bolt of lightning transversed the shadowy void between the blue sky and the menacing thunderhead.

"We need to wait until they leave," Kuruks said.

Some of the anger from the transformation resurfaced, quickly quelling my anxiety and stirred intense feelings inside me against the settlers. It was difficult to resist the urge to rush after them. Another rumble of thunder shook the ground.

"I won't go with them," I said defiantly. "I'll stand and fight with you."

"That won't be necessary," he replied.

The pioneers started to move again, adjusting their course to the south to avoid the worst part of the storm. While part of me breathed a sigh of relief, my anger was unsatisfied.

I realized at that moment that I had a new identity. I couldn't consider myself an American, at least not using the commonly accepted definition. To be transformed from an average white woman living on the edge of the frontier to the central role in some strange Indian prophecy in such a short period of time was quite a tumultuous, yet enlightening experience. The remaining fear and anger faded as I contemplated this enormous change within me. As we watched them completely fade from view, I tried to explain my profound, transformative epiphany to Kuruks.

"I was born with them, but I am more Pawnee now than they would ever understand. My home is with you." I took his hands and put them over my heart. "This is yours, Kuruks."

He smiled warmly. "I love you, Izzy. Now, if we hurry, we might make it back before the storm hits."

We wasted no time in gathering our belongings and made our way back to the village. Thunder and lightning drew closer and a cool wind blew behind us. A terrible downpour began to fall as we reached the village, soaking us from head to toe. The storm filled the air with crackling energy. I feared we would be hit by the blindingly bright streaks of lightning. We ducked into Sakuru's hut before the terrific winds began to howl through the village.

"Look at you two!"

"I hope we'll be safe in here," I said.

"Yes," Sakuru replied. "We build our homes to withstand the storms of the plains. But you won't be safe from catching a cold if you two don't get out of those wet clothes."

Kuruks started to strip his clothing.

"Do we have to remove everything?" I asked.

"I have already seen you naked," Kuruks replied.

"Yes, but—"

"Then I will make you more comfortable," he said, then resumed until he was fully nude, then put his clothes near the fire to dry.

I had seen him nude before, but it was incredibly awkward and embarrassing for him to be undressed in the presence of Sakuru. I reminded myself that it was perfectly normal to them. I stripped my clothing as well and placed it by the fire. Kuruks fetched a blanket and wrapped it around me.

"You'll have to excuse me - this is the first naked dinner party I've ever attended," I said, trying to bring some levity to the situation.

"I am not naked and I have no intention of removing anything," Sakuru said. "Being nude outside in the dark is completely different from having a brightly glowing fire in front of you."

I raised an eyebrow. "Have you not commented on my modesty before, Sakuru?"

"Of course. I am not modest. I simply won't subject you two to a fully illuminated display of the rigors that old age has placed upon my body."

"You are not old," Kuruks said.

"Isabella keeps telling me the same thing. You two are already beginning to speak like one another, you know?"

"Thank you," I replied. "Now, we were going to speak about the prophecy."

Sakuru shook her head. "You should know me well enough to know that I have no intention of discussing anything before dinner."

I knew she was right, so we went ahead and proceeded to eat. Sakuru had prepared yet another delicious meal of elk meat, squash, and maize. Throughout dinner, the thunder was so loud it was difficult to hear my own thoughts, let alone any conversation. I feared the heavy rain would start to leak through the hut, but Kuruks reassured me that the structure would hold. By the time we finished eating, the storm had subsided, leaving behind a gentle, soothing shower.

"I owe you an apology," Sakuru admitted. "I've kept the full prophecy from you for selfish reasons."

"You aren't selfish," I said.

"I have used many excuses to justify it. I thought that by steering you through this process and only giving you the details I thought you needed to know, I was both protecting you and ensuring its success. In reality, though, I was hampering you and appealing to my own interests. I am truly sorry."

"I have been frustrated," I replied. "But I am sure you were also looking out for me."

"Partially, yes. Thank you for making this easy for me. As you know, Isabella, we pass down stories, prophecies, medicines, and traditions via song and the spoken word. We do not write down our wisdom for the world to see as we are selective as to who we choose to pass on our knowledge. We want to ensure that it is treated with care and respect for our people and our ancestors."

"I understand," I replied.

Sakuru shook her head. "No, you don't. I mean that with no disrespect, but you come from a completely different mindset. You don't have to understand it now, but since you're now part of our story and marrying into our culture, you will. I had previously thought that since you didn't know our language you couldn't fully appreciate the prophecy, but that is obviously not the case. Before we continue, I must ask that you leave, Kuruks."

"He can stay," I replied.

"No, he cannot. What you are about to hear is for you alone."

"I do not keep secrets from Kuruks."

"This is not a secret. It is our way."

"I can't honor something that—"

"It is alright, Izzy, I will leave," Kuruks said as he stood and began to put on his clothes.

"His clothes aren't even dry, yet," I said.

"They are fine. I am not offended, Izzy. Come to me when you are finished."

I tried to reassure him it wasn't necessary for him to leave, but he ignored me.

"I wish you hadn't done that," I said.

"The prophecy is not for his ears."

"He already knows some of it," I replied.

"Yes, but not all of it. Please, Isabella, do not fight me on this."

I reluctantly agreed to drop my protest.

"You know what powers are foretold that the Child of Darkness will possess: accelerated learning, clairvoyance, and unmatched skill in any endeavor. I've neglected to mention that you now possess the skills of a battle-tested warrior and a powerful healer."

"My newfound skill in archery," I said.

"Indeed. And you will be quite proficient in matters of spirit, as your recent integration back into your body demonstrated. I will now sing you the prophecy. I am trusting you with this knowledge. Let the words wash over you and absorb their meaning."

I nodded in acceptance and listened intently as Sakuru sang in a beautiful voice:

In the shadow of the Sun, a daughter will be born. Her power drawn from behind the Veil. The Seed of Darkness grows in the absence of Light, yet is nourished in denial and exile. After shadows cross her path the Gift will bloom, dashing love and hope and sealing her fate. She fights the darkness and resists her Gift. She is fierce, wise, and yet unsure of herself. After the second shadow passes, she must face six tests of her strength and will.
She takes and restores life, protecting her family. She carries the burden of passing on the Song.

She repeated the words several times, but I was listening with such intent that it wasn't necessary for her to do so. When she finished, we sat in silence. I poured over each detail in my mind.

"It would normally take someone a while to memorize one of our songs, but I trust in your current state of mental acuity that you have committed it to memory?"

"I have," I replied.

"Do you understand it?"

"I think so. But only enough to know what I don't know."

Sakuru smiled. "A wise answer. Prophecy is open to interpretation. We must be careful to not read into it what we want. That is why you must have faith in yourself and your destiny."

"But it is not set in stone?"

"There are certain fixed points in our life, but there is no set path, nor guarantee that we will reach our destination. Given the threat we face, I hope you do fulfill it."

"It sounds like I will lead a miserable life."

"A happy ending for heroes is an unrealistic artifact of American folklore. If you fight with honor to defend what you love, you have a greater chance of success. But a righteous cause does not protect you from paying a price for that victory."

"I will pay any price to protect my family. Right now, that consists of Kuruks and you."

"I'm honored you consider me family," Sakuru replied.

"Six tests," I said, thinking out loud. "The first one was undoubtedly losing my parents."

"Your two confrontations with Paa may be your second and third. It is difficult to say until your story is completely told."

"I need to think about all of this," I admitted. "It's overwhelming."

"Yes, but you do not have long. I fear your next test is soon. Study the prophecy and consider it well, but don't let it completely rule your life."

"I would say I understand, but I'd be lying. I don't. I think I will, though."

Sakuru smiled. "You are growing wise, Isabella. You can only grow when you admit what you don't know. Go and be with Kuruks. But don't tell him what we discussed."

I was reluctant to agree to her request, but I signified my acceptance with a nod. I left Sakuru's hut and returned to our home. On my way there, I realized that I thought of his hut not as his home but our home. When I returned, I found him tending to the fire. I hugged him sat next to him.

"I am sorry I can't share this with you. It kills me to keep a secret from you."

"It is a secret that I want, and expect, you to keep," Kuruks replied.

"If you ever change your mind, let me know. It would be a great relief to me."

"It pains me to know it bothers you," he said."

"I promise that it will be the only secret I ever keep from you." □

Chapter 25

As we sat by the fire, my thoughts drifted to the sight of Kuruks in Sakuru's home. I was becoming quite aroused, but felt the need to tamper my lustful thoughts. I wanted to be close to him, to give myself fully to him, but I wasn't sure if I was ready. Sakuru seemed to think I was. Rather than keep my thoughts to myself and become lost in a loop of analyzing a million different options, I decided to externalize them.

"You have been incredibly patient with me," I said. "I am not sure what we are. By your culture, we are married. If I were to go by the standards by which I was raised, I am a whore for touching you as I have, and allowing you pleasuring me."

"That does not sound good," Kuruks replied.

"It isn't. And I'm beginning to think it's a steaming pile of horse... how do you say—"

"Manure?" Kuruks offered in Pawnee.

"Yes, but that's not the exact term I'm looking for. I only know it in English. Horseshit."

"I have never heard that word before," Kuruks admitted.

"It means manure, but with a different meaning. I heard a wide variety of words used around the word shit back in Independence. It can mean nearly anything you want it to mean, but it's always bad."

Kuruks nodded slowly in acceptance. "Shit."

I giggled at his nonchalant recital of the term.

"Is shit funny?" he asked.

"The word is quite flexible."

"I learned a new word of English today," Kuruks said proudly.

"Well, I wouldn't use it much. And don't tell Sakuru. She probably knows what it means and she wouldn't want either of us to use it. I didn't mean to get off on that topic, anyway. I'm just frustrated. After the wonderful feeling you gave me last night I cannot imagine how that could possibly be wrong. I have never felt more alive in my whole life. And, I've literally been dead before, so I can say that with confidence."

"It's never wrong to feel good unless it's at the expense of another," Kuruks said. "And I enjoy making you feel good."

"You're right," I declared. "It isn't wrong. And I enjoyed what I did to you, too. I won't make any more apologies for it. If we weren't meant to give each other pleasure, then it wouldn't be pleasurable."

"Then what is wrong?"

"I've thought about it a lot, and the only thing that really bothers me is that I don't know what I'm doing."

"It is not difficult. And I will be honest with you. I am a bit nervous about it, too."

It struck me as odd that Kuruks was nervous about anything. He seemed to handle even the most difficult of challenges with ease.

"Why would you be anxious about being with me?"

"The first time for a woman can be difficult. I don't want to hurt you."

"I know you wouldn't hurt me," I replied. "You don't have to worry about that."

"I know you want to get married."

"I do. I'm not part of that culture anymore, but it still means a lot to me. It doesn't have to be a complicated ceremony. Sakuru could do it."

Kuruks took my hands and smiled. "That's a good idea. I would be glad to do that."

"You would? I'm grateful you're willing to compromise on this tradition for me."

"Of course."

"I need to ask Sakuru if she'll do it," I said.

"Why don't we ask her now?"

I motioned to the door. "You don't have to ask me twice. Let's go!"

We eagerly headed to Sakuru's home. There was no way to knock on a Pawnee earthen home like on an American house, so I learned the only way to announce my presence was to start talking before I entered. Before I could say a word, Sakuru knew it was us.

"I hear you two," she said.

"I'm glad you're still up," I replied.

"An old woman like me doesn't need as much sleep as you do."

"You are not old," Kuruks corrected.

Sakuru shook her head.

"Ok, then, you're old," he said.

Sakuru motioned with her finger. "No, go back to telling me I'm young. I preferred that. Let me live a moment of illusion. Now, what can I do for you two?"

"Can you marry us?" I asked.

"I am not a Christian minister," she replied.

"No, but it is important to me that I am married."

"I thought we talked about that," Sakuru said. "You are as much joined to Kuruks as you will ever be. Love, not ceremony, binds you."

"And yet it was a ceremony that hastened the medicine within Izzy," Kuruks observed.

Sakuru smiled. "Years ago, I would not have let a young man make such an argument against me."

"You have taught me well," he replied.

"That's gracious of you, but I can't take responsibility for your wisdom, Kuruks."

"I would not ask you to do something that is against your religion," I said. "I do not consider myself a Christian, but marriage was around long before Christ."

"Pawnee celebrate a loving union, but not in the same way," Sakuru said. "You two are bound in love. Your heart already beats as one."

I sat next to Sakuru. "Yes, but some traditions are difficult to shake. I know we're already a couple, but I want to marry him. Finding a minister to do that is obviously out of the question."

"It would mean a great deal to us," Kuruks said.

I appreciated his kind words. I know he didn't consider it essential in the least, but I loved that he was willing to do it to honor me.

Sakuru paused in thought. "I'll be glad to."

"Thank you," I said with a hug.

"We can perform the ceremony by the pond where you assembled your medicine bundle. Won't that make a good spot?"

"Absolutely," I replied. "We'll be back tomorrow, then."

Before I had a chance to stand, Sakuru grabbed my hand. "Where are you going?"

"Back to Kuruks's home," I replied.

"The bride should not be seen by the groom until the wedding ceremony. I am surprised you didn't know this tradition."

"I had completely forgotten," I admitted.

"Being in love will do that."

It was more than just that, of course. My separation from American culture was becoming more permanent, and details like this were lost in my new existence.

"You will have to spend the night by yourself," I told Kuruks.

He held out his hand and pulled me up to him, then kissed me. I could feel the longing in his lips. Mine quivered in anticipation, and were reluctant to let him go. "It'll be our last night apart. Sleep well, Izzy."

"I won't be able to sleep."

"I know," he replied with a grin, then he left.

It was hard to see Kuruks go, but I knew our parting would be brief. I sat next to Sakuru and ate a small chunk of sweet potato.

"It's customary for you to have a bridesmaid."

"You certainly know a lot about our marriage customs," I observed.

"As I said, my father was a French trader."

"True. I love your accent. Pawnee with a twist of French is very interesting."

"So, who will you choose?"

"I don't have anyone," I said.

"What about Tuhre?"

"Well, she'd be fine, except..."

Sakuru raised her eyebrow, waiting for me to finish my sentence.

"She and Kuruks have been together."

"So?" she asked.

"So it would be awkward, don't you think?"

"No," she answered succinctly. "They don't love each other, and they aren't a couple."

It was hard to argue with her logic. "Maybe I will ask her."

"I'm sure Tuhre would be glad to perform the role. You should try to get some sleep, Isabella. You will need it."

"I can't sleep," I admitted. "Maybe I should go see Tuhre."

"It's late," Sakuru said.

"But she may make other plans tomorrow," I fretted.

"She may have plans tonight, like sleeping," Sakuru replied. She stared at me for a moment. "You're going anyway, aren't you?"

"Of course!"

Sakuru laughed. "If you hurry, you might catch her before she goes to sleep."

I had bolted out the door before she could finish her sentence. I had taken a fair number of steps before I realized I didn't know where she lived. I walked back and poked my head inside Sakuru's home.

"Third home on the left past the main hut."

"Thank you," I said, then eagerly followed her directions.

Tuhre was walking home, so I called out to her. "Tuhre! I'm glad I caught you."

"It's good to see you, Izzy. What can I do for you?"

"Kuruks and I are having a wedding tomorrow. Sakuru will perform the ceremony."

"A wedding?" Tuhre asked. "I'm very glad to hear this. What kind of ceremony?"

"Kuruks is honoring my tradition of having a marriage ceremony. I need a bridesmaid - an unmarried woman to stand with me."

"Interesting," she said. She took a deep breath and then looked away for a moment.

"Is everything alright?" I worried she might object, or even still have feelings for Kuruks.

"Yes," Tuhre replied. "I just… haven't considered marriage in quite a while. We are friends. But if you want me to be a part of your union with Kuruks, I will promise to give it some serious consideration."

I was puzzled as to why she had to give this simple task such serious thought, but I was relieved she didn't outright reject the idea.

"It will be at noon tomorrow. If you want to join us, meet me at Sakuru's home tomorrow morning."

Chapter 26

Somehow, I managed to sleep. An unidentified warm drink that Sakuru offered me might have played a role in my slumber. I awoke to Tuhre speaking with Sakuru. I wiped the sleep from my eyes and eagerly greeted her.

"After much consideration, I have decided to accept your offer, Izzy."

"That's wonderful!"

"I do have one condition, though."

"Alright," I cautiously replied.

"I will not join your family until next autumn. This will give you and Kuruks time to adjust and form a strong bond in your home. Perhaps you will even have a child on the way by then. Once that happens, I will bond with Kuruks."

I looked at Sakuru, then looked back at Tuhre. I am certain my expression was completely blank with shock and confusion. Eventually Sakuru broke the silence.

"I believe we have a considerable misunderstanding."

"That's putting it mildly," I added.

"Tuhre, did Izzy explain what a bridesmaid does in an American wedding?"

"She said I would stand with her while she married Kuruks," Tuhre replied.

"As a witness, not as a marriage partner," I corrected. "I didn't intend on you joining our family."

"Oh," Tuhre said. She seemed understandably shocked, but there was a hint of disappointment in her voice. "I am sorry, Izzy. I misunderstood."

"It was my mistake," I admitted. "No need to apologize."

"Despite the misunderstanding, it's a great honor, Isabella," Sakuru said, giving me an insistent glare.

"Yes, of course," I replied with hesitation. "Thank you, Tuhre, for considering it. And I am very sorry. I didn't mean to give you the wrong impression."

"It's alright," Tuhre said. I watched her carefully, but she was hiding her emotions better than she did with her initial reaction. "I will still be glad to be your bridesmaid. What do I need to do?"

"If it were a traditional wedding, you would have a dress and hand me a bouquet, but I don't have either." I paused as I remembered a warm memory. "My mother always said I could use her wedding dress. But it was washed away in that infernal river."

"I'm afraid you'll have to wear what you have," Sakuru said. "But we can do something about the bouquet."

"I'll make one," I said, then started outside. Sakuru stopped me. "You need to eat something, first."

"I can't eat. I'm too excited!"

"You don't want to collapse during your ceremony, do you?" Sakuru asked.

I reluctantly agreed and ate a quick bite of breakfast. Tuhre lingered a moment and then let us know she would meet us at the pond. After I ate, Sakuru and I took a bath in the nearby creek, and then we picked flowers for a bouquet. When we returned to her home, I used a small mirror that her father had given her to try to make myself look as presentable as possible.

Sakuru offered to braid my hair, and I was glad to accept her kind gesture. I hadn't worn my hair in braids since I had left Independence, so it was nice to indulge in a bit of vanity. As Sakuru created an intricate French braid down my back, I fondly remembered my mother braiding my hair before school or special occasions. We didn't speak a word while she worked, and I was glad because, for a brief moment, I imagined my mother in place of Sakuru, taking care of me before my big day. I handed her my mother's dragonfly comb, and she placed it in my hair.

"Thank you," I said.

"You have beautiful hair. It was a pleasure."

I hugged Sakuru tightly, and I nearly started to cry when she began to gently stroke my head. I'm sure it was just a coincidence, but she was performing the exact same gesture that my mother did when we hugged. When we pulled away from each other, she gazed at me.

"Is something wrong? Do I have something in my teeth?"

Sakuru chuckled. "No, Isabella. You look wonderful. I just want to remember this special moment." After a brief pause, she pulled away. "We'd better get to the pond before Kuruks thinks you've changed your mind."

"He wouldn't!"

Sakuru smiled. "No, he wouldn't. He's a kind, patient man. You two will have a wonderful life together."

While we headed to the pond, I asked Sakuru if she knew what to say at the ceremony. She reassured me that she'd think of something fitting. When we arrived, I was delighted to see Kuruks and Tuhre standing patiently at the water's edge. Sakuru gave me another hug, then proceeded to join them. I approached slowly, bouquet in hand, imagining my father walking me down the aisle. His missing presence made me misty-eyed.

"Are you alright?" Tuhre asked.

"Yes," I replied. "Just overjoyed." I handed the bouquet to Tuhre and Sakuru began officiating.

"We are gathered to join this man in woman in matrimony. The two of you share a deep bond, and the purpose of this ceremony will be to cement this bond for all eternity."

She turned to me. "Isabella, will you take Kuruks to be your husband? Will you honor, serve, love, obey, keep him in sickness and in health, and forsake all others for as long as you both shall live?"

I was astonished at how well Sakuru was reciting the marriage ceremony. "Yes."

"And Kuruks, will you take Isabella as your wife? Will you honor, serve, love, obey, keep her in sickness and in health, and forsake all others as long as you both shall live?"

"Yes," he replied.

"Repeat after me, Isabella. I take thee, Kuruks, as my husband, to have and to hold, for better or worse, for richer or poorer, in sickness and in health, to love and to cherish until death do us part."

I repeated her words, looking into Kuruks's beautiful dark eyes as I made my solemn vow.

"Repeat after me, Kuruks. I take thee, Isabella, as my wife, to have and to hold, for better or worse, for richer or poorer, in sickness and in health, to love and to cherish until death do us part."

Kuruks repeated his vows with a tender, loving smile.

"Then I now pronounce you husband and wife," Sakuru announced.

Before Kuruks and I could kiss, I heard a thud.

Horror crossed Sakuru's face. Eyes wide with fear, her olive skin paled as she took a small, stiff step toward us. A strange, blood-curdling noise escaped her lips and vibrated in the air between us as she gasped for breath. She fell into my arms as the arrow buried deep in her back came into view.

I screamed.

Kuruks rushed to help ease her to the ground. The arrow had impacted near the center of her back. I looked up and saw Paa no more than ten paces behind her.

"I hope I'm not too late," Paa said. □

Chapter 27

Everything faded to the background of my mind when I saw Paa's disgusting smirk. I wanted to pound that blisteringly smug grin deep into her skull. I left Kuruks to tend to Sakuru and stalked toward her.

"Paa!" Kuruks yelled. "What have you done?"

"I have kept the prophecy from an outsider's hands."

Paa nocked another arrow.

"Izzy, no!" Kuruks implored. I ignored him.

"Paa, if you shoot my wife, I will kill you with my own two hands."

I quickened my pace. As with my initial confrontation with Paa, time slowed. Before she could fire, I lunged, knocking her on her back. I took her bow and threw it as far as I could. I heard footsteps behind me.

"Get Kuruks!" Paa yelled. "I'll take this bitch."

Two women rushed to Kuruks with bows drawn. I punched Paa back to the ground, grabbed the arrow she had nocked, then ran towards one of them. One of the women was ready to fire, so I took the arrow by its shaft and lunged it into her chest. She screamed in agony as blood poured from the wound. I tried to pull the arrow out, but the arrowhead had become lodged between her ribs. She was still struggling to stand, so I kicked her in the stomach and pushed her to the ground.

I turned in time to see the other attacker releasing her arrow at Kuruks. I'm not sure if it was the distraction of her companion's screams or Kuruks's uncompromising charge, but she narrowly missed him. Once he had her on the ground, I noticed Tuhre was tending to Sakuru. In my moment of distraction, I suffered a swift kick in the back from Paa and promptly collapsed.

"You fool," Paa scowled. "You'll have to die after what you did to my friend!"

I managed to turn myself over and narrowly avoid a kick to the head that would have surely knocked me out. I sprung up, ignoring the shooting pain in my back, and swung at her as hard as I could. I missed and nearly lost my balance.

"The Child of Darkness is no lumbering fool," Paa laughed.

Paa was right. I had let my rage get the best of me. I took a second to collect myself, then successfully dodged her punch. A quick glance told me Kuruks had his attacker on the ground. I wasn't convinced he was out of danger, but I knew he could defend himself.

"You're a monster, Paa!" I yelled. "I understand you hate me, but Sakuru and your brother?"

Paa replied with some hateful nonsense about how everyone had worked to deny her what was so rightfully hers, so I used the distraction to kick her in the shin. Her screamed silenced her incessant monologue of pity.

"I should've killed you when I had the chance," I said as I hovered over her.

"Yes, you should have," she replied, then lunged upwards and delivered a firm punch to my stomach. I doubled over in pain and nearly choked as an intense wave of nausea washed over me. I knew I had just seconds to recover and get back on my feet, so I pushed away the pain and faced her.

Kuruks groaned in agony.

I was horrified to see that he had been stabbed in the back with a knife. Every bit of me wanted to rush to his side and defend him, but I knew that if I did we would both die. I fought the urge to save my husband and decided on the only course of action that could save us both. I struggled through the unrelenting nausea from the blow to my stomach and channeled all the strength I had into a powerful kick to Paa's side.

As soon as Paa tumbled to the ground, I rushed to Kuruks's and pulled the knife from his back. His attacker had already lost consciousness, but the one he had been fighting was still trying to hit him. I moved him out of the way, hovered over her, and plunged the knife into her chest. The woman cried out as the tip of the knife stuck into her sternum. I realized my mistake and pulled out the knife to slash her neck.

Her screams turned into gurgling gasps, then silence. Blood continued to pour from her neck, and soaked my arms, my clothes, and my victim. I remained transfixed on the bubbling pool that emerged from her body, and couldn't pull my gaze from it—not even to check on Kuruks. I dropped the knife and scooted away from her.

"Izzy!" Kuruks yelled. The sound of his voice brought me back to reality. Blood oozed from the wound on his back. I prayed it wasn't as bad as it looked. He propped himself up on his uninjured side and yelled my name again. Through the haze of carnage before me, I understood what he was trying to tell me. I whirled around to see Paa nock an arrow.

There wasn't time to rush her. I was unarmed. The initial decision I had made to ignore Kuruks was sound. Had I gone to his aid, we would have both died. At least this way one of us would live. I stood resolved once more at the tip of my sister-in-law's arrow, resigned to my fate. I closed my eyes, then heard a tremendous bang. I opened them to see Paa clawing at the gunshot wound in her stomach.

Chapter 28

I'll never forget the look on Paa's face. She always seemed to know what was going to happen next. Even if she didn't, she gave the impression she did, which gave her a commanding, determined presence. Yet it was plain to see that, with this turn of events, she was genuinely startled.

"How could you?" she asked.

"If you take another step towards my wife," Kuruks said, then coughed, "I will shoot you again."

She looked at her wound with a strange sort of detachment. She moved her hand from it and a small stream of blood began to flow. She covered it again and glared at Kuruks.

"At least it doesn't bleed much when I hold it."

I thought it was a peculiar thing to say, despite the shock of the situation.

"We can mend the wound," he replied. "But I will only save my sister's life – not the monster you have become."

Paa again removed her hand, then quickly put it back.

"It doesn't hurt that much," she observed. "Not like I thought. Maybe our parents didn't hurt much, either."

"Sakuru needs help!" Tuhre yelled in the distance. "She's not breathing right."

I turned back to Paa. "Why?"

"I had to," Paa replied confidently. "Now you will never be the Child of Darkness."

"You're too late," I stated. "She has passed the song to me."

"Oh no," Paa replied.

She lowered her head for a moment, then looked at Sakuru. Her eyes betrayed a sliver of remorse for what she had done. If I wasn't full of rage, I might have been convinced she was human.

"What will it be, Paa?" Kuruks asked.

"I love you, dear brother," Paa said. "Even after the wicked things you have done. Your whore of a wife killed my friends. You took away my destiny, Kuruks. You sold out our tribe for a piece of American trash." She paused then gazed again at Sakuru. "I loved her, too. But you both betrayed me. You made me do this!"

"What will it be, Paa?" I asked, sternly.

"You are not my family," Paa sneered.

I wanted to kill her. Did she not deserve to die? She had made me take a life, and tried to take two others, and even though Kuruks shot her to defend me, I knew he loved her.

All at once, a strange sensation ran through me. It wasn't of the physical world, rather it shook my soul to its very core. I wasn't sure if it was the trauma or a delayed reaction to learning the prophecy, but regardless, something was changing within me as I stood before Paa. It was not a violent transformation as before, but rather a reflective epiphany that came to me at the most interesting time. A sense of clarity and calm washed over me. The anger and anxiety of the present moved into the past, and I knew, at that precise moment, that the medicine that Sakuru had given me had firmly taken hold in my psyche.

"I am the Child of Darkness," I stated involuntarily.

"It is a curse, you fool!" Paa yelled.

"I have darkness within me," I admitted. "But I've reined it in. It will not control me."

"Darkness is all I have left," Paa replied. "Thanks to you."

"No," I said, extending my hand. "We can heal, together, as family, and possibly prevent further tragedy. You are my sister-in-law. For Kuruks's sake, I will not abandon you, despite what you have done."

Paa had a confused, almost disgusted look on her face. She shook her head, then took a few steps backwards. "Get away from me!" She hesitated a moment more, then ran away. I had no idea how she could move so swiftly with her injury.

"Paa!" Kuruks yelled, but she ignored him and eventually disappeared.

I rushed to my husband to inspect the knife wound on his back. He tried to keep me from seeing it.

"I'll be alright," he said.

I ignored his protestations and examined it more carefully. The cut was deep, but clean. It only bled when he moved.

"I don't think it hit an artery," I said.

"I told you I'll be fine," he replied as he stood. He was very wobbly, but with my help he managed to steady himself.

"Can you walk?" I asked.

"I think so."

As soon as I was reasonably sure Kuruks was going to be alright, I rushed to Sakuru. Tuhre had moved her onto her side and had already removed the arrow. She had her fingers over the wound.

"Her breathing doesn't sound right," Tuhre said.

"Why did you remove the arrow?" I asked scornfully.

"It's not bleeding much. See?"

She removed her fingers and demonstrated there was no blood. But from what I had learned about human anatomy in my schooling, I knew this wasn't necessarily a good thing. Sakuru took a deep, jagged breath, and a few bubbles emerged from the wound. I tried to rouse her, but she was barely conscious and didn't respond.

"It may have hit her lung," I said.

"What do we do?" Tuhre asked.

"I don't know," I replied. I picked up the arrow and examined the arrowhead. "It may heal on its own, but even if it does, this poison is going to be a problem."

"I can make a litter to carry her," Tuhre offered.

Kuruks started to pick her up. "There's no time. We have to get her back to the village."

I stood and pulled him from Sakuru. "We have to get you *both* back to the village."

"I told you," he began, then winced in pain. "I will be alright."

I stood over him and pointed. "We are getting you both back to the village, and you're not carrying anyone."

"There is no choice," he said, leaning down again to pick up Sakuru.

I stopped him. "Kuruks, I am your wife. You just promised to obey me. I will carry Sakuru, and Tuhre can help you walk."

Before Kuruks could protest, I picked up Sakuru. I had never carried a person before, and I wasn't about to let him see that I struggled. I shifted her so that it was more comfortable, but it didn't help much. As we walked back to the village, his gait became erratic and his steps increasingly labored. We barely made it to Sakuru's home.

Chapter 29

Sakuru let out a moan as I gently laid her on her side. I felt terrible for the pain she was in, but at least she was still able to make a noise. Kuruks grunted as Tuhre helped him sit.

"I can clean Sakuru's wound if you will to tend to Kuruks."

"Thank you," I replied.

I took a cloth and soaked it in water, then applied it to the lesion in his back. Even though he was trying to restrain his response, he still shook as I cautiously continued to clean the wound. I hated causing him pain, but I knew it was necessary.

"Do you have any other healers in the village?" I asked.

Tuhre shook her head. "No, though Paa was studying the art."

I restrained myself from saying anything negative for Kuruks's sake. He must have sensed the tension in the air. "I have no sister now."

I made a simple bandage and tied it around his shoulder. "I don't know how well this will stay, so you'll need to be as still as possible."

He subtly shifted his shoulder and winced in pain. "I can be still."

"I have cleaned it as best I can," Tuhre said.

I helped her fashion a bandage. "The poison has likely entered her blood. From personal experience, I know it doesn't take long."

"You survived the poison," Kuruks said. "So will she."

"All we can do is wait," I replied.

By late afternoon, Sakuru started showing signs of a fever. I tried to get Kuruks to lie down, but he said it was too painful. He eventually drifted off to sleep lying on his side. When I stepped outside to take a break, Tuhre followed me.

"I'm sure this is not what you imagined for your wedding day," she said.

"I should have seen it coming. I grew too complacent, and Kuruks and Sakuru have paid a price for my shortsightedness."

"It is not your fault," Tuhre reassured me. "We all knew Paa was insane."

"Perhaps," I replied.

"I'll watch them if you want to take a bath in the creek," she offered.

"Why would I do that?"

Tuhre looked confused. "The blood. There isn't a dry spot on you."

I had completely forgotten about the blood. I don't know why because it was everywhere – it completely covered my hands, arms, and even streaked down my legs. My clothes were completely soaked.

"I didn't realize Kuruks and Sakuru had lost that much blood," I remarked.

"That's not theirs," Tuhre corrected. "That is from the one you killed with the knife."

"I… suppose I was trying to forget about that," I replied.

"I don't think you will. I will go home and get a change of clothes for you."

"I don't have time to wash —"

"You need to, Izzy." Tuhre put her hand on my arm. "Don't pretend like it didn't happen."

"I'm not, but —"

"I will be back soon."

Tuhre left my blood-soaked-self standing there, not giving me time to protest. She was right, I needed to come to grips with what I had done. I killed a person. I killed two people. It was self-defense, sure, but I was brutal. I was angry. I ripped apart her throat like it was a piece of meat. With just a simple twist of my knife I cut the arteries that supplied her brain with blood, ending her misguided allegiance to her friend Paa. I didn't even know her name.

I went back inside and checked on Sakuru and Kuruks. They were both still sleeping. I wiped Sakuru's forehead again and checked her breathing. I was surprised that it sounded better, but her fever raged. I felt helpless.

"Here you go," Tuhre said, startling me. She handed me a beautiful deerskin dress with bright red beading in the shoulders with fringe at the bottom. "I do not need it anymore. It is yours."

"I didn't even know their names," I said as I accepted her gift.

"The one you killed with the knife was named Chakira," Tuhre said. "I did not know the other one."

I wasn't sure I wanted to know, but once Tuhre uttered her name I vowed to never forget it.

"Chakira made a lot of bad choices."

"She will never make another bad choice," I replied.

"You did what you had to do," Tuhre said. "You have taken on an incredible burden; one you can only hope to begin to ease by washing her blood from your body."

"It will never go away," I said.

"I hope not. At one point, I considered her a friend."

I immediately looked away, then left Sakuru's home without saying a word. I couldn't make it to the creek without bursting into tears. I removed my clothing and threw it haphazardly on the bank, then submerged myself. I thought the darkness of the water would calm me, but instead it only brought my internal dialog to the forefront. I saw Chakira's face, first angry, then scared, then terrified as I gutted her like a fish.

I decided that I had no right to live after what I had done. And yet, I knew what Tuhre said was right – I had no choice. How could I possibly reconcile this moral battle raging inside of me? Both sides made equally defensible cases, and my instinct, that very instinct that saved Kuruks's life, committed two women to die. I screamed, cursing Paa's name so loudly she could have heard me no matter how far she had slithered from the scene of her crime.

I splashed the water over me in an attempt to rid myself of evidence of my horrendous deed. Gradually the red departed from my pale skin, but I knew that no matter how hard I scrubbed I could not ever fully be clean again. When I was finished, I put on the clothes that Tuhre had so kindly given to me and stood by the creek.

Something compelled me to return to the scene where Kuruks and I said our vows. I had to do it, like pinching myself in a dream. Had the traumatic event really happened?

Fresh horror consumed my mind as I returned to the gruesome scene – but that was not at all what consumed me.

The bodies of the two women who died at my wedding were gone.

Chapter 30

Paa was nowhere to be seen, and she was clearly in no condition to move the bodies. I pondered the situation in utter confusion, then rushed back to Sakuru's home. Kuruks and Sakuru were asleep, so I motioned for Tuhre to come outside.

"Chakira and the other woman's bodies are gone and there's no sign of Paa."

"I don't understand," Tuhre replied. "Kuruks shot her with your gun."

"Maybe it wasn't a fatal wound," I replied. "She'll have to get the bullet removed. She doesn't have any sympathizers in the village, does she?"

"No. Sakuru is a loner. She is both respected and feared by the village."

"Feared? Why?"

"A healer dances on the edge of death far too often for some people's taste. They rely on her strong medicine, yet are also intimidated by it. They were also distrustful of Paa for similar reasons. The only person I know that had anything to do with her was—"

"Chakira," I said. Tuhre looked down and sighed. I put my hand on her shoulder and added, "I am very sorry about her."

"She attacked us."

"I regret that you lost someone who was once a friend."

"Thank you," Tuhre replied.

"How are they?"

"Sakuru's fever is raging but her breathing is better. Kuruks snored a few times."

"Oh really?" I asked with a chuckle. "He once commented on my snoring. I'll have to talk to him about this."

Tuhre smiled. "How are you, Izzy?"

"Sore, but I will manage."

Tuhre looked deeply into my eyes as if she didn't believe me.

"I am in pain," I admitted. "But I will recover."

"I will stay with you and help as long as you need," she offered.

"I appreciate that. I am going to wake Kuruks. He needs to eat."

Tuhre and I went back inside, and I leaned next to Kuruks and gave him a gentle kiss on the cheek. "My love, you should eat."

He mumbled something, then opened his eyes. "I'm not hungry."

"You have to eat something. You lost a lot of blood. You need to regain your strength."

I handed him a few pumpkin strips. "Eat these for now. And maybe later some fish?"

Kuruks nodded and began to eat the strips. "How is Sakuru?"

"She is still fighting the poison," I replied. "But her breathing has improved, so that is a good sign. How do you feel?"

"The same."

I laid my head on his chest and gave him a hug.

"I'm sorry!"

He took his other arm and put it around me. "It's not your fault. It's alright now."

I looked carefully in his eyes to determine if he was telling the truth. "I promise, I'm fine," he said.

"You will be," I replied. "That won't take long to heal. But we have to keep it clean."

I debated telling Kuruks that Paa's accomplices were no longer at the scene. I thought it might give him hope that Paa was still alive. I knew that he had disowned her just hours ago, but I was sure that some part of him still cared for his sister. Before I could reach any decision, Sakuru made a noise and started to move.

I called out to her and her eyelids fluttered. She coughed several times and then tried to sit upright. Tuhre and I helped her make slow, careful movements to avoid injuring herself further. She coughed again and spit out a lot of blood. Once she regained her breath, she looked at me and gave me a strange smile.

"Sakuru?" I asked, both delighted that she was awake and confused by her expression.

She started to speak, but immediately began another coughing fit. She grimaced in pain with each movement. Eventually she settled down and managed to utter, "You must..."

"I must what?" I asked. It was clear she couldn't say anything more at the moment, so I helped her back down and wiped her forehead again. "Save your strength, Sakuru. You have to fight the poison."

She shook her head at me and then closed her eyes, then returned to sleep.

I glanced at Kuruks. "Did I wake any time while I was poisoned with Paa's arrow?"

"You talked in your sleep a few times, but we couldn't understand you."

"She was trying to tell us something," I said.

"Or she was dreaming," Tuhre replied. "Her mind is plagued with fever."

"Maybe."

The pumpkin must have increased Kuruks's appetite, because after he finished the strips he wanted fish. I took the largest one I could find from Sakuru's fish rack and cooked it for him. His eyes grew wide when I handed it to him.

"This looks very good. Thank you, Izzy. Have you eaten anything?"

Even though I had pestered him to eat, I had neglected to do so myself. I picked up a pumpkin strip and nibbled on it.

"You need more than that," he said.

"You're right, but I've been too nervous. I was worried sick about both of you." I looked at Sakuru. "I still am."

"I'll be fine," Kuruks replied. He handed me a leftover portion of the fish.

I clutched my stomach. "I can't. I'm nauseous."

Kuruks touched my stomach and I withdrew from him. "Did Paa injure you?"

"She hit me pretty hard."

"Is your stomach bruised?"

"I haven't looked. When I was in the river I didn't see anything on me but blood."

"You need to check yourself," he insisted.

"I will at first light," I said.

My new dress was not in two pieces so I would have had to completely disrobe. I know the Pawnee thought nothing of it but I still wasn't comfortable doing so in mixed company, especially considering Tuhre's past with Kuruks.

I laid my head on Kuruks's chest and released a heavy sigh. "I never thought I'd want my wedding day to be over with. But I just want this miserable day to end."

Kuruks held me and kissed my forehead. "I'm sorry."

"You did this for me. If I hadn't insisted on this ceremony you wouldn't have a knife wound and Sakuru wouldn't be fighting for her life."

"Paa would have attacked no matter what," Tuhre said.

I couldn't argue with Tuhre's logic. "You're right."

"Do you want me to stay the night?" Tuhre asked. "I don't mind."

"There's no need. I'll manage," I replied. "You've helped more than I could have ever asked."

Tuhre put her hand on my shoulder. "It is the least I could do for both of you, and Sakuru. If you need me in the middle of the night do not hesitate to come get me."

I embraced Tuhre and thanked her again.

She gave Kuruks a hug. "Your new wife needs you, Kuruks. Get well soon, my dear friend."

Kuruks smiled. "I will. Good night, Tuhre."

Not long after Tuhre left, Kuruks admitted he was in considerable pain. He was grimacing earlier and I knew he was trying to hide it, but now it had reached a point where he couldn't maintain his needless stoic facade. He pointed to some bark Sakuru had used to help relieve pain, so I fetched it and prepared it in some tea.

"It's from a tree that grows south of here," he said as he sipped the warm drink. "Hard to find around our village."

"Willow bark?" I asked.

"I am not sure its name."

I tasted a tiny piece of it. "Yes, it's willow. It always took care of my headaches."

He pointed to my stomach. "Maybe it will help you, too."

I took a piece and began to chew on it. "I don't mind the taste."

Kuruks shivered in disgust.

"You mean to tell me that my big strong husband can't stand the taste of willow bark?"

"I prefer it in tea," he replied. "Izzy, you need to see if you are cut or bruised."

I knew he was right, but I didn't want to. I bargained that I couldn't do anything about it if I was injured. My stomach was eased by the willow bark, but I was sore all over.

"It can wait until morning."

Kuruks shook his head. "No, you need to check now."

I rolled my eyes and gave in, knowing that arguing with him would be useless. I stood near the fire and took off my dress. There was a considerable bruise on my stomach, and numerous smaller bruises on my arms. There were a few cuts, but nothing serious. I started to put my dress back on, but Kuruks stopped me.

"Your body against the fire looks amazing."

I smiled at the compliment, then walked over to him and stood at his feet. "I thought you were in pain, my love?" I asked with a mischievous grin.

"My body is in no shape to do what I want right now," he admitted. "But my mind…"

"I know exactly what you mean," I replied.

Kuruks motioned with his finger to come closer. I leaned over him and put my hands on his chest. I thought about all the wonderful things I wanted to do with him as I ran my fingers over his muscles, but I could only indulge in my fantasies for just a moment before the pain in my stomach became unbearable. I grunted as I repositioned myself next to him. Fortunately the pain eased to a manageable level.

"I have to be careful what I do," I said.

"We'll feel better soon," he said as he kissed me. "And then we'll make up for lost time."

His suggestion brought a smile to my face. "I like your idea."

"Despite having the most beautiful woman in the world next to me, completely naked, all I want to do is rest."

"I understand, love. I am happy here, in your arms. There is nowhere else I want to be."

Chapter 31

Something, or more precisely someone, was trying to reach me in my sleep. Someone called my name. As their volume increased, I realized it was Sakuru. She called me by my full name, Isabella, as she always had, not the more familiar Isabelle or Izzy. I wanted to respond to her weak voice, but I didn't know how.

I could tell it was taking every ounce of Sakuru's strength to initiate contact. I tried to call out, but I wasn't in control of the dream. My unconscious mind couldn't make the connection alone, it needed help. I jerked awake with my sweat-dampened skin and left Kuruks's embrace so I could be next to her. Her breathing hadn't changed, but her fever seemed a bit better.

"How do I respond to you, Sakuru?" I whispered as I put my arm on her shoulder.

And then it hit me. If I was going to reach her, it would not be with words but through meditation. I recalled the moment when I slipped into her mind. I could perceive the world through her eyes and yet retain some aspect of me. Sakuru had mentioned that meditation was the key to connecting with her in a similar way, but my experience with it was extremely limited.

I took some of her tobacco and smoked it in her pipe. I used the technique that she had shown me, and became momentarily dizzy. I connected to her spirit in this moment of disorientation. I heard a stream of faint, unintelligible words.

As I immersed myself in the flow, I began to see faint silhouettes of images float by. They had no clearly defined borders like a painting or a photograph, but instead were nearly life-sized windows into an alternate reality. I examined the images carefully, and as my perception increased, they became more clearly defined. When I intensely focused on one, it stopped, and though it was translucent I could make out what was happening. I realized the objects in these apparitions were moving. I was watching events through my connection to Sakuru's mind.

The first scene that caught my attention appeared to be in a Pawnee hut. Sakuru was hugging a Pawnee man. The timeframe seemed recent as she appeared to be the same age as she was today. Both she and the man were completely silent and seemingly unaware of my presence.

In the next scene, Sakuru wore an older-style European dress, and put her arm around a man I presumed to be her father. She had said that her father was a French trader, and though I wasn't completely sure of the man's heritage, he was certainly Caucasian. She sat outdoors in a beautiful grove of trees. The foliage seemed different from the plains, so I wasn't sure of the location.

Another picture materialized, rapidly displacing the previous image. In this one, Sakuru was dressed in Pawnee clothing. She seemed to be the same age, yet this time she tended to an older woman. The other woman seemed to bear a familial resemblance to her. It could have been her mother or grandmother.

Clearly, images from the timeline of Sakuru's life were being shown to me, though the sequence was incorrect. She could not have been tending to her mother, or even grandmother, and appear to be the same age she currently was. It was also highly unlikely she would have ever worn a European-style dress from the eighteenth century. She continuously made remarks about being old, but she wasn't as old as she claimed. She had few wrinkles and her hair was only slightly gray. I doubt she was over forty years old.

The next scene was of a Pawnee woman out in a field, holding a newborn baby. The child was still uncleaned and joined to her mother via the navel-string. She and who I presumed to be her husband fawned over the new addition to their family. It was difficult to make out a lot of detail because the light was low. It appeared to be just before sunset. Within moments, light was restored to the image and it was now daylight. The baby was born during a solar eclipse.

"Do you understand now, Isabella?"

There was no need to telepathically reply that I knew what she was telling me. Her question was purely rhetorical. Since I had first learned of this prophecy I had assumed that the medicine was something I was born with. In truth, that was only part of it.

"Your journey has just begun, Isabella. The medicine in me has run its course. It's your turn, now."

Her telepathic voice sounded tired and her words were colored with a dark shade of resignation. I was overcome with a massive wave of grief. At first, I thought it was from her, but it wasn't – the emotion was mine.

"You are healing from your wounds," I assured her.

"What little medicine that is left in me has defeated Paa's poison."

"Of course it has," I replied. "Your breathing is better. You will make it."

"I need rest, Isabella. I am tired, and old."

Her exhaustion was understandable. She had been through a lot. I emerged from meditation and checked her breathing and pulse and noticed that they were roughly the same. I wiped her forehead again before returning to Kuruks's side.

As I laid there, watching Sakuru sleep, I thought of her words and the tremendous responsibility she had passed on to me. I thought of the historical images that she had projected and wondered just how powerful the medicine of the prophecy was. Had she somehow traveled through time, or had she lived longer than her middle-aged appearance showed? There was so much more I wanted to ask her, but I knew she needed to spend her energy healing instead of answering my endless stream of questions.

I pondered for hours the incredible telepathic experience Sakuru had provided for me. Eventually I lost the battle against my fatigue. The warmth of the fire and the slow rise and fall of my husband's chest lulled me to sleep.

Chapter 32

"Izzy, wake up!" Tuhre nudged me. I was exhausted and I didn't want to move, so I buried my face into Kuruks's side.

"You have to get up!"

I bolted upright when I realized it might be about my new husband or Sakuru and immediately checked them both. Kuruks was asleep and seemed to be free of fever. Sakuru's fever had broken and her breathing was still a bit labored. The bandage on the wound on her back had already been changed.

"Don't worry, I've taken care of that," Tuhre said. "Kuruks's will need to be changed, too."

"What is so urgent?"

"The chief would like to speak to you," Tuhre explained.

I was surprised and didn't know what to say. "Really?"

"Yes. He'll be here soon."

"Alright, I'll help him however I can," I said, then sat and patiently waited for him.

Tuhre grinned as she handed me my dress. "You might want to wear this."

I couldn't believe I had forgotten I was nude. Even the modesty and social standards I had been raised in were giving way to my new culture. I stood and dressed as quickly as I could.

I had barely finished dressing when the chief entered Sakuru's home. He was tall and wore an elegant feathered headdress. He had red paint under his eyes and wore a beaded necklace that had a small medallion. His robe was made of white fur with a prominent, dark, fuzzy neckline.

Kuruks was still asleep, so I nudged him. He wiped the sleep from his eyes and tried to stand. The chief extended his hand towards Kuruks, motioning for him to stay seated.

"I am Piita," he pronounced plainly in Pawnee. "You are Isabella, correct?"

"Yes. It's an honor to finally meet you," I replied, holding out my hand. He extended his hand cautiously and I shook it.

"Sakuru showed me this strange custom," he recalled.

"I'm not sure why we," I stopped and corrected myself, "why Americans do it, either."

He raised an eyebrow. "You consider yourself Pawnee?"

I was surprised by the directness of his question. "Yes," I answered without hesitation.

Piita sat near the fire. Kuruks, Tuhre, and I formed a circle around him.

"Isabella, you do not have our blood," he observed. "You are not Pawnee."

"No, but I am–"

"The Child of Darkness does not make you Pawnee."

"But Sakuru said–"

Piita looked at Sakuru then back towards me. He lowered his voice and replied, "Sakuru is very wise. But she does not know everything."

"I do not have to have Pawnee blood to be Pawnee."

"Your skin is pale, your hair and eyes are lighter than ours. Have you seen any in our village that look like you?"

I didn't reply to his rhetorical question. He paused a moment then added, "I do not say this to hurt your feelings, Isabella."

"I know. You are simply stating a fact. My parents were not Pawnee. But I respectfully disagree with your assessment. I am Pawnee."

Kuruks looked at me with surprise. "Izzy, it's not a good idea to contradict the chief," he cautioned.

Piita laughed. "It's even more foolish to correct your wife in public."

I couldn't help but grin. Kuruks looked down for a moment. "She's not used to our customs."

The chief shook his head. "No, she is not. Tell me, Isabella, why are you Pawnee?"

"My life is now with my husband. I speak your language and I am learning your customs. My children will be members of this village, and I'll raise them to be Pawnee."

"And yet just as you've begun that life, you've shed the blood of two Pawnee women."

"They were trying to kill us."

"Now we are getting to the heart of the matter," Piita said. "You have killed to protect Pawnee life. It is rare, perhaps unheard of, for a white person to do that. But that act alone does not make you Pawnee."

"None of us here are Pawnee," I proclaimed. I surprised myself with that argument. I knew what I meant to say, but I didn't intend on spouting that so directly.

"Explain," he replied.

"We are humans," I said. "Our skin, eyes, and hair are different, but we all have the same color blood. We have the same feelings, and many of the same thoughts."

"Then I must ask, Isabella, why are your kinsmen killing us?"

I lowered my head and sighed. "I cannot answer that in a way that will appease you."

"Try," he insisted.

"Best I can understand; they think they are entitled to this land. They think you use it poorly and that they know what is best."

"Do you agree with them?"

"Of course not. They are misguided. My mother taught me that it's ignorant to make assumptions about people they didn't know. So even though many in Independence thought that you are savages, I try my best to reserve judgement about people until I've had a chance to meet them."

"Your mother was a wise woman," Piita stated. "So I'll ask again, why do you consider yourself Pawnee?"

I took Kuruks's hand. "There is nowhere else I would rather be. This is my home."

The chief smiled. "That is the exact same answer Sakuru gave me when I asked her the same question."

"Why did you ask her that?" Kuruks asked.

"She never told either of you, did she? Sakuru was born to Pequot parents in what America now calls Connecticut."

"She isn't… Pawnee?" I asked after a moment of confused silence.

"She is Pawnee in spirit. As you said, Isabella, this was her home. She, and you, are Pawnee."

I looked at Sakuru, lying unconscious on the floor while we talked about her, and wondered what other secrets she had yet to reveal about herself.

"I came to ask you if you will take over Sakuru's role as our healer?" the chief asked.

"No, I mean... wait... she will make it through this. I do not need to replace her."

"I hope you are right," Piita replied. "But our numbers are not as strong as they used to be. America keeps expanding, and before long we may have to move, or worse. We already rely on other tribes, such as the Omaha and Lakota, for far more than we have ever had to in the past. Opportunities to marry inside our village are few."

"Sakuru will pull through," I stated again.

"Even if she does, we need a replacement. She will not live forever."

I narrowed my gaze. "You speak of her as though she were a tool to be discarded after she had served her purpose."

"Izzy!" Kuruks put his hand on my shoulder.

"I respect Sakuru and value her work. She is kind and caring, and has saved my life on more than one occasion. I want her to live. But I am the leader of our village. It would not be wise of me to ignore our need for a healer."

"I hadn't considered that," I admitted. "I apologize for my assumption."

Piita shook his head. "No apology necessary. I appreciate your candor. She and I have not always seen eye to eye, but she tells me what she thinks even when she knows I won't like what she has to say. You remind me of her, Isabella."

"Thank you," I replied. "I graciously accept, though I should mention I am not a skilled healer. I was educated to be a teacher, not a physician."

"Sakuru was the Child of Darkness, and now she passed on the medicine to you."

"The prophecy does not state I will be a healer."

"No, but strong medicine is within you. That, combined with skill, will save lives and make our tribe strong."

"I appreciate your confidence in me," I replied.

Piita stood. "I know you have much to do, so I will leave you to your work." He smiled and clasped my hand. "Welcome to our tribe, Isabella."

"It is an honor."

"Kuruks, you have done well for yourself."

"I know," he replied with a grin. "Every time I look at her I remember how lucky I am."

I am certain that my pale face turned bright red. His public compliment caught me completely off-guard.

As the chief left Sakuru's home, he turned to me. "I have had visions of a great trial for your family. I fear it is soon. Be cautious, Isabella."

Piita's warning sent a chill through me. After he left, Kuruks hugged me. "I am so proud of you, Izzy."

I took his hand and looked up at him. "Sakuru will make it."

He gazed at her a moment.

"You don't think so, do you?" I asked.

"I don't know," he admitted. "I have to be honest – I do not have the same faith in her recovery as you do."

I was shocked to hear that from him, but nevertheless appreciated his honesty. I leaned next to her and took a stray strand of hair that had fallen across her face and brushed it back with my fingers.

"I can't stand to lose anyone else. Neither one of us can. We have had so much loss, Kuruks. I need that faith."

He knelt and put his arm around me. "After you lost your parents, you had no faith. I suppose I gave mine to you."

"It is hard. Oh, so hard," I admitted with a tear in my eye. "Before I left on this journey I didn't believe in anything beyond what I could see. Now I have seen more than I ever thought possible. There is a reason for everything, Kuruks. I see that now." I took his hand and squeezed it. "We are a team now, my love. If one of us is lacking something, we provide it for the other. I have enough hope now for both of us."

Chapter 33

After the visit with Chief Piita and a light breakfast, Kuruks and I took a nap. Neither of us had a truly restful sleep from the previous night, so we curled up next to the fire and drifted into a pleasant, refreshing slumber. When we awoke sometime in the midafternoon, I changed Sakuru's and Kuruks's bandages.

"Your wound is healing nicely," I observed as I finished applying the clean dressing. "In a few more days you may not even need this."

"Good," he replied. "It annoys me. But I know it is necessary. And how about you?"

"I haven't checked today. I suppose I should. I wasn't nauseous after breakfast, so I think that's a good sign."

I stood and lifted my dress high enough to see my stomach. The bruising had spread a little but it was significantly lighter in color.

"May I see?" he asked.

"It looks bigger," he said.

"Hey!"

"That's not what I mean. The bruise."

"It is a lot lighter. It will go away soon. Don't worry, love."

He took his hand and put it on my stomach. "Do you mind?"

After my nod of approval, he gently pressed with his fingers. It had hurt the day before, but there was only a slight twinge now.

"Much better," I said.

"Are you sure?"

"Yes, I promise."

"Alright," he replied. He looked below my stomach and grinned.

"I thought the same thing," I replied. "But… not here."

He quickly removed his hand. "Sorry, I wasn't thinking."

"No need to apologize." I lowered my voice to a whisper in case Sakuru could hear what we were saying. "I have longed for your touch."

Kuruks raised an eyebrow. "Sakuru is sick. She needs us. And your stomach – I don't want to hurt you."

I took his hand and dragged him to the far corner of the hut. "My discomfort has come from wanting you desperately."

"Tuhre said she'd sit with Sakuru," Kuruks eagerly suggested. "But you still hurt a little."

I ran my fingers over his shoulder. "And you still hurt, too. I see you wince when you reposition yourself."

Kuruks smiled. "I'm sure we can manage. Do you want to get Tuhre, or shall I?"

"I'll wait for you. I need to run a brush through my hair and make myself somewhat presentable for you. I want your first time with me to be special."

He wrapped his arms around me "Being with you is what will make it special."

"You are sweet, love," I replied. "But no matter how much you try to convince me otherwise, I know I look like a cow chewed me up and spit me out."

Kuruks chuckled, then left to fetch Tuhre. I ran my brush through my long, tangled hair. It was a mess, but I knew I didn't have time to wash it and let it dry, so I did the best I could. When Tuhre arrived, I thanked her for looking after Sakuru, then we politely excused ourselves and made our way back home.

"We're married, we're alone, and no one is trying to kill us," I observed. "That's great, but not exactly what I imagined my first time to be like."

Kuruks smiled and took my trembling hands. He pulled me close and held me. "There is no need to be nervous."

The more I tried to calm my nerves, the more it increased my anxiety.

"We have been together, alone, in each other's arms many times before."

"But not like this," I replied.

Kuruks raised an eyebrow. "I remember some very intimate moments with you."

"It's not the same."

"Tell me your greatest fear," he said.

I nervously shrugged. "That I'll do something wrong."

"How can you do something wrong?"

"I don't know," I replied. I wanted to pace around a bit, but he held me still.

"We'll both make mistakes, because it will take a while for us to learn exactly what the other one wants."

His advice was simplistic, but completely accurate. Even though he had experience, neither one of us knew quite what to expect.

He held up my hand. "You are not shaking anymore."

I ran my hand through his hair. "You've put me at ease, love. You always do."

I raised my hands and allowed Kuruks to remove my dress. He set it aside and smiled as he stared at my body.

"You are beautiful, Izzy."

I loved that he found me attractive. The way he looked at me was not mere appreciation - I could tell he adored me, and it felt wonderful. We kissed, and then I tugged at his clothing. He removed his shirt and I removed his pants. I ran my hands along his muscular shoulders as we continued to kiss, being careful to avoid his wound. He stopped and held my face in his hands, smiling.

"I love you."

Before I could reply, he walked behind me. He stopped for a second, and then wrapped his arms around me. I could feel how excited he was, and it was erotic and empowering to know how much he wanted me. The feel of him against me took my breath for a moment. I arched my back to press closer to him. His hands caressed my breasts as he kissed the back of my neck and shoulders. I leaned forward onto the blankets, and he ran his hands along my waist and bottom. After several kisses on the base of my spine, he gently maneuvered me onto my back.

Kuruks showered my neck, breasts, and stomach with slow, tender kisses. I expected him to come back up to kiss me, but instead he remained at my abdomen. He ran his hands along my waist, and then proceeded to kiss my legs. I instinctively parted them, and his kisses began to work their way up my inner thighs. I twitched with a brief rush of nervous energy.

"Are you alright?"

"I just… didn't expect you to do that."

He took his finger and gave me several teasing strokes. I propped myself up on my elbows and gave him a playful look. "I know I've earned this teasing, but–"

Before I could finish the sentence, he ran his tongue in one long, steady movement between my legs. I made some noise that could probably be roughly described as a surprised moan.

"Kuruks!" I managed. He looked up at me and replied, "If you are uncomfortable…"

I was horribly embarrassed that his mouth was hovering less than an inch away from an area that I had trouble accepting was remotely appealing.

"Why do you want to do that?" I asked.

"Did you hear the sound you just made?"

The look in his eyes was even more intense, more hungering than when he was admiring my figure.

"I thought it was awkward," I admitted.

"You explored every bit of me. Now I want to do the same to you."

I couldn't argue with his logic. It was plain to see that he was eager to be there. My muscles relaxed a bit and I cautiously nodded for him to resume. I was completely surprised with the intensity of pleasure each movement of his tongue provided. Before long, every bit of the apprehension I had melted away. I leaned back, closed my eyes, and thoroughly enjoyed every moment of bliss he so skillfully delivered.

After a while, a yearning strengthened from within me. I knew I wanted him inside me, but he continued pleasuring me with his tongue. The lack of him became something of a tease, but the wonderful sensations I experienced made me almost forget that unfulfilled need. Before long he drove me over the edge. I could barely contain myself as I experienced powerful and exquisitely blissful contractions. My legs shivered around his head as the sexual tension completed its release from my body. Even though the tension had diminished, I still wanted him. And I was ecstatic to see him crawling back up to my face.

"You can explore every bit of me anytime you want, love," I said.

"I'm going to remember that," he replied with a grin. "Are you ready?"

"More than ready."

Kuruks leaned up and slowly guided himself into me. I was so excited, and so relaxed from what he had just done that it wasn't as bad as I had feared it would be. There was discomfort, but I trusted him, and the patient, caring gaze in his eyes kept me distracted enough until it subsided. Once pain became pleasure, the craving was completely fulfilled, and I relished the ultimate closeness I could now finally share with him. I was surprised to find my hips moving precisely in time with his motions. I fell completely in line with his rhythm - our rhythm.

His face filled my field of vision, and I became consumed with the intimacy we shared. His pleasing, masculine scent that I adored filled my senses. I was feeling an undeniably new set of sensations, yet the melding of our two bodies was extremely familiar. In our motions, in our proximity, and in spirit, we became one. His presence completed me, and I could tell, solely by the look in his eyes, that I did the same for him. Absolutely nothing else existed for me, for us, in that moment.

Kuruks's chest gleaned with a thin layer of sweat, and his breathing became faster. He started to moan and hold me even closer. The veins in his neck bulged and the muscles in his shoulders tensed, and he began to thrust vigorously. I gripped him tightly as he released into me. It was clear by the look on his face that he was just returning from the same realm of blissful unawareness that he had so easily taken me to on multiple occasions.

He collapsed between my breasts, and I ran my fingers through his hair as he recovered. After he caught his breath, he rolled to my side and we held each other. There was no need for words, as we communicated all we needed to express with the closeness of our bodies and the adoring gaze we shared.

I rolled over on top of him and gave him a sly look.

Chapter 34

"You didn't eat your dinner," Daniel says as he enters the room.

It's sweet how he worries about me. "What I'm about to do requires total concentration. You know that. Food is the last thing on my mind."

"Yes, but you have to keep your strength up to get through this."

"Have I told you how Sakuru told me my powers of clairvoyance would heighten. I wasn't sure if I believed her at first because I didn't seem to have any warning of Paa's attacks upon me or Sakuru. If I had known what she was planning, I would have not had a wedding. I feel terrible that my attachment to my own customs put her in harm's way. Tuhre told me that Paa and her followers were to blame, but it's undeniable that had the ceremony not taken place, the gruesome attack would have been averted. We were all caught unawares."

Daniel puts a cup of fresh tea in my hand. "Drink. And stop punishing yourself for your wedding. You didn't know."

"There are a lot of things I didn't know," I say as I reject the tea. "But it's time to correct that. I need to know exactly what happened to Paa. For the story. It has to be accurate."

Daniel's worried expression would be comical if I didn't know how concerned he really is. "You know how this goes, Daniel." I offer him my hand. "Help me get ready."

I pick up my favorite skin that Kuruks gave me and hold it close, taking in the smell of our home in the Nebraska plains. I spread it on the floor and Daniel helps me sit.

"I hate to see you upset," he says. "You've paid a great price for your gift… for the life you've lived. The journey back is difficult, especially to gaze into someone else's past. Are you up for it?"

"It must to be done. I'll see you in a bit. Tobacco, please. And the pipe."

I close my eyes and hear Daniel close the door. I take several deep breaths from the pipe, then settle into a state of complete relaxation. I focus my mind on my target. Hazy figures appear in the darkness, and then distinct images form.

***

Paa stood over the bodies of her friends. Seeing their savage scars stirred a vicious anger within her. She felt terrible about their loss, but knew there was no time to grieve. She didn't want anyone else to handle their burial, but there wasn't a way she could attend to both bodies by herself in her current state. She decided she would have to hide them until she could return, so she dragged them to a dense grove of trees along the shore of a creek. She knew it wasn't a perfect hiding spot, but it would have to do.

Dragging the bodies with just one arm put a tremendous strain on her muscles. The pain inside her body was almost more than she could bear. She sat by the creek and took a break while she considered her next step. Anger toward me, her brother, and the entire village clouded her mind. She could see nothing but hate. She had long given up on obtaining her goal. From that point forward, she was solely focused on revenge.

Her wound was beginning to clot, but Paa knew she needed the use of both of her arms. She took some clothing from one of her friend's bodies and fashioned it into a crude bandage, then wrapped it around her stomach. It would have to do until she could find a more permanent solution. She desperately wanted relief from the pain, but she knew that eating some willow bark would increase her bleeding, so she resisted the temptation.

Paa tried to stand, but was too wobbly. She sat back down and tried again, this time managing to steady herself. She didn't make it out of the grove before her head started spinning. She grabbed hold of a tree, but all it did was slow her descent. She fell on her back, looking up at the sky. Her abdominal muscles were so sore that sitting upright was simply impossible.

Paa was determined not to give up, but there didn't seem to be a way for her to get on her feet. She hoped that her energy would return with a brief rest, so she relaxed her body and tried to breathe through the pain. The view went dark, so I assume that Paa had lost consciousness. The next image that followed was the face of a middle-aged American man looking over her with great concern. It was blurry, but I could make out a rifle in his hand. He leaned in for a closer inspection, and then everything faded to black. □

**

The remaining images rush through my mind at dizzying speed. Her hopes, her anguish, and her indescribable pain pour through me.

"I see now, Paa. I see everything."

Chapter 35

The next morning, I rushed to check on Sakuru. Her condition was unchanged. I worried I had let her down or done something wrong for staying away from her for so long. I was extremely grateful Tuhre had stayed the night with her.

"The bleeding has stopped," Tuhre observed.

"She's probably dehydrated," I replied. "Dripping water into her mouth is not enough. A good solid meal would help, too."

"Her breathing sounds better," Tuhre said. "I don't understand."

"I'll attempt to connect with her spirit again. Maybe she can help us help her."

"May I participate?" Tuhre asked.

I hadn't considered asking for her assistance, but I realized it certainly might prove valuable. "Of course. Thank you staying with her all night."

"I don't mind. Sakuru is like a second mother to me."

"I hope I'm able to repay you soon."

"The healer usually has an assistant," Tuhre noted with a grin.

"You're hired! Though, I can't pay you."

"We don't work for pay," Tuhre replied. "We work to gain knowledge and wisdom."

"You'd get far more knowledge from Sakuru," I admitted. "I have a lot to learn."

"We can both learn. Maybe you could teach me some English?

"I'd be glad to," I replied. "When I first met you, I had hoped that you'd teach me Pawnee. Even though I know the language, I still have much to learn about the culture."

"I can help with that, too." Tuhre pointed to some food near the fire. "I cooked breakfast. There should be enough for you and Kuruks."

I gave her a hug. "You're already the best assistant."

Tuhre returned a shy grin. "I need to return home. Is it alright if I come back later this afternoon?"

"Sure," I replied. "I'll wait until you return to try to contact her."

After Tuhre left, I left to go wake Kuruks so we could eat breakfast together. I wanted to wake him up with more than a kiss, but I was afraid of leaving Sakuru alone for more than a few minutes. I coaxed him out of bed with the promise of a warm meal, and we returned and enjoyed Tuhre's wonderful cooking.

"Tuhre is a much better cook," I admitted.

"She is just more experienced with Pawnee food," Kuruks replied.

"She'll be my assistant. She's been wonderful, Kuruks. I owe you, Tuhre, Sakuru, and our village so much. I'm excited to be a part of it. For a while I was only known as the Child of Darkness. Now I feel like I have purpose beyond the prophecy, beyond being your wife—" Kuruks raised an eyebrow. "Of course, I love being your wife."

"I understand," he replied. "I'm proud of you."

I hugged Kuruks. "I love you. I go to sleep thinking that it isn't possible to love you more, and then I wake up in your arms and realize I was wrong. You make me so incredibly happy."

"You make me happy, too. And last night…"

I flashed a sly grin. "The first of many nights just like that."

Kuruks rotated his shoulder. "I thought I would be sore this morning—"

"Why?" I asked in a deliberately innocent tone.

Kuruks smiled. "Anyway, my shoulder actually feels better."

"Good!"

"We are both very lucky," he admitted.

I put my hand on his shoulder as he drifted off in thought. I had the distinct intuitive sense that he was thinking about Paa. It was more than just knowing him well – I caught a brief glimpse of his thoughts. I hated that he was in turmoil. Eventually he broke the silence. "We have our whole lives ahead of us."

I took his hand and gave it a loving squeeze, then nodded in agreement. I was concerned that he wasn't vocalizing his concern for his sister, but knew there was little I could do about it. He looked around the room. "I've been thinking about expanding this home."

"Expanding?"

"Well, since you're now the healer, we'll probably move here. We'll need more room."

"Sakuru's home is bigger than many of the other huts," I said as I gestured around the room. "How much bigger are you talking about?"

Kuruks paced to the far side of the room. "Our buildings are cool in the summer and warm in the winter because they're built with mud and grass and surrounded by earth. But everything is in one room. They are not built with privacy in mind."

My heart warmed. "I love it that you respect my privacy, Kuruks."

"I will get started tomorrow," he declared.

"Are you sure that you're up to that?"

"I've been sitting around resting for too long," Kuruks said.

"What will become of our home, then?" "We could —"

"What?"

I laughed at myself. "I was going to say sell it. Sorry, an old habit."

Kuruks walked back to me and put his arms around me. "No need to be sorry. That is how you were raised."

"Tuhre looked at me strangely when I said I couldn't pay her for being my assistant."

"We work for the good of the village," he said. "Past that, we only have joy to give others."

I smiled. "Then it'll give someone great joy to have our old home. Maybe Tuhre would be interested."

"Women do not generally leave the home until they are married," Kuruks replied. "But there is no harm in asking her."

I looked down at Sakuru. "Tuhre and I are going to try to contact Sakuru again."

"Good," he said. "Do you mind if I participate?"

"Of course not," I replied. "The more help, the better. Tuhre will be back this afternoon."

"Alright. What should we do until then?"

I stared at him intently, trying to ascertain the seriousness of his question. There was a little glimmer, a sign so subtle that only an observant wife would notice. I wrapped my arms around his head and gave him a lingering kiss that quickened my heart.

"But…" I said, motioning towards Sakuru.

Kuruks grabbed extra blankets and pointed to the corner of the room. I eagerly followed him to the edge of the hut. There wasn't much light from the fire, and we didn't have much headroom.

"It's still weird," I admitted, despite her being turned away from us in the other side of the room and having ample blankets above us. As soon as Kuruks began caressing my body, I dropped my protest. □

Chapter 36

Paa saw a faint light in the darkness. Eventually she could make out blurry shapes around her. A voice emerged from the silence.

"Hey, are you awake?"

She wasn't sure. Everything felt like a dream. She was weak, her vision nearly useless, and her head was filled with a high-pitched tone. A series of fuzzy lines waved across her field of view.

"Can you see me?"

After some intense focusing, Paa saw a hand waving across her face. A man with short, brown hair and a well-trimmed beard was sitting at her side.

"There you go. Easy now."

She tried to lean up but her head spun. She laid back down and closed her eyes.

"Your head took quite a wallop," he explained. "Well, actually, your whole body took a wallop."

Paa put her hand over her stomach.

"I got the lead out of you and bandaged you right up."

"Thank you," Paa slowly managed.

"You've got to be in a lot of pain," he said. "That bullet went deep, but I don't think it hit anything too bad."

"Where am I?"

"In my guest bedroom, ma'am. What's your name?"

"Paa," she replied. "No, I mean where are we?"

"You speak good English, you know? You sort of sound French."

"I was taught English by… a friend," Paa explained. "Are we near the river?"

The man nodded. "Well, yes. The Missouri River is less than a mile from here."

"How far?"

"From where I found you? About a three-day horseback ride."

"The creek," Paa said as she tried to stand. "I need to return. My friends —"

He put his hand in front of her. "No ma'am, you're not going anywhere. And I've already buried your friends. I don't know if it was proper to Indian custom, but they're in the ground at least. You need rest. And good food to bring back your strength. I'm a single man so you're out of luck on the food, but at least you can have rest."

"What's your name?" Paa asked.

"Timothy. Or Tim."

Paa had a confused look on her face. "Which one?"

"Tim will do fine," he replied with an awkward chuckle. He reached behind him and fetched a plate. "Are you hungry? It ain't much, just hardtack and raspberry jam, but it's something."

Paa nodded and accepted the plate. "Thank you."

"You must be thirsty. I'll fetch you some water."

Paa dutifully chewed the hard tack. She was just about to swallow when he returned. "Those crackers will sure make you thirsty."

"I haven't eaten since, well… it's been a while," she said, taking a drink from the tin mug. She used the cracker as a scoop and loaded it with jam, then took another bite.

"It's better like that, eh?" Tim asked.

"Yes. I appreciate it."

"No problem. Mind if I ask you some questions?"

"Go ahead."

"I don't mean to pry, but it's not every day you find a pretty Indian girl near death from a gunshot wound. Who shot you?"

Paa took a deep breath. She didn't want to divulge too much, at least until she could figure out if she could trust him. "I don't know."

"How can you not remember something like that?"

She put her fingers to her head and closed her eyes. "I'm confused. I don't know."

Tim lifted her hair to expose a small lump. "You busted your head pretty good. Maybe when you collapsed. Either way, I suppose you're lucky to be alive, let alone remember anything."

"Maybe it will come back to me," Paa said.

"I hope so. You remember your name, so that's good."

Paa handed him the empty plate. "That was delicious, thank you."

"You've got great manners, Paa. That wasn't good food. I'll try to cook you something proper this evening."

"It was fine. I like raspberries," she replied, then took the cup and finished it. "I was so thirsty."

"I imagine so," Tim said. "Do you remember what tribe you are from?"

Paa paused. "Pawnee."

"I reckon I was near your village, then. I've heard about one to the west of here."

"I think so, yes. My head is spinning, I don't know my directions."

"What about your family? They must be worried sick about you."

"I don't have anyone that cares about me."

"Everyone has someone," Tim replied.

"I have a brother," Paa said. She was reluctant to tell him more. She laid her head on the pillow and closed her eyes.

"Here I am talking your ear off," Tim said. "I should let you rest."

"If you don't mind," Paa replied. "But if that offer of dinner is still available—"

"I'll wake you up in time, don't worry. I haven't cooked for two in a good while. I'm looking forward to trying."

Tim left the room, and Paa drifted off to sleep.

Later that evening, Paa awoke to an empty, dark room. "Hello?" she called out in Pawnee, her voice broken with emotion. The high-pitched tone in her inquiry was almost childlike. She called again in English, then tried to sit upright, but the pain from her wounded abdominal muscles forced her to compromise by propping herself up by her elbows. "Tim?"

Paa heard footsteps, then a strange rasping sound. Suddenly, a brilliant light flared across the room. Within seconds, it died down into a small flame.

"I'm sorry, I should have brought a lamp in here," Tim said as he carried the candle to the nightstand. "I suppose this will have to do." He paused and looked at Paa in the candlelight. "I didn't mean to frighten you," he added.

"What was that?" Paa asked.

"It was a match. You haven't seen one before?"

"No. May I?"

Tim handed her the burnt stick and she examined it carefully. "Why not use a flint?"

"I do, sometimes. When I run out of these handy things. I'm a fool and let the fire go out while I was out fishing. I caught some good ones."

Paa tried to get up again, and this time she was successful. She sat on the edge of the bed, panting from the pain.

"Careful now."

"I will clean the catch and help cook them."

"I told you I'd do that. You need to rest."

"I can't stay in this bed forever," Paa said.

"You're in pain. I don't expect you to–"

"It's easing up some."

"Maybe you can sit in the chair over there," Tim said. "But I don't think you should be walking around. At least not today."

Paa looked at the chair, then back at Tim. She finally relented. "Maybe I'm trying to do too much."

Tim chuckled. "Well of course you are. I've been trying to tell you that. I've got an extra lamp - I'll bring it in here so that you don't have to sit in candlelight."

"I don't mind," Paa replied.

"You were scared when I came in here."

"No, it was just your... fire stick thing."

"Match?"

"Yes, match. It startled me, that's all."

"It's alright to fear the dark, Paa. Look, I grew up in Chicago. I never thought I'd see so many stars and such pitch darkness until I came out here. It scared me a little, and I don't get scared."

"I'm not scared of the darkness," Paa insisted.

"Ok, that's fine. Now, do you want to get in the chair?"

Paa tried to stand, but she got dizzy and immediately sat back on the bed. She used her hands to steady herself. "I think I'll stay here for now."

"That's a good idea," Tim said. He fetched the lamp, lit it, then blew out the candle. "Now this is much better, isn't it?"

"Thank you, but I—"

"I know, I know, you are not afraid of the dark. I'll be back with some fish in no time."

Paa started to say something, but Tim left the room. She rocked back and forth as she tried to keep her mind occupied. It became clear the darkness was not what she feared.

She was afraid to be alone.

Chapter 37

Kuruks, Tuhre, and I sat comfortably in a semi-circle around Sakuru. I had let the fire die down a bit to reduce the light in the room, but the flames were still bright enough to cast our shadowy silhouettes along the walls. I puffed on some tobacco and passed it to my husband and then Tuhre, then took their hands.

"We will reach her," I declared, projecting my will to bolster my hopes of a successful outcome.

Kuruks smiled and nodded. Tuhre did well to hide her trepidation.

As I softened my focus, shadows appeared to dance along the corners of the room. I was reminded of the telepathic ritual that Sakuru had initiated before I even reached the village. I closed my eyes and called out to her.

"Sakuru, we need your help."

There was nothing. The darkness in my vision was cold and empty. And then suddenly, I heard a voice emerge from the darkness.

"You are here, Isabella."

Sakuru's voice came through loud and clear, without the weakness I had previously heard from her. I thought it odd that she said that I was here, rather than acknowledging her presence.

"I fear you're slipping away from us, Sakuru. What do we do?" I asked.

"It was a privilege to help give birth to the Child of Darkness. I waited so long to meet you."

Though it was encouraging to hear her voice, I was eager for her help.

"What do we do?"

"You have beautiful children with Kuruks. You train your eager new assistant. You help your people. Above all else, you live your life."

"That is good advice, Sakuru, but it's time to help you."

"I have something to tell you. But it is for you alone, not for the others. Walk with me."

"I don't understand," I said.

"Stand up and walk outside."

Before I could voice my concern that the ritual would be disturbed, she added, "Trust me, Isabella."

I cautiously did as she asked. I opened my eyes and saw Tuhre and Kuruks still in a deep, meditative state. I released their hands, walked outside, and was suddenly whisked to another place. I found myself standing in a field of golden wheat, surrounded by rolling hills. The gentle landscape nestled a small lake in the distance. The sun was bright and there was a hint of salt water on the breeze.

Before I could ask where I was, a hand rested on my shoulder. I turned and saw Sakuru in a beautiful white dress. Her skin was noticeably lighter.

"Where are we? And why do you–"

"Look different? The Child of Darkness is a chameleon. The medicine within us causes us to gradually change in appearance to match those around us. We are in a field outside my home in what you would now call Prince Edward

Island." She took a few steps forward and then inhaled deeply. "This was always my favorite spot. I missed it later in life."

"Why did you leave?"

Sakuru grinned. "The usual reason women do foolish things - the love of a good man." She paused. "I have left too many favorite spots behind. That is the curse of living for centuries."

"You were the Child of Darkness. Why didn't you tell me when you first explained the prophecy to me? And you said it was a Pawnee prophecy. You are not Pawnee."

"Did you not have that discussion with your new chief?" she asked. "I am Pawnee. I am French. I have been American, too. I am a member of whatever culture I choose to live with at the time. The curse of a tremendously long life has its benefits."

I shook my head. "No, Kuruks knew the prophecy. Paa knew it."

"I shared it with them. I took old prophecies handed down through the tribe's history and modified them."

"But why?"

"Partially in a vain attempt to explain my purpose, but it also helped to train Paa. I had hoped that she was born close enough to the eclipse, but I was wrong."

"You should have explained all of this before," I said.

"You do not become the Child of Darkness overnight, Isabella. I gave you the information as you needed it. Perhaps a bit late, at times. You are the first, and last, Child of Darkness I will ever train."

"Last?"

"I have passed on the legacy to you. I have fulfilled my purpose."

"There is still much for you to do," I said.

"Yes, but not in this realm."

"Realm? Sakuru, what do you mean?"

She put her hands on my shoulders. "Isabella, it is now your time. I know you are here to save me, and that warms my heart more than you could possibly know. But you are wasting your time."

I shook my head. "That's not true. I know I can save you."

She took a few steps back and extended her arms. "I am healed. I have never felt better. Isabella, you saved me when you let me pass on this tradition to you. Don't you see?"

I looked away. "No. There has to be a way."

"My time in your realm has ended, Isabella. But I will not leave you. The spirit of every Child of Darkness will be with you until you pass on this tradition, and then you will move on as well. Do you remember those who danced in a circle in your first vision with me?"

"Yes," I answered.

"They are our predecessors. And there will be more after you."

My eyes twitched as I tried to hold back tears. "I am not ready to lose you, Sakuru. I can't. Not now. There are still things you must show me."

Sakuru dried a tear that had managed to escape my increasingly futile efforts to contain my emotions. "Isabella, you are ready. You know everything you need to know now. You will learn more as time progresses, and you will receive inspiration."

"I need you," I implored, with tears freely flowing.

"I am privileged to join the ranks of those who watch over you. Your parents, your grandparents, and guides from lineages deep within your family tree. I will be here. In spirit."

"No!" I fell to my knees and grabbed her dress as I sobbed uncontrollably. She kneeled and held me.

"It is the way of things. You will see something out of the corner of your eye, hear someone calling your name as you drift off to sleep, or catch a glimmer in an animal's eye that tells you more than a thousand words could ever explain. We will be there for you in your darkest hour, and watch in awe as you triumph. It is a difficult task to watch over someone, but it is one I accept with great honor."

Sakuru kissed my forehead, and took the sleeves of her dress and dried my tears. "It is time. When you return to your present, I will be gone. This will be hard for Kuruks, too. I need you to be there for him."

I nodded, trying to prevent erupting back into tears.

"I love you, Sakuru."

She held me and stroked my hair, doing her best to soothe me. "I love you, too, Isabella. You truly are the dragonfly."

I hugged her tightly, and after a few moments that passed too quickly, my vision faded to black. I returned to the ritual, still holding hands with Kuruks and Tuhre. I opened my eyes and watched Sakuru's chest, hoping to see her take a breath.

I waited.

Nothing.

Chapter 38

Paa ate a bite of fried fish. "This is delicious."

"Fish is about the one thing I can cook," Tim declared with cautious pride. "And sometimes cornbread. But that's hit or miss. How are you feeling?"

"Better. Just having food to eat helps my spirits."

"You're lucky. I wasn't sure you were going to make it, and here you are, sitting upright eating," Tim said, shaking his head in disbelief. "You know that bullet missed your liver by just a hair? You must have a guardian angel or something looking after you."

"Maybe," Paa replied. "Either way, I would have died if you hadn't come along."

"Now that is correct. But I ain't saying that for praise. It's just a fact. You were well off the trail. Probably not another soul passing by for miles."

"Do you live alone?" Paa asked.

"Yes ma'am I do," Tim replied. "I am from Chicago, but I got the gold bug."

Paa gave him a strange look. "Did you recover?"

Tim laughed. "It ain't a sickness like you're thinking, but no, I never recovered. The Missouri River and its branches around here are excellent for panning. I've been fetching enough gold out of the water to pay my way. Just enough to keep a chronic case of gold fever. But I haven't hit it real lucky yet." He put the last bite of fish in his mouth and motioned to Paa with his fork. "But I will, though."

"I don't understand," Paa said.

"Oh, that's right, you Indians don't have money, do you?"

"We trade for what we need."

"Well, we do too, but with money. Or gold. I prefer gold. A lot of people are heading further west but I figure they've got it all wrong. You see, I prefer to look where there ain't a lot of competition."

"Makes sense," Paa replied.

"You are a smart girl. But most people aren't smart. They think you gotta do what everyone else does. The first few people to follow a smart man may be smart, but after that they're just dumb. You've got to make your own way in life."

"You live off the land, just like we do," Paa observed. "The water provides fish and gold for you."

Tim nodded. "You're right. I hadn't thought of it like that. I'm like a farmer. A prospecting farmer, that is."

"You are a wise man, Tim."

"I wish my family could hear you say that. They think I'm a fool."

"That is something we share," Paa replied.

"Is that why they shot you?" Tim asked.

Paa was caught off guard. "No. Wait, why do you ask?"

Tim laughed. "I've been wondering who did that. You pretty much confirmed it, there. Since it ain't common for a parent to shoot their kid, I'd reckon your brother or sister did that to you. Am I right?"

Paa sighed. "I don't want to talk about that."

"I'm sorry they did that to you. I've been in a few fights with my family before. And only one of them involved a rifle."

Paa raised an eyebrow. "It seems like you made it through the ordeal."

"Yea. My mother never aimed the thing at me. But our kitchen cabinets were never the same after that."

Paa started to ask, but decided against it.

"Anyway, you don't want to hear about my family squabbles."

"You wanted to hear about mine," Paa retorted.

"Good point. So what does Paa mean, exactly? In English, it's what we call our father."

"That's pa," she corrected. "In Pawnee, paa means moon."

"So, you were named after the moon? Interesting." Tim pondered that a moment. "So if your name means moon, how do you say sun in Pawnee?"

"Sun in Pawnee is sakuru."

"Paa, moon, sakuru, sun," Tim said. "Hey, at this rate, I'll learn your language in no time."

Paa's skepticism was evident in her expression, but she dipped her head to hide it. "Of course. Like I said, you are wise, Tim."

Tim had a huge grin on his face. "That's awfully nice of you to say. Teach me some more words."

Paa was tired and growing weary of the conversation, but she didn't want to disappoint her new benefactor. "I'm tired, Tim, but I will teach you one more phrase. It is a phrase that describes you, Tim. You are a tuhre."

"Tuhre? What does that mean?"

"Tuhre means a good person."

"Oh, well, you are determined to flatter me, aren't you?"

"I didn't—"

"I'm not complaining," Tim said. "Don't stop."

"You rescued me from certain death. Only a good person would do that."

"I'm not so sure. Bad people do good things sometimes, too. Especially if they think it will get them something."

"I have known a great deal of darkness in my life and I've become quite adept at spotting it. You, Tim, are good."

Tim nodded with delight. "I ain't gonna argue with someone who is paying me a compliment."

Paa relaxed into the bed. "Thank you for everything you've done."

"Don't mention it. Now I'll stop yapping and let you go to sleep."

Tim put out the light. "Good night, Paa."

Paa soon fell asleep. Her dreams were filled flashes of seemingly random images. Time passed so quickly while she was asleep. Eventually, from the din chaos of her unconscious mind, emerged an image of a knife sticking out of Chakira'a chest. After much distress, the nightmare concluded.

The rest of Paa's sleep was relatively undisturbed. She awoke to bright morning sunlight pouring into the window. After a moment of regaining her bearings, she listened intently to see if she could hear any sign of Tim. The house was silent.

"Tim?"

Paa heard no response. She sat up in bed with only minimal discomfort, then attempted to stand. The pain from her abdominal muscles was intense, but she pushed through and managed to steady herself on her own two feet. She called again to Tim but to no avail. She took a few successful steps only to be stopped by a near fall. Hanging onto a dresser was the only thing that kept her from crashing helplessly to the floor. She cautiously took a few more steps, making sure she kept a firm grip on the furniture until she made it to the door.

Paa held onto the doorframe for dear life as she tried to peer into the other rooms that were connected to the small hallway. Her long, slender arms gave her some leverage, but the layout of the home prevented any meaningful inspection. She awkwardly darted to the opposite doorway and grabbed its frame to steady herself. The main room was empty, and a check of the other bedroom revealed only Tim's unmade bed. She limped into the main room and took a seat on a chair. She gently rocked, and stared at a painting on the wall.

Paa didn't want to be alone.

Eventually, the rocking ceased, and she closed her eyes, then put her hand over her abdomen. Her mind was remarkably silent as she meditated.

Paa ventured outside with little difficulty and found a well. She took off her dress and began washing it in a basin just beside it, vigorously trying to remove the blood stains. Just as she finished, she heard an approaching horse. She had barely put her dress back on when Tim rode up to the house and put away his horse. His face was red, and he avoided eye contact.

"You're back!" Paa walked toward him.

"I see you're feeling better," he replied. "I didn't expect you to be on your feet so soon."

"Thanks to you," she said with a smile. "What's wrong?"

Tim looked away. "Oh, uh… I might have — "

"Might have what?"

He sighed in frustration. "I saw you naked. I'm sorry, I didn't mean to, but — "

"I was washing my dress. I was naked, so that makes sense," Paa replied. "There is no need to be embarrassed."

"I'm just not used to…"

"You must have seen me nude when you removed the bullet from me."

"Well, uh, just your stomach. I made sure not to look at anything else. I am not perfect by any means, but I try to be a gentleman."

"I do not know that word," Paa admitted.

"A gentleman is, well, gentle. He doesn't act harshly or dishonor a woman."

"Then I agree. You are a gentleman."

Tim grinned. "I appreciate that. I promise I didn't try to look. My eyes just — "

"It is alright. There is nothing to worry about."

"If you say so."

Paa eyed the small crate that Tim was carrying. "What is that?"

267

"Oh, I got a few things from the general store. Lookie here!"

Paa leaned over the crate and examined the items one by one as Tim pointed them out. "Cornmeal, for starters. I didn't have enough for that cornbread I was threatening on making. A few eggs, some salt pork, and a treat for you."

"A treat? What's in that bag?"

Tim shook his head. "I ain't showing you 'till after dinner. It's sweet, and my mom always told me to not eat sweets before dinner."

Paa offered to help cook, but Tim adamantly declined. He insisted that if the cornbread was going to be a failure, he was going to take full credit for it. Paa sat and watched him cook, then the two ate the fruits of Tim's labor.

"This is good!" Paa exclaimed, taking another hearty bite.

"It ain't bad," Tim replied. "Yea, I did pretty good. I wish I had some butter, but they were out."

After they finished, Tim pulled a brown bar from the pouch that he had, until now, kept a mystery and encouraged Paa to take a bite. Her eyes grew wide with surprise.

"This is... amazing!" She eagerly finished the last bit of the bar she had. "What is it?"

"It's called chocolate. They don't always have it, but I buy some every time they do. It ain't cheap, either. But I've got a good sized credit at the store from my last find."

"It's hard to describe," she added. "I've never had anything like it."

"It's good, eh? I tried some back in Chicago and my life hasn't been the same since. You wanna go sit outside?"

"Sure," Paa replied.

The two moved out to the porch, and Tim offered the bigger rocking chair to Paa. Her slight frame made the chair look considerably oversized.

"It's much cooler out here," Tim observed.

Paa smelled the air. "It won't be long before snow falls."

"Snow? It's only September 24th. I figure a freeze is at least a month away."

"No, it will be soon. Do you have anything in your garden?"

Tim laughed. "A single man can pan for gold or raise crops, but he ain't got time to do both."

"What would you do if you didn't find enough gold?"

"I've always been lucky enough," Tim said. "I get a steady stream from the river. And when I've run a bit dry, I just fall back on a little savings I have. I ain't gettin' ahead but I don't get behind, either."

"Get ahead?"

"Well, I want to strike it rich," he replied.

"What would you do with the money?" Paa asked.

"Fix up this place, for starters. I don't plan staying single forever, and I'm sure a future wife would want it to be a touch nicer to raise some children in."

"And she could plant a garden."

Tim nodded. "She could. Free, fresh vegetables sounds good to me."

"Couldn't you just skip all of that and plant your own garden?" Paa asked.

Tim paused a moment, then chuckled. "Fresh vegetables would be great, but I'd like a little female companionship."

"I am female."

"Uh, no, that's not what I mean. Yes, of course, you are, but I meant a wife."

"Oh, yes. I didn't know exactly what you meant."

"You know some pretty big words in English, but you don't know exactly what they mean sometimes, do you?"

"A friend of mine taught me. I spoke it exclusively for about a year while I learned. But I do not know all your sayings. To me, companionship means a friend."

"I see what you mean," Tim said. "I should be more clear."

"It's not your fault," she replied.

"It's nice to know you consider me a friend," he said.

"I do."

Tim paused a moment. "Paa, something is bugging me. I gotta know what's going on with you."

"Going on with me?"

"Yea. It don't make sense for an Indian girl to get shot by another Indian."

"Do white men not shoot other white men?"

"Well, yea, but—"

"It is no different."

"You had other injuries, too," Tim said.

"I thought you didn't look at my body any more than you had to?"

"Well, I didn't. But I had to remove some of your clothing to tend to your wound. Someone beat the hell out of you. Who did that?"

"My brother," Paa admitted.

Tim waited for her to expand on her thought, but she didn't. "Mind if I ask why?"

"Yes, I do. It is an uncomfortable subject."

"I understand that, but, it ain't right for a man to beat up on a woman like that."

"He is my brother, and I forgive him."

"That's mighty big of you," Tim said. "But if you—"

Paa stopped rocking and looked directly at Tim. "Are we friends?"

"Well, yes, of course."

"Then respect my wish to not discuss my brother. Would a friend not grant that request?"

Tim sighed. "You are right. I'm sorry."

A moment of uncomfortable silence passed between them.

Paa resumed her rocking.

"I'll honor your privacy. But I can't ignore something else strange, friend or no friend."

"What is it?" Paa asked, trying her best to restrain her annoyance.

"What happened to those two dead Indian women by the river?" □

Chapter 39

The funeral for Sakuru was an intense experience. It's fair to say all funerals are, but seeing the death rituals of another culture adds a surreal layer to the painful event. It was usually the healer who led the funeral. Though the village understood that I was new to the job, the somber duty fell upon me, and I had no intention of rejecting it.

It was unfair to have Kuruks be my surrogate into this unfamiliar aspect of Pawnee life, as Sakuru had become a mother to him. Regardless, he showed his usual selfless strength in guiding me through what I needed to know. Since Sakuru held a high status in the village, her funeral was to be more elaborate than most, so I wanted to make sure I did the best I could for her memory, and the benefit of the village.

Kuruks, Tuhre, and Chief Piita helped me apply the sacred burial paints and ointments to Sakuru's body. We dressed her in her finest clothes, the same she had worn to my wedding ceremony when she was mortally shot by Paa. With a skillful patch and a thorough cleaning, the dress was presentable. As we finished preparing her body, I had flashbacks of the moment she was hit by that wicked arrow.

The next morning, with the entire village in tow, we carried Sakuru's body to the burial site. Despite the gloomy event, it was a beautiful day. The sun shone brightly and a pleasant breeze danced across the plains – a stark contrast to the dark mood that so pervasively hung in the air. Words were few and movements were slow and deliberate, as though everyone had drawn inward to process their grief.

Since I was not familiar with the words commonly spoken at this ritual, the chief spoke immediately before the burial. His words were recited in a reverent and eloquent meter that I would have been oblivious to had I not known the Pawnee language.

"Sakuru's path in this life led her to our village, and she choose to dedicate her life in faithful service to its health and mental wellbeing. She was honored in life, and will be honored in death. She will ascend to the heavens and take her place as another point of light in the night sky. She will be missed."

With that, much as in my birth culture's tradition, various people approached the body to pay their last respects. One by one they filtered away, until it was just Kuruks, Tuhre, Piita, and I. The chief nodded at me, then walked toward me. He put his sturdy hand on my shoulder for a moment, then left. I was comforted and honored by his reassuring touch.

Tuhre gave me a hug, then hugged Kuruks, then told us she would be there if we needed her.

"I will leave you alone if you like," I said to Kuruks, wishing to give him a private moment with Sakuru. I moved my hand, and he gripped it harder. It was as close as he could come to telling me he needed me, so I dispensed with any notion of leaving. He tried to hold back tears. I wanted to tell him it was alright to let go of the sadness that welled up inside him, but instead I listened to something inside me that told me to remain silent.

I gently squeezed Kuruks's arm, and opened my heart to him, letting him know in our beautifully complex telepathic language that I was there for him. I'm glad I chose not to speak, as verbal communication would have sullied the message I was trying to convey. I wrapped my love around him as his stoic countenance gave way to freely flowing tears.

As a couple, we paid our last respects to a woman who had meant so much to us. As we walked back to our new home, I worried about Kuruks. I had dried his tears, but the violence that Paa had visited upon us still gravely wounded him. The physical scars were healing, but his emotions concerning his sister were still far from resolved.

At home, we spoke little. Instead, Kuruks held me by the fire. We stared into it for quite some time, and we then drifted off to a late afternoon slumber. I awoke after sundown and made a light dinner. The smells of my cooking roused him, and we shared a pleasant meal.

"There's no need to add any more room to this home," Kuruks admitted.

"I think we might need an extra room if we're going to have a little Kuruks running around here," I said.

"Our children will sleep near the fire during the winter. We don't usually have more than one room."

"That is just my old culture talking," I replied. "I had my own room in Independence. If I had a sister, I'm sure I would be sharing one with her."

"Even a large family can share a single home, especially as large as this one."

"I should get used to that idea," I said. "But how will we ever have privacy?"

Kuruks smiled a bit, the first time since the funeral. "Our kids will find plenty to do outdoors."

I giggled and then leaned my head against his shoulder. "I can't wait to fill our home with little feet prattling around."

"We are going to have many beautiful children, but only if they take after you, Izzy."

"Hey now, you are very handsome."

"If they are only half as strong as their mother was for me today, I will be proud."

I hugged him. "I love you, Kuruks."

"I love you, Izzy. I want to make a pact with you. Today has reminded me again that life is fragile, and sometimes short. If something happens to me —"

I tried to interrupt him, but he continued. "If something happens to me, you will find another husband."

"No, I can't. I cannot love anyone else like you."

"That is true," he said, "but you can love someone else should that happen. You deserve to be happy."

"I don't want to talk about this. The thought of you dying —"

"I am older than you —"

"Not that much older," I protested.

"Promise me," he insisted.

I saw the look in his eyes. He was serious. And yet I hoped humor could escape me from this unpleasant conversation. "After a suitable mourning period. Several hundred years, perhaps?"

Kuruks sighed. "I will accept that as a promise."

"And what about you? If I die, will you find someone else?"

"After a suitable mourning period, yes. One, maybe two moons."

He said it without a hint of a grin on his face. Only with my playful protest did he break into laughter. We rolled around in the floor, tickling each other in playfighting. We needed the release from the dreary and emotional day. After several more hours of intimate conversation, we peacefully fell asleep.

Chapter 40

Paa had no immediate answer prepared to explain the bodies of her two departed friends. While Tim was gone, she had plenty of time to come up with stories, but this one had slipped her mind. She cursed herself for being so careless while frantically searching for something that sounded halfway plausible.

Since Tim was obviously in the dark about the situation that resulted in their deaths, there seemed to be nothing specifically to hide. She had lied so often that it not only was comfortable, but expected. The truth just wasn't something she was comfortable with, even when it didn't pose any direct threat to her.

"Did your brother kill them, too?" Tim asked with a hint of incredulity.

Paa walked in front of him so she could better gauge his reaction. "Why do you ask in that tone of voice?"

"It just seems strange to me that you would leave out that detail."

Paa scoffed. "It seems strange that I would remember anything. I'm still a bit hazy."

Tim ran his hand through his hair. "I suppose you're right. I didn't mean nothing from it, I couldn't understand why you left that part out. But you've been through enough without me hounding you about it."

Paa relaxed and sat back down. "I'm sorry. I should have told you. I guess I'm still a bit defensive."

Tim nodded. "Understandable. There's no need to apologize."

Paa gazed into his eyes to see if he truly bought her crudely executed diversion. His replies seemed genuine. "It is difficult when your own blood turns against you."

"All things considered, I'd say you are handling things pretty well," Tim observed. "I know if one of my family killed any of my friends and took a shot at me, I'd be mighty angry."

"I do not think it's fully sunk in yet."

"Do you think he'll come after you?" Tim asked.

"He probably thinks I'm dead."

"Maybe. Well, either way, if he comes here, I won't let him hurt you."

Paa was shocked by the notion that he would defend her. "Why would you do that?"

"I don't want anything to happen to you," Tim replied.

Paa didn't know how to respond.

"You haven't ever had anyone defend you before, have you?"

Paa took a deep breath and looked away.

"Now that don't make any sense. I haven't known you long, but you're nice enough. I wouldn't just share chocolate with anyone."

Paa grinned slightly. She was still turned away, so Tim couldn't see it. "I am used to people not trusting me, or even wanting me around."

"I find that hard to believe," Tim said.

"I can be… difficult."

"Everyone can be difficult. I ain't met an exception, yet."

Paa gave a slight shrug.

"You're welcome to stay for long as you need to."

"I can't intrude on your hospitality forever," Paa said.

"Well, once you're fully recovered, maybe you can help out some if you feel like you have to earn your keep."

"I do," Paa replied. "I'll cook breakfast tomorrow."

Tim shook his head. "Not until you're fully healed."

"I feel better."

"Only when you're good and ready. And you can't do all of the cooking, 'cause I like to cook, too."

"I'm sure I can find something else to do around here," Paa said. "Your home is not ready for winter, and it will snow in just a few days."

Tim scoffed. "I'll believe it when I see it."

Paa raised an eyebrow. "You do that. I will be preparing for winter." She yawned. "Tomorrow, of course."

"I don't know what to make of you sometimes, Paa."

"Why would you make anything out of me?"

Tim laughed. "I don't mean literally. I just don't understand you. Not quite yet."

"No one has understood me," she replied, then walked back into the house.

She proceeded to the guest room and prepared for bed. As soon as she slid into the covers, she heard Tim outside the door. "Are you decent?"

"If you mean clothed, then yes."

He stood in the doorway and took a deep breath. "I hope you didn't take offense to what I said."

"What do you mean?"

"Oh, well I guess you didn't. About not understanding you."

"No, I didn't take any offense. I am not the best with conversations."

"I can't say I am, either," Tim replied. "I can talk a plenty, but most of the time that doesn't work to my advantage. Sometimes I don't know what to say."

"That is something we share," Paa said. "I seem to never pick the right words, so I usually just stay quiet. I think it's part of the reason people don't trust me."

"I trust you."

Paa was genuinely touched by his gesture. He was the first person to ever treat her as a normal person, and accepting that kind of trust and friendly discourse was awkward to her. She realized it would be best to return the sentiment.

Paa smiled. "I trust you, too. Good night, Tim."

"Good night, Paa. Sleep well."

Paa put out her lamp then contemplated the night's events. She replayed the conversation in her head, still frustrated that she wasn't prepared to answer Tim's question about her friends' bodies. She knew she'd need to have better explanations for her recent circumstances and vowed to make sure her story made more sense. She stared at the ceiling for close to an hour as she decided her next move. Eventually, she drifted off to sleep.

The next morning Paa awoke to find that Tim had already left for the day. She had a surge of panic as she realized she was alone, but then soothed it with a quick moment of calm meditation. When she opened her eyes again, she recalled all that she had planned to do, so she used the remaining twinge of nervous energy as a catalyst to start ticking items off her to-do list.

Paa ate a simple piece of bread for breakfast, then immediately set to work with a scrub brush and pail to thoroughly clean the kitchen. Though Tim wasn't overly messy, she still was still able to remove months of cooking residue and accumulated dust from nearly every surface she touched. Her injured muscles ached throughout the work, but she pressed on through the pain, knowing there would be plenty of time to rest and recover later that evening.

Paa surveyed the windows and doors of the home, looking for any loose boards or cracks that could let in cold air. She gathered straw and mud from outside and plugged the spaces. Though her technique seemed a bit unusual to use on a wooden structure, she smoothed the patch surface until it was not obvious. A simple test with her hand assured her the leak had been fixed.

The fireplace between the main room and the kitchen was in deplorable shape. Though it drew air, the walls and floor of the fireplace were caked with considerable soot and ash. Paa took the brush and vigorously scrubbed it clean, then relit the fire. After resting a moment by the newly refurbished hearth, she cleaned the main room. By the time she had finished, the house looked wonderful.

She wanted to cook dinner, but she wasn't familiar with using wheat flour. She knew that meat was her easiest option, but she wasn't certain where the river was, so she decided to hunt. She sharpened a stick and headed out into the fields, and before late afternoon she had caught a rabbit. By the time Tim had returned, she had the rabbit dressed and cooked.

Tim's eyes were wide with surprise when he looked around his home. "I swear, I think I've got a new house."

"Now it is fit for winter," she said as she handed him a plate.

"And dinner, too. This smells great. It's been a while since I've had rabbit. You didn't have to do all of this."

"I can't just sit here all day," Paa replied.

"Just because you feel better doesn't mean you shouldn't take it easy."

"I'm sore, but I'm happy to have accomplished something."

Tim looked at everything in more detail. "The fireplace. It looks great."

"You are lucky that soot didn't catch fire."

"Well, I can't thank you enough," Tim said.

"You saved my life. A day of cleaning will hardly make up for that."

"You don't owe me anything," he said, taking a bite of rabbit.

"If it bothers you, then pretend that I did it for myself. I wanted rabbit, and if I'm going to be stuck here for the winter I'd like it to be warm."

Tim laughed. "I thought you were crazy, but you're right – we might just get snow. I heard at the general store that some folks a bit north of us have already had a dusting. And there's a sharp wind out there. How'd you know?"

"Nature tells us what it plans to do," Paa replied. "You just have to listen."

"You're going to be stuck here all winter, huh?"

"Looks like it. With your permission."

Tim shook his head. "Not at all. The winters out here are awfully lonely. And I think you can teach me a thing or two."

"Certainly," Paa replied, then took her first bite. "We both have a lot to learn."

Chapter 41

I hadn't given a second thought about losing Kuruks until he wanted me to promise I'd find someone else should I outlive him. Sakuru's funeral left me drained, so I didn't give serious thought about it until the next morning. He likely mentioned it because I had shared the details of my spiritual encounter with Sakuru. The reality that I would likely outlive him was settling in for both of us, and yet his first thought was of my happiness after he died.

My heart was warmed by his selfless gesture, but I didn't want him giving too much thought to that morbid possibility. I wanted to shield him from worrying about that. I felt that by ignoring it we would be able to focus on our lives now, not what may be in the future. Regardless, his honest question forced me into this reality – the inequity of our lifespans and the fact that one of us would eventually be alone.

As I did my morning chores, I started to fear what life would be like absent Kuruks. A life without him was unfathomable. I looked at him, still peacefully asleep, and let the thought sink in of how much he, and my love for him, had changed me. My new world was not something I could ever see myself leaving. His words weighed on me heavily throughout the day.

After Kuruks and I ate breakfast, Tuhre came and said that one of the villagers was sick and needed help. They were too sick to come to our home, so I gathered my medicine bag, some herbs that Sakuru had in her collection, and then Tuhre and I walked to their home. When I arrived, there entire family was inside their hut. Their two children were chasing each other around, the mother was busy cooking, and the father was pale and leaning on his side near the fire.

"Hello," I said. "I am Izzy."

"I know who you are," he snapped. "I am Askue."

"He hasn't eaten this morning, and he was vomiting all night," his wife said. "He hasn't been feeling well for several days."

"She sent for you. But I'll be alright. It's just something I ate."

"Probably so," I replied. "But I will do what I can."

"No English woman can help me."

I felt as though I were blind, and his lack of confidence in me didn't help. I ignored his comment and looked through my bag of herbs. I remember that my favorite, chamomile, soothed and calmed a nervous stomach. I wasn't certain what exact ailment he was suffering from, but I knew reducing his symptoms would help. I took some of the plant I had and made him some tea.

"Drink this, Asuke," I said and offered it to him.

He looked at the cup with caution, and glared at me. I smiled and made a motion encouraging him to drink. He timidly took some of the liquid, then snarled his nose a bit. Reluctantly he finished the cup, then sat upright.

"Feel better?" one of his children asked him.

"No," he said flatly.

"It's only been two minutes," I replied.

"Patience is not one of Asuke's virtues," his wife retorted.

I did my best to hide a smile while I observed his slightly annoyed reaction.

The younger child, who couldn't have been older than three, came up to me and touched my face as he stared into my eyes.

"Hello, there," I said to him. He didn't respond.

"He doesn't talk much yet," Asuke said.

After a moment, as in defiance of his father's prediction, he said, "Hi."

"He doesn't usually speak to strangers," Asuke added.

"Hopefully I will not be regarded as a stranger for long," I replied.

"Some in the village think you will leave as soon as you tire of our ways," Asuke said.

"Then those people are wrong."

Asuke managed a decidedly non-committal grunt of acceptance.

"Is daddy okay?" the quiet one asked.

"Of course," I replied.

I waited a few more minutes. "Do you feel better?"

"Maybe a little," he replied. "It comes and goes."

I took out my remaining stock of chamomile and mint. "Take these in a tea whenever you feel bad. They will help settle your stomach. Let me know if it doesn't get any better."

Asuke accepted the herbs with a kind nod. His wife tried to offer us some breakfast, but I told her I had already eaten. Tuhre, however, accepted some pemmican, and she ate it as we walked back to my home.

"I appreciate your help, Tuhre. I feel lost. I didn't go to medical school, and I only know a fraction of the knowledge that Sakuru had amassed."

287

"You did what Sakuru would have done. She would give me mint, chamomile, and sometimes marshmallow root to soothe my stomach."

"I didn't think of marshmallow."

"I hope he feels better soon," Tuhre said. "He looked very pale. If Sakuru thought something serious was wrong, she would do a ritual to drive out the evil spirits from the body."

I am ashamed to admit I had a dismissive reaction to the notion at first, but that was simply a matter of my previous cultural conditioning. I knew that spirits could inhabit another body from the experience I had, so it was foolish of me to scoff at the idea of spiritual issues creating disease. I shoved the last vestige of my disbelief aside.

"I don't know how she did it, exactly, but with most spiritual matters I have learned it is not the precise technique but the intent behind the action."

"You also have to fully believe in what you are doing," Tuhre added.

"You caught that flash of rejection, didn't you?" I asked. "You're very perceptive. I came from a culture that would laugh at what you just said, yet think nothing of buying patent medicines that claim to cure every possible aliment known to man and chase them down with a desperate prayer."

Chapter 42

As late afternoon approached, a brisk, chilly wind blew from the north. I remarked to Kuruks it was weather that would usually encourage my mother to start making wonderful stews. I carried on the tradition by putting together a bison stew. I didn't have the same vegetables that she used to add, but I did have onions and plenty of aromatic herbs, so I added them to a big pot of bison cuts and allowed them to simmer so that the wonderful, deep flavors would begin to merge.

"It's a bit early for such cool weather," I remarked to Kuruks as I stirred the pot.

"I don't think so. The days have been getting shorter. And the trees are turning."

"Yes, but it's only…"

I suddenly realized I had no idea what the date was. Kuruks looked at me strangely while I struggled to finish the statement. I had been disconnected from American culture for so long that I had lost track of the days. I knew that fall had settled in, but I had given scarcely little consideration to the change in seasons. Worse, I had completely omitted keeping track of the calendar. I didn't even know the day of the week.

"I have no idea," I finally admitted. "I always used to know the date. I don't know if it's a Friday or Monday."

"I do not understand the purpose of naming days," Kuruks said.

"It helps people keep track of them."

"The earth, moon and sun tell us all we need to know about time."

I tried to think of why Pawnee would ever have a need to know the day, and outside of periodic celebrations and planting, I couldn't arrive at a valid reason.

"You don't know the day you were born, do you?" I asked.

"It was a few days after a full moon in the middle of winter," he replied.

"I won't know when to wish you happy birthday."

"When you are connected to the land, it tells you what you need to know. If you listen to it closely, it says when to plant and when to harvest."

"This cold wind was no surprise to you, was it?"

"No. The village has been preparing for winter. We have been injured and out of the normal preparations, but you will notice our stockpiles of meat have increased."

"I feel so foolish for not having paid attention," I said.

"You were focusing on Sakuru," Kuruks replied. "In addition to nursing your own wounds and taking care of me. When members of our village are having problems, the rest come in and help without being asked. If they do their job correctly, your absence is hardly noticed."

"I owe everyone thanks."

Kuruks shook his head. "No. You thank them by helping them when they need it. You are the healer, now. When someone is sick you tend to them. When we face a problem that is of spirit, we come to you. That is your place, your task. You are already doing your part."

As I absorbed his words, I realized that had joined more than a culture. A group of people I barely knew, some of who still felt I was not reliable, or that I would leave as soon as I grew bored of them, had been covering some of my needs and looking ahead on my behalf without my conscious knowledge. I was impressed, and my heart was warmed upon realizing the size and strength of my new family.

"I would still like to know your birthday," I said.

"We have but one birthday," Kuruks said. "And it is a joyous occasion when our village welcomes a new life."

I took his hand and smiled. "They will have reason to celebrate with us soon enough."

Kuruks's eyes widened and a grin instantly spread across his face. "Are you with child?"

I laughed. "No, that's not what I meant." There was immediate disappointment in his expression. "I'm sorry, I didn't mean to give you that impression. I meant that it will soon be our turn to bring a new life into the world."

"No need to apologize. I made a bad assumption."

I gave him a hug. "I think it was adorable. I loved your expression. You'll be an excellent father," I said right after I sampled some of the stew.

"Is it ready?" he asked.

"Not quite. It's good, but it'll be even better tomorrow."

"I don't think I can wait," Kuruks admitted.

"We still have enough food left over from lunch," I explained. "Trust me, this will taste wonderful tomorrow."

After sunset, the air grew even colder. We heard strange noises as the wind assaulted the roof of our hut. Smoke from our fire was drawn out at incredible speed. Soon after we finished eating, we went outside to survey the skies. After just a few minutes, Kuruks noticed that I was shivering.

"Your dress isn't enough for weather like this," he observed.

"This is all I have," I replied.

"Sakuru's fur cloak would be nice and warm. She would want you to have it."

I knew the one he was referring to, but I had left it in the corner along with a few other of her belongings. I had not yet gathered the emotional courage to go through her things. I went back inside and fetched her beautiful fur wrap. I held it in front of me for a moment, thinking of her and how she would tell me that there was no use in letting a nice piece of clothing going to waste.

I could feel her presence on the garment, and caught a whiff of the tobacco she used in meditation. I already felt unworthy of holding her previous position, and wearing her beautiful, handmade clothing seemed more than I could bare. Kuruks walked in behind me, took the cloak, and put it over my shoulders.

"You look beautiful in it," Kuruks said. "Sakuru would be proud."

"I don't feel very prideful in my work. I still stumble to follow in her footsteps."

"That is to be expected," he replied. "But you will grow and learn every day."

After donning warmer clothing, we returned outside to check on the weather. A few drops fell on my head. "It's raining."

Kuruks showed me his outstretched palm and pointed out a few snowflakes. "It's more than rain."

Bigger flakes started to mix with the wind-driven sheets of rain. "The ground is too warm for it to stick."

"We should get back to the fire," Kuruks replied.

I was glad that we had a well-built home and a roaring fire to keep us warm. We snuggled up to chase away the cold. A few lingering kisses quickly led to a sudden increase in temperature. We had soon shed the clothing that we had just put on to get warm, and within moments Kuruks was over me.

Our previous conversation about having children must have partially inspired him because we made love numerous time throughout the evening. I was delighted by his endurance, but eventually the warmth of the fire and the sweat from our vigorous activities had left me drained. We fell asleep naked by the fire, holding one another through the cold night.

Chapter 43

Paa woke to unusually bright light shining through the window. She worried that she had overslept and missed preparing breakfast, so she bolted out from under the covers. When she landed on the floor from her small, yet enthusiastic jump, she felt a twinge of pain in her abdomen. She had considered her wound healed, and dismissed it as leftover soreness. She shook off the discomfort and headed immediately to the kitchen.

Paa was relieved that Tim wasn't up yet. She felt a strong need to take care of him as repayment for what he had done for her. Cooking breakfast seemed a good way to fulfill that desire. Before she began, she peeked outside the window and was not at all surprised to see at least a foot of snow on the ground. She grinned with pride at her successful prediction, then proceeded to make a nice meal for the two of them.

Breakfast was ready, but Tim wasn't up, so she went to wake him. She knocked on his door, but there was no answer. She walked inside and saw him snoring, so she approached and called his name. Her voice interrupted his snore, but he wasn't fully roused, so she put her hand on his shoulder. He opened his eyes and smiled.

"You're a wonderful sight to see first thing in the morning."

"I made something for us to eat."

"I'll be right there," he said. "Just have to get dressed first."

Paa retreated to the safety of the doorway. "I'm not naked - there's no need to run away," he added.

She was even more embarrassed. She tried to reply, but was unable to form any cohesive response. She returned to the kitchen and plated their food. After a moment, Tim joined her, and they began to eat.

"I didn't mean to embarrass you," Tim said. "It's just nice to have company. I'm glad to have you around."

"It snowed," Paa announced, trying to change the subject.

"I saw that. You were right," he admitted. "Looks like I won't be finding any gold today."

Tim finished his breakfast, then noticed that Paa had barely finished a quarter of her meal. "What's wrong?" he asked.

"I am not as hungry as I thought I was."

"You really outdid yourself. You need to rest today."

"I have rested enough. We've been over this."

Tim shook his head. "Now how did I know you were going to say that? I've seen men take months, sometimes years to recover from injuries like that. I think you're being a bit hard on yourself."

"I don't need to rest!" Paa yelled, then looked away.

"I'm concerned about you."

"I know," she admitted in a softer voice, having reined her temper. "Keeping busy helps keep my mind off what happened."

"Makes sense," Tim replied. "But please be careful."

As Tim began to clear the plates, Paa regretted her outburst. "I'm sorry."

"It's alright. If someone told me to rest for a whole day, I'd give 'em lip, too."

"I'll go get some more firewood," Paa said.

"I can do that. It's pretty heavy," he called after her, but she had already shut the door behind her.

Paa walked outside and looked out over the snow-covered field. She tried to enjoy the peace and serenity of the beautiful scene in front of her, but all she could think about was her churning stomach. She swallowed hard and trudged a path to the wood pile. She barely made it back inside to put the logs near the hearth before she was overcome with nausea. She rushed outside and lost her breakfast in the snow.

After Paa regained her breath, she noticed streaks of blood in her vomit. She buried it with more snow then walked back inside as she held her stomach.

"I heard you out there. You aren't fine. I should've carried that."

"I won't argue with you," Paa admitted.

Tim grabbed Paa by her shoulders. "You can get mad and yell at me all you want, but I am not going to let you hurt yourself. You need to rest, and I won't take no for an answer."

"You're right."

"What?"

"I need rest," Paa admitted.

"Yes, but I expected—"

"I'm too nauseous to get mad at you, Tim."

Tim helped her back to bed. "I wish I had a proper nightgown for you."

"I would be worried if you had women's clothing," Paa replied.

He chuckled. "You are too sick to yell at me, but not too sick to tease me."

"That means I will live," she replied. "Like you said, I need rest. I can heal on my own."

Tim stood in the doorway and glanced back at her with affection.

She was touched by his protective nature. "I'll be fine."

She worried about the blood. She attempted to soothe her concerns by reaffirming to herself there was a good chance she could heal herself. She admitted she had a lot more healing to do before she was ready to declare herself fully recovered, but didn't want to worry Tim, so giving into his requests that she rest was good cover. She pulled the covers up over her, closed her eyes, and entered a deep meditative state.

Chapter 44

"Izzy, wake up!"

I could make out Tuhre's face through blurry vision. I must have ignored her and briefly drifted back to sleep because she called again, then shook me. I bolted up and looked around as I tried to get awake. I realized that Kuruks and I had fallen asleep naked. I was covered, but me sitting upright had jerked the blanket off Kuruks. The cooler air and commotion stirred him awake.

"You've got to hurry! Askue is bad!"

"I'll get my things and meet you there," I said, wiping the sleep from my eyes.

"Hurry," Tuhre insisted.

As soon as she left, I quickly got up and dressed.

"Don't forget your cloak," Kuruks said.

I noticed the temperature fell just a few feet away from the fire, so I knew it was cold outside. I finished dressing and leaned down to give Kuruks a kiss.

"Do you want me to come with you?"

"Sure, if you want," I replied.

While I gathered my things, Kuruks dressed and we headed outside. I was shocked to see at least a foot of snow on the ground. He took my supplies from me and held my hand.

"I'll be alright," I said as snow crunched beneath my feet.

As we walked, I realized I must have looked horrible. A quick survey of my hair with my fingers convinced me that rat's nests were kept in a more presentable condition. I tried to make it at least somewhat passable but soon gave up.

"You look good," Kuruks said.

I love that he knew what I was thinking. I didn't have to say a word. Despite his reassuring sentiment, I knew it wouldn't do. I fetched a small string from my bag and tied my hair back. Kuruks looked puzzled. I realized he hadn't ever seen me with my hair up. He gave me an adorable grin, one that made me forget, for a moment, the serious nature of my trek out into the snow on that cold autumn morning.

When we arrived, I was shocked to see Asuke's condition. He was lying flat on his back near the fire, and the color in his face had all but vanished. I leaned next to him and examined him. His eyes were closed, his skin hot, and his breathing was shallow.

"He was awake most of the night, and then he finally slept," his wife said. "But I haven't been able to wake him. Something is not right."

Kuruks and Tuhre did their best to calm her while I continued my examination. It took me a while to find his pulse, and when I did, I could feel that it was clearly weak and erratic. I tried to piece together his symptoms as though they were clues, but I came up with no ideas. I lacked medical training.

I sat back and stared at Asuke, feeling helpless. And then I remembered the one tool I had left – the same technique I had used for Sakuru. I didn't have time to prepare a ritual or even light a pipe. Instead, I lit some sage to purify the air. I put my hands on Asuke's arm and closed my eyes, then entered a deep, relaxing state.

It was difficult as I was quite worked up from the stress of the situation. The more I chased that treasured lush, dream-like state, the more it eluded me. Frustrated, I realized I had nothing to lose by trying the reverse – letting the calm seek me. I remained open and receptive to it, but didn't try to force it. As soon as I released control and let my mind begin to float, deep meditation overtook me.

I attempted a connection to Asuke's spirit. I hoped he would be able to give me an indication as to what was wrong with him, and more importantly, how to resolve it. After a moment of waiting, I sensed the presence of his spirit.

"Help me, Asuke. What has made you so ill?"

Instead of a reply in words, I saw, in my mind's eye, a silhouette of his body. I could see the various organs inside, and saw a great multitude of tiny yellowish-green points of light flowing throughout his body. I wasn't quite sure what they were, but it was clear that they weren't supposed to be there.

Though I wasn't sure precisely what a normal human liver should look like, I got the sense his was inflamed. Upon closer look, a structure underneath it, presumably the gallbladder, was the source of the numerous invaders in his body. I reached the conclusion that the stones had blocked and inflamed his gallbladder, causing it to rupture. I am not sure if I arrived at the final diagnosis myself or I was aided by his spirit, but given the lack of medical training I had, it is reasonable to give credit to the spiritual realm for this discovery.

Now that I knew what was wrong, I needed to figure out how to solve his problem. I suspect a doctor might have performed surgery to remove the malfunctioning organ, but this seemed pointless due to the transmission of toxins throughout his body. My only recourse was to try to fight the contamination that was raging inside of him. I had herbs that could help with inflammation, but nothing powerful enough to remove it without killing Asuke.

The only tool I had at my disposal was my mind. I had done some admittedly incredible things with my mental abilities, but removing toxins from a body, especially one so weak, was not something I had any confidence in being able to do effectively. I knew that confidence in any act was key to its success, so I tried my best to shove aside my doubt and proceed with the task at hand.

I heard voices around me, presumably Tuhre and Kuruks trying to help keep Asuke's family calm and focused, but I was so deep in meditation that I couldn't process their words. I had confidence in them to help provide me the space and time needed to heal Asuke, and was grateful for their assistance.

I envisioned pure, white light flowing through me, then flowing into Asuke's body. I imagined the light chasing down the particles of toxins in his blood, nullifying them of their poisonous power and returning his blood to a natural, healthy state. The stream waned while my concentration slipped. I continued until I felt a change in his body.

The toxins still circulated, but the chaos and disorder that undulated throughout him had calmed. I was bolstered by the fact that changes occured, so I continued the flow of healing light as strongly as I could. When the point of maximum effect had been reached, I slowly backed out of my meditative state and opened my eyes.

Tears streamed down his wife's face. I smiled warmly and reached across him to take her hand.

"What is wrong with daddy?" I heard from Asuke's son.

The child might as well have stuck a knife through me. Ice ran through my veins as I realized what had happened. I couldn't bear to look at Asuke. Instead, my heart ached with profound sorrow as his wife sobbed. Kuruks's put his hand on my shoulder, and I heard Tuhre say something, but neither could break me away from being lost in her tears. "He has moved on," Kuruks told the boy.

"To where?"

"To the sky. To the world of spirits. It is all the same."

"Will he be alright?"

"Yes," Kuruks replied. "Izzy guided him home."

Chapter 45

"I need a moment," is all I could manage before I left Asuke's hut. Kuruks followed immediately behind me.

"What are you doing?" he asked.

"I'm a fraud!" I yelled in English. I'm certain others in the village heard me, but might not have understood what I said.

Kuruks put his hand on my shoulder. "No, you aren't," he replied in Pawnee. "Why would you say this?"

"I thought I had helped him," I replied, switching away from English.

"You did help."

"No, I didn't. I didn't help him move on. He–"

"He couldn't be saved," Kuruks stated.

"I gave his family false hope and dismissed his previous symptoms as a simple stomach ailment. If anything, I killed him."

"Don't say that," Kuruks insisted.

"It's true. I am not Sakuru. My healing arts might be able to help a cold, but they can't do anything serious. I am of no use here."

I started to leave, but Kuruks caught up to me. "I have never known you to walk away from a responsibility."

"I can't do it, Kuruks."

"You're walking away from your most important task: provide comfort to his family."

"Tuhre knows them better, she would—"

"Isabella!"

I was surprised he used my actual name. To my knowledge, it was the first time. I turned to see a frustrated and disappointed look on his face. I don't think I had ever disappointed him before. I felt horrible for letting him and a grieving family down.

"Go help them," he said, pointing to the hut. "It's the healer's job."

His tone was firm, and I didn't like him telling me what to do. "You are not my father, Kuruks."

"No, but you are not thinking clearly. Be mad at me now if you wish, but if you walk away you will never forgive yourself."

My gut told me he was right. The pain of the situation, my lack of confidence, and his disapproval hurt me, or more precisely, my ego. My knee-jerk reaction of anger faded as I realized that he was right. I took a deep breath and walked back inside.

"I'm sorry, I—"

His wife's embrace stopped my words. She was a slight woman, but I could feel the weight of her grief hanging on me as though she carried a ton of bricks. My eyes misted as I held and consoled her, and then I cried even more when Kuruks explained to the two kids where their father had gone. He was always looking out for me, even when I didn't deserve it.

"Kuruks told me that when a child is born, the entire village celebrates. I feel compelled to remind you that the entire village is here for your loss. We feel it with you, and all of us will help you through this."

"Thank you," she replied.

Kuruks give me a warm smile.

Tuhre left to tell the chief and the rest of the village what had happened. Soon, the entire village began shuffling through her home, offering to help the family with whatever they needed. Baskets of food were delivered, and men stacked extra firewood to keep the home fire toasty warm. Though I meant what I said, within moments the village, my village, had made good on what is usually offered as a well-meaning platitude.

Several of my fellow Pawnee made it a point to thank me for my help. Some went out of their way to make sure I knew that I was appreciated, even though I feared my contributions weren't nearly enough. I was touched by how much help the family received. It felt good to be part of that community, that family. And yet, despite all the support, I still couldn't help feeling, deep down, that I wasn't what they thought I was.

I returned home, and Kuruks followed shortly afterwards. I looked through Sakuru's belongings, taking each item and absorbing as much as I could from it. I could feel echoes of her in each item - her hairbrush, some of her jewelry, and even a handkerchief. If she'd shown me her European-style handkerchief when I first met her, I would've had a lot more questions.

Thinking back, though, I understood why she didn't tell me everything at first. I had to go through an initiation, of sorts. If she'd dumped everything at once on my plate, I would've rejected it as utter nonsense. I wasn't ready, and she knew that. Though her time after passing the prophecy to me was cut short, she made the best of what she had. She trusted me, and I knew that I had to trust myself. After what had just happened with Asuke, that was extremely difficult.

Kuruks sat behind me and put his arms around my shoulders. "I have two things to tell you, Izzy. I am proud of you, and I am sorry."

I nestled my face against his hand. "You have no reason to apologize. You were right. And you weren't proud of me."

"I am proud of you all the time. You may not be perfect, but neither am I." He looked through a few of the things I had been holding. "Sakuru once told me something. She said that most of our time is spent learning, and most of the time we won't even know it is happening."

"An interesting observation," I replied.

"That is what is happening with you. If Asuke had a much less serious illness, you may have been able to heal him. But the lesson for you today had nothing to do with that. You were shown that the most powerful way you can help is with the heart, not with the mind."

"You showed me that."

"No, I just pointed you towards a lesson I knew you would learn."

I turned and hugged him. "You're a wise man, and I'm blessed to be your wife. I treasure you every day."

"And I you," he replied.

Chapter 46

Paa awoke the next morning with a strong chill. Worried that the fire had gone out, she made her way to the living room to check on it, despite intense pain in her stomach. After she discovered it still roared, she tried to return to her room, but stumbled over the footing of the fireplace. She caught herself, then dozed off in the rocking chair next to the hearth.

"You're burning up!" Tim said with his hand on her forehead.

"I'm cold," she replied through chattering teeth.

"You must have an infection. I need to see your stomach."

Paa pulled up her dress. There was considerable redness and swelling around the wound. Tim pushed gently next to it, and she screamed in pain.

"I'm sorry, I'm sorry," he said. "I needed to see how far the infection has gone. I think it's deep."

"Cold," she said again. "Blanket."

"Right, but… you're already burning up."

"Please."

Tim fetched a quilt and placed it over her. "Is that any better?"

She nodded.

"My mother made this for me. She told me she sewed love into it as she made it. It has always made me feel better."

"I feel it," Paa replied.

"You do?"

"Mmmhmm."

307

"Ok, I need to fetch the doctor."

Paa grabbed his hand. "Don't leave."

"I have to. You are sick and need medicine. I don't know what else to do."

Paa knew he was right and didn't have the strength to argue. Tim fetched some water and made her drink a few sips, then brushed her hair aside and held her cheek a moment as he spoke to her.

"It's going to take me most of the day to get back, but I will hurry as quick as I can. Your job is to rest until I return."

"Alright," she replied.

Tim reassuringly squeezed her hand, put a ladle in the water bucket near the chair for her, then put on his coat and left. Within moments, Paa's feverishly hot eyelids slowly closed. She awoke when the doctor had arrived. She remained silent while he examined her, and then he looked at Tim, and back at her. He stepped away with Tim and discussed the situation. She couldn't make out exactly what they were saying, so she suspected the prognosis wasn't good.

"Can you help me?" Paa asked when they came back.

"I'm afraid there isn't much I can do, young lady," the doctor replied. "You have a case of surgical fever. It is very common, though given how long it's been since Tim operated on you, it is unusual that it took this long to set in."

"She's a fighter," Tim said. "She kept it away this long, maybe she can finish this fever off."

"There is a possibility. Strong, healthy people have about a twenty percent chance of recovery from an infection like this. You must keep the wound very clean."

Paa didn't understand what twenty percent meant. She perceived math in a different way. "Twenty?" she asked.

"Oh, yes, I suppose the natives don't know fractions and figures."

"She speaks two languages, doc. She's smarter than you think."

"Je parle trios langues," Paa said. "I speak three languages."

"Impressonnant!" the doctor replied. I studied some French in college. A beautiful language, but my Latin studies had to take precedent, unfortunately. He turned to her. "Vous êtes intelligent pour un indigene. You are smart for a native."

"Et vous êtes adéquat, pour un médecin," Paa replied.

The doctor snarled his nose and took a quick, snooty breath. He patted his knees then stood. "She has a quick tongue. If she redirects that effort towards healing, she might pull through."

"I told you she was a fighter," Tim said. The doctor left some medicine and grain alcohol for cleaning the wound, and Tim paid him for his services.

"I wish I could do more," he said before leaving. Tim bade him goodbye and returned to Paa.

"Twenty percent chance, Paa. That means one in five."

The ratio made more sense to her. "Not good odds."

"I think he's wrong. I say it's more like eighty percent. With this medicine, and the best care you can imagine, I will have you good as new."

"Thank you," Paa replied. "I do not deserve your kindness."

"Nonsense. Here, take this medicine the doc gave you. He said it'll help with pain."

After she drank some of the liquid, she laid her head back against the rocking chair.

"That ain't gonna do," Tim said and went to get a pillow. He gently lifted her head and guided her onto it. "That feel better?"

Paa nodded.

"What did you tell that doctor? I don't speak French."

"That he was adequate, for a doctor."

Tim laughed. "Yea, serves him right after that rude comment. If I didn't need his help to fix you up again, I would have rearranged his face a little."

Paa smiled. "You do not have to do that."

"Do you think there's anyone in your tribe that can help?"

"Maybe. But she may be dead now."

"Who? What's her name?"

"Sakuru, our healer."

"Well, maybe we won't need him."

"Her."

"Sorry."

"It is alright," Paa replied. She began to feel a bit swimmy-headed. "I am sleepy."

"It's probably that medicine kicking in."

Within seconds, Paa had closed her eyes.

Tim placed a loving kiss on her forehead. "Get some rest, Paa."

Chapter 47

I presided over the funeral of Asuke, the second death to befall our tiny, close-knit village in a matter of weeks. It was a somber event, yet I was more confident in the proceedings. Instead of being one of the principal grievers and woefully unprepared for my responsibilities, I understood my role and provided comfort to his grieving family.

To say family is a misuse of the word. Yes, he had a wife and two children, but he had an extended family that was larger than many of us can fathom. I felt so connected to the Pawnee, and was privileged to have such a treasured and respected position in our group. Our mutual strength helped give his wife the courage she would need to face the brutal mourning process.

On the day after the funeral, Kuruks went with some of the other men of the village and hunted, and returned with a successful haul. I went to one of the other huts and learned how to process and preserve meats with some of the older women. They were patient in showing me what I needed to know without condescension. After we finished, they gave me enough meat to last Kuruks and I at least a week.

Though I was a bit less depressed after a day of pleasant social interaction, I was still preoccupied with what had happened with Asuke. After dinner, I could tell that Kuruks wanted to make love, but for the first time since we had wed I reluctantly declined his advances. I hated to disappoint him, but I knew I couldn't concentrate on either of our pleasures. I rubbed his sore muscles from the hunt, and we slept well throughout the night.

Intermittent snow showers and bitterly cold wind continued for the next few days. This would have been a horrendous week for me had we still been traveling the Oregon trail, or even in our old home in Independence, and yet, here in my earthen hut in the plains, I was scarcely inconvenienced. I was removed from every trace of what most Americans would consider normal civilization, and yet I was warm, safe, loved, and most importantly, free.

Shortly after noon a few days later, Kuruks and I heard some commotion. We hurried outside to see the Chief Piita and a few elders pointing towards the eastern horizon. After shielding my eyes from the bright, reflected sunlight, I saw the object of their interest - a man riding toward us.

"That is a white man," one of the villagers noticed.

"I will go get our pistol," Kuruks said.

I put my hand on his shoulder. "Wait."

Several of the elders drew long rifles. "It is prudent to defend yourself," Piita said.

I had been afraid of previous sightings of Americans, but my instinct told me that he was not a threat. "We have nothing to fear."

Several of the men looked at Piita for confirmation, and he motioned for them to lower their weapons. I took a few steps towards the rider and closed my eyes, listening to the wind for any clues. I was startled to see a brief flash of an empty rocking chair, the same chair in one of the dreams I had before we reached the village. By the time I had opened my eyes, the man was upon us. He stayed mounted, but raised his hands. He was exhausted, and it was clear that something grave troubled him.

"I mean you no harm," he said.

"You'll find only peaceful people here," I said in English. Kuruks translated what was said into Pawnee. I looked back at the chief to make sure I was not speaking out of turn. He nodded in approval.

"My name is Isabella."

"I'm Tim. You are white."

"I am."

"Where are you from?"

"Independence," I replied.

"But, you—"

"I am Pawnee, now," I interrupted.

He looked confused. "Does Sakuru live here?"

"She did," I replied with a sigh. "She died."

"Oh, no," he replied, then dismounted. "No, no, no."

"Did you know her?"

"No, I… I need help. I was told she was a healer."

"She was. That is now my responsibility."

"So, maybe you can… but wait," he started, then looked at me closely. "How can you heal her if you aren't…"

"There?" I asked, correcting his implication that I wasn't Pawnee. "I have plenty of herbs and remedies, and can–"

He shook his head and turned away from us. "No, that won't do. She needs more than herbs. This is serious. Even the doctor couldn't help her. No, I need Sakuru."

"My wife was trained by Sakuru," Kuruks said.

"I've heard that Indians have mysterious ways of healing. That's what I thought she meant."

"You are referring to medicine, and yes, we do."

"Who is she?" Kuruks asked.

"An Indian girl I rescued near the creek. Not too far from here, maybe a day away."

"Paa!"

"Yea, that's her. She's real bad sick and needs help. Do you know her?"

"She's my sister."

Tim's countenance immediately changed. His face turned red and he reached for his saddle bag, grabbed a pistol, and pointed it towards Kuruks. "You rotten bastard, you did this to her!"

Chapter 48

Within seconds, several rifles and arrows were at the ready, surrounding Tim. I should have been horrified at the prospect of him hurting my husband, but I wasn't. Just like when Paa aimed the arrow at me, I knew no harm would come to anyone that day. With a calm demeanor, I approached him.

"There is no need for any of this," I said.

"If it weren't for Kuruks, Paa wouldn't be sick. He shot her!"

"He did," I replied. "But Paa killed Sakuru, and tried to kill others. You only know part of the story."

Tim was confused for a moment, then stiffened his resolve. "Liar!"

"Izzy, stay back," Kuruks said. "If he wants to fight me, I will give him his wish."

"There will be no fighting today," I said.

"Oh, I ain't gonna fight you, I'm going to kill you!" Tim yelled, pushing his gun further towards Kuruks.

Tim's hand shook, and his finger became fidgety. I held my hand out and asked for the gun, but he ignored me.

"If you fire at Kuruks, the rest of these men will kill you, Paa will still need help, and we won't know where to find her. Is that what you want, Tim?"

He swallowed hard, and his hand began to steady. "I don't trust you."

"No, but you will," I said.

I wasn't sure if my confidence was from the medicine of the prophecy or a result of my own spiritual growth, but I especially appreciated it in tense moments like that. I reached for the barrel of his pistol. His frantic breath had left a thin film of condensation on its highly polished, icy cold metal, one that my fingers cleared as I extended my hand around the weapon. After I settled his shaking with my calm, yet firm grasp, he looked at me strangely. I kept my gaze transfixed on his, and in a deliberate, yet non-confrontational voice, I repeated my demand.

"Hand it to me."

Tim shook his head a few times, then released the gun into my charge. I heard multiple sighs of relief before the elders restrained him.

"Make sure he does not have any other weapons," the chief ordered.

"He doesn't. He's scared and needs our help," I said.

"Pointing a pistol at us is not the way to get it," Kuruks remarked.

"What is wrong with Paa?" I asked.

"She's real sick," Tim replied. "She got shot with a belly full of lead by this man," he said, looking at Kuruks, "But I got it out. Doctor said she's got surgical fever, though. She's burning up and has the chills. She said Sakuru might be able to help her."

"She killed Sakuru. But I can help."

Tim frowned. "Like I said, I don't trust you."

"You do not have a choice," Kuruks said.

Tim had lost what little bit of control he had over the situation.

"Do you think you can save her?"

I am ashamed to admit my first reaction was to say no. Not because I didn't think I could, but because I didn't want to. I admit it was selfish, but that was how I felt. My life with Kuruks had just achieved a modicum of stability, and having Paa back in our lives would greatly complicate things, as well as create a risk of physical harm to us and our village. Rather than go with my gut emotional reaction, I was fortunate to have the wisdom to not provide an immediate answer.

"Isabella is a capable healer," Piita said, and Kuruks translated. "But Paa has visited much grief upon her and Kuruks, as well as this village. It is not good to hold a grudge, but the wound is still fresh. It is her choice to make."

Tim sighed and relaxed against the men holding him. "I don't know what happened between all of ya'll, but it don't change the fact that a woman is sick and needs your help." He turned to Kuruks and emphasized, "Your sister, dammit!"

I watched Kuruks for any reaction, but his expression didn't betray his thought process.

"Come on!" Tim yelled. "You aren't just going to let her die, are you?"

A big part of me still wanted to say no – to take the easier road and to keep my life simple, but I couldn't. How could I live with myself if I had not tried to save her?

"No," I replied, then handed his pistol to Kuruks. "I cannot let her die."

Kuruks put his hand on my shoulder. I took his hand and we walked a few paces away to speak in private.

"You do not have—"

"I do," I interrupted.

"Not for me."

"No, but for me," I replied.

"How will it help you?" Kuruks asked. "She has brought you nothing but misery."

I put my hand on his face and smiled. "I appreciate your stoicism, my love, but I know you think about Paa. I see your mind wandering, and I can hear whispers of your thoughts. I know you don't mention her to protect me. But I don't need protecting from her anymore."

"I will always protect you," Kuruks replied. "I will never trust her."

"Don't trust her, trust me," I implored. "I need to do this."

"Are you sure this is what you want?"

"I am."

We returned to Tim, who barely contained his impatience. "Will you help her?"

"Yes," I replied.

Relief washed over his face. "Thank you. But we have to hurry!"

"There are a few conditions," Kuruks said. I turned to him and raised an eyebrow, but his demeanor indicated he wasn't interested in negotiating.

"What?" Tim asked with frustration.

"I'm coming with you, I will keep your pistol until we are safely there, and if you do anything to harm Izzy, I will not hesitate to kill you."

Chapter 49

After hurriedly packing some supplies, Tim, Kuruks, and I started our journey east on horseback. Tim didn't say a word while we rode, though it would have been useless to try to converse for the constant noise of the wind and the galloping horses. The remainder of the day was clear and sunny, but the bitterly cold breeze from the north chapped our faces and pulled the moisture from our skin. Though I was eager to get to Paa as soon as possible, I looked forward to sunset so we could stop for the evening and light a fire.

We rode until the last remnants of sunlight completely faded, then stopped and lit a small campfire. We were careful to save as much of our rations as possible, though we insisted that Tim have a bit more than us as he hadn't eaten since he left his home. After ample hydration from melted snow and a solid meal, he looked better. Our conversation after dinner would barely qualify as small talk. It was clear he wasn't interested in communication. That seemed to suit Kuruks just fine, but I wanted answers. I considered pressing him further, but was too drained.

The blankets we brought couldn't keep out all the frigid night air. I bundled my cloak around me, snuggled under the blanket, and held Kuruks as tightly as I could to conserve our heat. After a difficult night of sleep, I rose before Kuruks and Tim and prepared a simple corn porridge for breakfast. We returned to the trail and rode hard throughout the day. The wind died down, so we made much better progress, I was even more determined to get answers at camp that evening.

"Tim, I know you're frustrated, scared, and tired, but I would be grateful if you could tell me more about what happened with Paa. The last time we saw her, we were in a fight for our lives to defend ourselves. She shot Sakuru with an arrow, and she and two of her friends tried to kill both Kuruks and I. She wandered off and we had no idea what happened, so please understand all of this caught us by surprise."

"You thought she was dead, didn't you?" Tim asked.

"I don't know. I suppose. She is very resourceful, so we weren't sure. You don't know what she put us through."

"I don't know anything about all of that," he replied. "That's between ya'll. I saw a woman nearly dead, and I knew I had to help."

"I would've done the same thing," I replied. "I'm not passing judgement. I'm just trying to explain our reaction and initial reluctance."

"Tim, I would like to know what happened after you rescued Paa," Kuruks said.

Tim relaxed his guard a bit and gave an overview of Paa's rescue and the time he spent nursing her back to health.

"Thank you for saving my sister's life," Kuruks said. "I am sorry I had not already told you that."

Tim chuckled. "That probably has to do with the fact that I was pointing a gun in your face and threatening to kill you."

Kuruks didn't laugh. "I would like to know if you are in love with my sister."

It was a horrible time to be drinking a sip of water. I nearly choked. Kuruks's directness was always something I admired, but this time it took me by surprise. It was charming to hear his protective nature emerge.

"I, uh… well, I care for her, if that is what you mean," Tim replied.

"Not quite. You know what I mean."

Tim paused a moment. "I do, and I guess I hadn't really put much thought into it. At first, I just wanted to save her life, but she is nice, and kind of grows on you, ya know?"

At the time, the idea that Paa could be kind or even endearing was a completely bizarre notion to me. But after having seen the visions of what went on during that time, I could understand how Tim could have seen that in her.

"I have issues with my sister, but she is still family. I care about her, and do not want her to be hurt."

"I understand that," Tim replied. "But you have nothin' to worry about with me. I wasn't the one who tried to kill her."

The silence that ensued after that was only amplified by the cold night air. I took another sip of water, then waited for Kuruks's reply. The two men stared at each other for a moment until Tim finally started to grin. I feared that Kuruks would be angry, but instead, to my surprise, he started to laugh. I was confused as they both cackled, seemingly bonding over this strange, macabre humor. I suppose they were releasing a lot of tension in their awkward hilarity.

"Do not break her heart, Tim," Kuruks said.

"I won't," Tim replied. "And don't shoot her, alright?"

The two fell into another fit of cheerful laughter. I shook my head and watched as they eventually settled down into a more somber tone.

"Are you two done?"

"Sorry, ma'am, I know it's not something we should be joking about. I'm just so worried about her."

"I can see how much you care for her."

"I do," Tim replied as he gazed into the fire.

"I promise you I will do everything I can to help her," I said. It brought him a brief smile, but he quickly returned to his contemplative stare.

We all agreed to retire early that evening in hopes of getting a fresh start the next morning. Thanks in large part to the calm wind and slightly warmer temperatures, I slept much better. I awoke shortly before sunrise feeling rested. Tim and Kuruks soon rose, and after a quick breakfast we resumed our journey. Our early departure put us slightly ahead of schedule, causing us to arrive at Tim's house late that afternoon.

After tying up our horses and unloading the supplies I had brought, we dashed inside to find the main room empty. A quilt was haphazardly tossed next to a rocking chair near the hearth, and a trail of blood led into the kitchen. I followed it to find Paa lying on the floor, clutching her stomach.

Chapter 50

"Paa!" She was still alive, but barely conscious.

"Good heavens! I didn't mean for her to get up. I hated to leave her alone, but I didn't know what else to do." He was clearly frazzled at the sight of her in such distress.

Kuruks picked her up and placed her in a bed.

"I'll get some clean cloths and fresh water," Tim said as he scurried out of the room.

Kuruks held her hand as I examined her. "What do you think?" he asked.

"It's good that it's draining," I replied. "But she's burning up, her color is terrible, and her pulse is weak."

Her eyes opened and she stared and us.

"Can you hear me?" Kuruks asked.

Paa opened her mouth, but couldn't talk. Her lips were dry and cracked.

"She's probably dehydrated," I said. I took a ladle full of water and helped her drink. She was reluctant at first, but eventually took several sips.

"The doctor gave her this," Tim said, handing me a bottle. It appeared to be a preparation of morphine.

I realized the doctor had no hope for her to get better, and simply resigned to ease her suffering until she died.

"Do you think you can you help her?" Tim asked.

I took the cloths he provided and cleaned and re-dressed the wound, then helped her drink some more water. "I'm going to try my best."

I knew that no known medicine or herb could cure her. If I was going to save her, it was going to have to be with the powers within me.

"Just tell me what you need," Tim said anxiously.

"I know this is going to sound strange, but I need to be alone with her," I said.

"What are you doing?" Tim asked.

"This will take some time," I replied. "Please keep this room as warm as you can."

"Alright," he replied, then turned to Kuruks. "Do you understand what on earth she's doing?"

"She must embark on a spiritual journey with Paa to bring her back from the brink of death," Kuruks answered. "Come, Tim, let us give them some privacy."

After they left, I lit some sage and cleansed the room, forming a sacred space to do my work. I waved the bundle above her, laid it on the end table, then laid next to her and took her hand in mine. I closed my eyes and took slow, deep breaths, allowing the sweet, cleansing smoke from the sage bundle to purify me. The calm space of deep meditation consumed the myriad of stray thoughts and doubts that constantly plagued me. Eventually, from the darkness, a shadowy figure emerged.

"We have much work ahead of us, Isabella."

I immediately recognized the voice. It was Asuke. I was so startled that it almost brought me out of meditation.

"I know you did not expect to see me again. I am one of your guides. I have come to help you."

I was curious as to how that could possibly be. He had been dead for such a short time, and his death was related to my inability to heal him. I had feared I had earned his hatred, and even worried that he might haunt me. Instead, he was here, offering to guide me with his wisdom. I was deeply moved.

"We have done this before, Isabella, and we will do it again. Though this lifetime will be unique, and last for much longer than usual, you will eventually return to our group."

"Our group?" I asked.

"We have known each other in many lifetimes. It is the way of things. At one point, you were one of my guides. It is now my turn to repay the favor."

"But wait - you said group. Who else is part of it?" I asked.

I believe Asuke was about to answer me, but then decided against it.

"Someday you will rediscover this knowledge. But that is not the task at hand."

I was disappointed at his reply, but understood. Saving Paa was my priority. "What do I do, Asuke? How can I heal Paa?"

"The key to healing her lies in understanding what is wrong with her."

"The doctor said surgical fever."

"That is one way to put it. An infestation has corrupted the wound. Normally, her body would fight this invader, but it is unable to do so."

"Why?" I asked.

"She is too weak, and the attack is too strong. She needs help."

"When I tried to heal you, I saw the same thing. I tried to attack the toxins inside you."

"That is one way to do it, but not the only method, and certainly not the most effective one. She is beyond conventional treatment."

"You make it sound hopeless," I observed.

"There is always hope. I am here to help you – to show you another way."

Suddenly I was in the deep woods. I couldn't tell where, exactly, but I was surrounded by tall, moss-covered conifers. The grassy ground was blanketed with pine needles and dotted with small ferns, and a faint smell of salt lingered in the air. I was in a clearing, and in the center of this clearing, directly in front of me, was a large pile of branches and sticks covered with moss. At the top, the pile was smoothed into a cradle-like shape, filled with a thick layer of leaves.

I turned to see Asuke standing next to me, fully healed, and dressed in clothing that was remarkably different than what he wore as a Pawnee. His hair was long and flowing, and he wore off-white robes that were accented with a gold-colored belt.

"Where is this?" I asked.

"In a far-off land," he answered as Paa appeared in the natural wooden cradle in front of me. She was nude, and the wound looked even worse in the sunlight that filtered through the trees. "Now we are ready to begin."

I still had questions about my surroundings, but Asuke was focused and insisted I do the same, so I reluctantly put my curiosity aside and followed his lead.

"Everything that ever was, is, or will be is brought into being by consciousness. That is the power of creation. With effort, you can change your own perceptions. With even greater effort, it is possible to change reality."

"Are you trying to tell me Paa is sick because she believes that she is sick?" I asked.

"In a manner of speaking, yes."

"I can understand changing reality in a dream. But this can't be done in the real world."

Asuke laughed. "I am in the real world. You are in the dream. Humans believe the land of spirit is make-believe, but I tell you it is more real than anything."

"If that is true, then can you simply think whatever you want to happen into existence?"

"Isabella, I tell you, it is possible to manifest whatever is in your mind. But nobody truly believes this is possible – not at their core. That is the reason we live our lives on Earth, to grow and learn lessons that are impossible to truly experience otherwise. For this to be possible, you must be lost in the dream, the waking dream of life."

Chapter 51

I understood the task before me, but was unsure as to how to accomplish it. Asuke sensed this indecision in me and provided further instruction.

"Changing yourself requires belief. Changing what you call reality requires will. But before you do this you must know yourself."

"I know who I am," I replied.

"Only in a rudimentary way. You are not Isabella. That is your name in the dream, but in the spirit realm, you are a soul. You have a name, but it is not pronounceable or even meaningful at this level of existence. Our souls know each other not by name but by an inherent quality that is undeniably unique. In spirit, we are drawn toward each other. The distinction is important."

"Can't Paa use her own will?"

"Yes, but will requires strength, and she is drained of strength. The spirit realm has no concept of good and evil, light and dark – but this realm does, and to change between those extremes, a strength of will is required."

I began to have a deeper understanding of what Asuke was trying to tell me. "Then how do I proceed?"

"You must eliminate all doubt in your mind that your true nature is a soul-filled being, and that you will, accomplish your task. This requires more than just visualizing and imagination – this requires filling yourself with unquestionable certainty. This normally requires a long time for someone to acquire this much certainty of will, and many will not reach that level. The magic within you helps make this possible. I have given you what you need."

And then Asuke slowly vanished. I stared at Paa and felt intimidated by the sheer weight of the responsibility before me. I shook off the initial layer of doubt. My intimidation melted into firm resolve. I put my hands on the wound and examined it, not with my eyes, or even my sense of touch, but rather in spirit. As my fingers inspected the gentle eddies of vibration that made up the physical structure of her abdomen, the disruptions became apparent. Invaders, in numbers too numerous to count, had taken up residence in the wound and thorough her body.

There was no way I could fight those malicious invaders that assaulted Paa's tissues and organs. Instead, the only way to interrupt their devastating action was for them to be eliminated from her body. To do this required not the forceful act of microscopic combat, but rather using my will, bolstered by the medicine within me, to deny its very existence.

I visualized the complete disappearance of the toxins. My thoughts were no longer in words, but rather an intricate set of symbols – those made by particles whizzing around the vibrational structure of Paa's body. By sheer mental force, I began to will the infestation to not exist.

I heard a faint voice in the corner of my mind. "Let me go." It was Paa.

"No, hang on," I replied.

Images from Paa's memory were thrust upon the common telepathic connection we shared. I could feel the sheer guilt, despair, and anger within her as these events surfaced. The emotion distracted me from my efforts.

"I need your help, Paa," I pleaded. "I can't do this alone!"

"I am not worth saving," she replied.

"You must deal with these emotions. I cannot do this for you."

My concentration slipped further. "Come on, Paa! Help me!"

Suddenly, there was a shift in our connection. Rather than ignoring the torrent of emotion, Paa began to face the images.

My concentration returned as she confronted the darkness within her. I poured every ounce of myself into the construction of a new reality, a reality where the toxins didn't exist in her body, and her strength was restored. An intense pulse of energy moved throughout me, and then Asuke returned to the clearing with a smile.

"I did it," I said.

"You knew you would. You understand the nature of the dream."

Paa and the cradle disappeared. Asuke and I remained in the clearing.

"You will someday see this place in the dream. Remember what you learned."

"I cannot ever forget, Asuke."

"You have many other tasks ahead of you in this life. Use it well."

"Will I see you again?" I asked.

"Not like this. The point of this waking dream, this reality, as you previously called it, is to experience it, not to stay mired in the mundane existence of the spiritual world. There is great polarity in which you will immerse yourself. You will have such great joys, and profound sorrow. You will bring new life into the world, and guide those who have finished this time here onto the next existence."

I reached out towards Asuke. "I need guidance. I can't do this alone."

He extended his hands into the air, and at their apex, a multitude of people appeared around him. My heart sprang out of my chest in indescribable exuberance when I saw my father, mother, and Sakuru among them. My mother approached me with a warm smile and hugged me. I began to sob tears of profound joy.

"You are never alone, Isabella."

We uttered no more words, but untold volumes of wisdom, thought, and compassion were exchanged between us. The experience was unlike anything I had encountered before, or since.

Chapter 52

I have no idea how long I stayed in the meditative state with Asuke and my departed loved ones. It seemed like a few moments, but when I woke, the sun had long set. I was relieved to find that Paa's fever had broken. I sat on the bed next to her and reflected on the experience until she touched my hand.

I took Paa's hand in mine. She was pale, but the energy around her was much stronger and more stable. I smiled. "You're going to be alright."

"I know," she replied. "I'm so thirsty."

She leaned up just enough to take a drink, then promptly finished the cup of water I had handed to her. I poured her another from the pitcher in the kitchen and she nearly drank all of it as well.

"You might want to be careful," I said.

Paa tried to lean up all the way, but it was a struggle. She grunted in pain for a moment, then returned her head to the pillow.

"You're going to be sore for a while. You need rest."

"Why would you save me?" she asked.

"You are my husband's sister, and part of his life. I would do anything for him and his family. And it is my job. I am a healer."

"Where is Tim?" she asked.

I peered into the main room then returned to her bedside. "They're both sound asleep. I can get them."

"No, let them sleep."

"Tim rode as hard as he could to get Sakuru. He didn't eat, and I doubt he slept. He really cares about you."

"I know," Paa replied. "I saw Sakuru."

I raised an eyebrow. "You did? How?"

"She came to me while Tim was gone."

"It must have been a dream," I replied dismissively.

"The Child of Darkness would dismiss a vision?"

I looked away, biting my tongue. I wanted to say something in spite.

"She cared about me, too," Paa said. "She forgave me."

Her reply did little to soothe my displeasure. "Sometimes we see what we want to see."

"Perhaps," Paa replied. "Either way, the beautiful wheat fields near her home in Prince Edward Island were a nice distraction from the pain."

There was no way she could have known that. I had to admit her vision with Sakuru was likely true.

"Then you know Sakuru died, then," I said.

"Yes. It is not fair. After what I have done, I am the one that should be dead."

It was nice to hear Paa admitting her sorrow for her actions, but the wounds were still fresh in my mind.

"I have wronged everyone. Including Tim. I kept the truth from him. He should know the monster that I am."

"Nonsense!" Tim said as he slipped into the room and sat on the other side of the bed. His hair stuck nearly straight up

335

from the awkward position in which he fell asleep on the chair. There was no force powerful enough on earth to remove the smile from his face. "You cured her!"

"The infection is gone, but the wound needs to heal. She's going to need rest."

Tim brushed Paa's hair from her face. "That's wonderful! Paa, you're gonna be alright."

Paa saw Kuruks behind me. I stood and let him take my place.

"How do you feel?" Kuruks asked.

"Horrible," Paa replied. "But I will live, thanks to Isabella. How are you?"

"I am well."

"Kuruks, I—"

"We will talk later."

"I want to say something now. I am sorry for what I did, both to you and Sakuru. Neither of you deserved it."

Kuruks sighed. "You killed her, Paa. She was a mother to us."

I motioned to Tim, and the two of us left the room.

"Thank you again, Isabella," Tim said to me. "I have something for you."

He took a decorative box from above his mantle and unlocked it with a small key from his pocket. He removed a small gold bar from it and handed it to me.

"It's pure. Should fetch close to twenty dollars. It's all I can spare now, given the rough winter we'll probably be facing this year."

I examined the bar. It was beautiful. Even though it had smudges and small imperfections, it was still a sight to see. For a moment, I thought about keeping it. I reasoned that twenty dollars could help get Kuruks and I through the winter. And then I realized that the lump of metal I was holding was merely a symbol of my old culture.

"I appreciate this, but I have no need for it," I said as I handed it back to him. "You can put it to much better use."

Tim shook his head. "You and your husband put your lives on hold to do this for me, and I will always be grateful. You could buy a new horse with this, or several rifles and enough ammunition to last for years. It's the least I can do."

"Paa's her brother. She's family. And I have all I need. Again, thank you, but I must decline."

Tim was confused, but he relented. "If you insist."

"I do."

"Then will you settle for a home cooked meal? I ain't a half-bad cook."

"Now I won't turn that down," I replied. "I think you'll be a good influence on Paa."

"A good influence? I figured it'd work the other way 'round. I may seem like I am settled, but let me tell ya, I—"

"No need to explain, Tim. You love her, and she needs someone like you."

Tim didn't respond, but it was clear he was thinking about what I said. I looked inside the doorway to Tim's room and was relieved to see Kuruks with his hand on Paa's shoulder. I tried to walk away before he noticed, but it was too late.

"You can come in, Izzy," Kuruks said.

"I want to talk to you," Paa added.

"Come help me cook us up something," Tim said to Kuruks.

"Have you made things right with your brother?" I asked her.

"It will take some time, but I think we can mend our wounds. I do not know where to start with my apology to you, Isabella. I am not really good at apologizing."

"It doesn't matter where you start. It matters that you try."

"I was so hateful to you. I wanted you dead. I don't know what is wrong with me. I shouldn't have been so angry, but I was."

I sat on the edge of the bed. "A stranger comes into your village and essentially assumes your identity. That can't be easy."

"Don't make excuses for me."

"Believe me, I'm not," I replied. "But I do understand some of the anger."

"You have truly become Pawnee. I thought you were foolish for trying to pretend you were one of us, but I see how wrong I was."

"I didn't know what I was doing at first," I admitted. "And to be honest, I still don't feel like I completely fit in."

"I understand that feeling," Paa replied.

"But our village is strong because our people are strong. And it's an honor to be a part of that."

"They will never take me back after what I have done," Paa said.

"I don't know about that. I think if you're willing to show that you have changed —"

"I'm not sure I have."

"You have. I don't feel the anger in you that I used to."

"Maybe you healed that too," she reasoned.

"Paa, regardless of what has happened, you are my sister. I don't know what the future will hold for us, but I am open to finding out."

"I would like that," she said.

We heard Tim and Kuruks fussing and banging pans in the kitchen. It sparked a grin on both of our faces.

"Tim cares for you a great deal," I said.

"I know. I have a confession to make, though. At first, I was simply using him. I was grateful, but I knew I needed more time to recover, and he was glad to provide it."

"Maybe, but I saw how you looked at him when he came in here, excited to see you."

"Yes, well, I suppose things didn't work out quite like I thought. I went from manipulating him to thinking of this as our home. I don't understand what happened."

I giggled. "You fell in love is what happened."

Paa had a blank expression on her face. She had never considered the possibility.

"The love of a good man can change you more than you could ever imagine. Kuruks has taught me and helped me so much, and yet at the same time given me room to grow as a person. He's been a wonderful influence on me. You have changed,

Paa, and you can continue to change and be a better person. But it is a lot easier to do with the help and love of a good, supportive partner."

"He is a good man," Paa replied.

"Yes, but is he a good cook?"

"Actually, he is. Why?"

"Because I think if I don't go in there soon those two men are going to tear the kitchen down."

Paa burst out into laughter. I was the first time I had ever seen her genuinely happy. Unfortunately, her laugh turned into pain, and she clutched her stomach.

"Thank you," Paa said. "For giving me another chance."

Chapter 53

Despite my misgivings of the combined culinary talents of Kuruks and Tim, we enjoyed a wonderful meal. Rather than eating at the dining room table, we all carried our plates into Tim's bedroom and sat around the bed with Paa so she wouldn't be excluded. It was a reassuring sight to see her eat a few bites of food.

"You should stay the night at least," Tim said. "It's almost midnight."

"Thank you for the offer," Kuruks said. "After the difficult journey here, we need rest."

"They can stay longer, can't they, Tim?" Paa asked.

"Of course. I didn't mean you could only stay tonight. Our home is open to you as long as you wish."

"Our home?" Paa asked.

Tim looked a bit sheepish. "Well, I, uh… I suppose I consider it ours. Unless you object."

Paa blinked several times, then looked at me before answering. "That is fine."

I couldn't help but to smile, and I even noticed a miniscule grin on Kuruks's face. I made a mental note to offer Paa a primer on expanding her romantic communications.

"We can stay a few days, can't we, Kuruks?" I asked.

"I would like that," he replied.

"And we'll only be a few days away by horseback, so we can visit at least several times a year," I added.

"Why, that'd be wonderful," Tim said. "You and Kuruks can sleep in the guest room, and I'll sleep in the living room. And Paa, if you need anything, you let me know and I'll be right here, alright?"

Kuruks and I left the room to prepare for bed. I remade it with fresh linens, an experience that I admit was strange after having regularly slept in a Pawnee home. When I was done, I heard Paa call for me, so I hurried to her room to see what was wrong.

"What is it? Are you OK?"

She could see that I was worried about her, so she quickly tried to diffuse the concern. "I'm alright. I just wanted to talk to you a moment. I need your advice."

It was strange to hear her utter those words. "I'll do my best."

"I don't want to sleep alone tonight. I want Tim in here with me."

"Then why don't you ask him?"

"I am concerned he'll get the wrong idea. This would be less of an issue if he were Pawnee, but you understand Americans better than I."

"I admit that it's unusual in his culture for a man and a woman to sleep in the same bed unless they are married, or at least romantically involved. But he cares for you and has proven he has your best interests at heart. I think he'd love to sleep in here with you."

Paa smiled. "That is reassuring."

"Kuruks and I had quite a few cultural issues to resolve. Still, there are times where our backgrounds clash, but talking about it before it becomes a problem is always best."

"You are right."

"Do you want me to tell him you want to see him?"

"Please. I will discuss this with him. Thank you, Isabella."

"Good night, Paa."

Before I returned to bed, I told Tim that Paa wanted to talk with him. He seemed delighted to have a reason to see her again.

We slept late into the next morning, and after breakfast I washed all the linens and thoroughly cleaned Tim's house. Kuruks hunted while Tim chopped firewood and removed the snow from his roof. By the end of the day, we were all exhausted, but the house looked and smelled much better, and most of the chores had been caught up so that Paa and Tim would have a much easier burden while she recovered.

The next day I cooked as much as I could without completely draining Tim's supply of food, hoping to provide enough baked goods and preserved venison from Kuruks's hunting to last until they could resupply. That evening Kuruks and Paa had a lengthy conversation while I gave Tim pointers on adjusting to Pawnee culture. Later, before we went to sleep, my heart was warmed when Kuruks told me that he and Paa were well on their way to rebuilding their relationship.

We awoke bright and early the next morning and were pleased to find that most of the snow had melted. There was still a cool breeze from the north, but it was no longer so bitterly cold. We agreed it was time to leave, so after informing Tim and Paa, we gathered our belongings and prepared our horses for the journey. Tim insisted that we have a farewell lunch, so we were once again treated to his excellent cooking. We were all pleased that Paa felt well enough to sit at the table.

Tim helped Paa outside so that she could help see us off. She and Kuruks exchanged a long hug while Tim thanked me again for my help.

"I'll always be grateful to you both," he told me. "Our home is open to you."

I hugged Tim. "I appreciate it. Paa is going to need a lot of patience and understanding. You both have a big adjustment ahead of you."

"If I need any help, I know where to find you."

Paa insisted on standing on her own without Tim's help, then walked towards me. Kuruks and Tim gave us a moment alone.

"I am afraid that I can never make up for all that I have done to you."

"You've helped me understand so much more about myself," I replied. "Because of your interference, I pushed myself to become who I am."

"It did not have to be like this," Paa admitted.

"Maybe not, but we can't change any of that. You are now my sister, and a permanent part of my life. From what I have recently learned, it is likely our souls meet in various lives to help teach each other lessons."

Paa sighed. "Then this must be my chance to experience profound remorse."

I took Paa's hands and smiled. "And mine forgiveness."

Paa pulled me close. I felt the sorrow within her, and its depth brought me to tears. If I had any doubt that our souls already know the people we meet in our lives, it was erased that instant. I was moved, and unable to speak. Paa eventually pulled away from me and wiped a tear from her eye as we mounted our horses.

"We will return in the spring," Kuruks said. "Be well, both of you."

With a gentle flick of the reins, we started our journey home.

Epilogue

I want to write *THE END*, but can't.

I've successfully written an entire manuscript detailing a pivotal time in my life, and yet, after all these words, the last six letters are seemingly impossible to type. Somehow, it doesn't seem appropriate to bookend that incredible period with such a simple, oft-repeated phrase of finality.

I close my laptop and stare out the window at the cold, rainy winter day. Writing this book has stirred so many memories. Memories that now circle around in my mind. I take a sip of tea and set mug softly onto the table, then close my eyes and allow the emotions to overtake me. I smile as I recall the warmth of Kuruks's arms around me, the peaceful look of my daughter nursing at my breast, the joy of seeing my child marry a good man, and the many happy years spent with the love of my life.

And yet the darkness of my gift, the curse of immortality, claws at that warmth, using time as its ally to slowly but surely take away everything I ever loved. It strives to fill my heart with a cold, empty longing. It takes so much from me, yet I persist, despite its dreadful assault. I know the only way to resume the march of time is to pass on my gift.

Then, I will finally be free.

A knock at my office door pulls me from my daydream.

"Good morning, Isabella. Sorry I'm a bit late, I was stuck in traffic."

I hug him and flash an incredulous look. "Daniel, our busiest intersection in town is patrolled by a four-way stop sign."

"I really was, I promise," he insists.

I shake my head.

"I didn't miss anything, did I?" he asks.

"We have an appointment later in the day. It's Mrs. Sharp."

"Oh," he sighs.

"No, don't *oh*. We must respect our patients. She needs our help."

"But she won't ever leave."

"Some people need a bit more help than others," I reply.

"I suppose she pays well."

I shake my finger. "You have been my apprentice for nearly four years now. You should know better than to say something like that. We accept payment only because most have nothing else to trade. It is an uncomfortable reality of living in this age."

"I didn't mean it like that. I… you're right. She just frustrates me."

"Why?" I ask.

"She's been coming for healing nearly as long as I have worked for you. She is much better than when she first came, but she has plateaued. I don't think we're helping her anymore."

I pause to consider Daniel's words. "You're right."

Daniel is startled. "I am?"

"Yes. I would've normally told her there was no more I could do for her, and that the rest was up to her. But I've been so wrapped up with my book, and your training, that I've let my attention slip. You've grown wise."

"I wish you could make my parents believe that," Daniel says. "They think I'm wasting my college years. My dad says I'm going to graduate with a useless degree in *mumbo-jumbo*."

I laugh. "Your dad doesn't know what a privilege it is to be so intimate with the creative source."

"Oh, to hear him tell it, he does that every Sunday at church."

"Every path to a spiritual life is a valid one." I say. "Some take a bit more time, and some stop off at the attractions along the way. There is nothing wrong with this. Delaying your walk in a garden to smell a rose is not a waste of time."

"I wish he had a teacher as wise as you," Daniel says. "You have taught me so much. You speak with the wisdom of an old sage."

I roll my chair to my desk. "I finished my book."

"Oh really? Will you let me read it?"

"Yes. I need your help to name it. I was going to call it *Child of Darkness*, but that doesn't seem quite right."

"Why name it that?"

"Well, it follows the story of a young woman who was born during a full eclipse."

"Like me?" Daniel asks. "Interesting."

"If you give me one of those UBS things–"

"You mean USB?" Daniel pulls one from his pocket.

I copy the file and hand the drive back to him.

"You've been keeping this from me for years. I can't wait."

"Go home and read it," I say. "The timing couldn't be more perfect."

"Now?" he asks. "Are you sure?"

"I can handle Mrs. Sharp by myself."

"In that case, I'll see you tomorrow!"

***

The next day, Daniel returns to my office with a large thermos of coffee.

"You look terrible," I observe.

"I was awake all night."

"You read the whole thing?"

"Yes," he replies as he takes a seat next to me. "I… I don't know what to say."

"I imagine you are just as surprised as I was."

"That's an understatement," Daniel replies. "Why didn't you tell me sooner?"

"As you know, I asked Sakuru the same question. I didn't understand her answer then, and I don't know that you will now, but I will tell you nonetheless. You weren't ready."

"But who was she to judge?" he asks.

"She was my teacher. And I'm yours. We all have a right to judge, and the duty of a teacher is to determine when her student is ready for their next lesson."

Daniel takes the USB drive out of his pocket and twirls it between his fingers as he ponders the answer. "Am I ready?"

"I would not have let you read the manuscript had I thought otherwise."

"So, after you pass this magic to me, what will happen to you?"

"My aging will resume," I reply. "And then I will grow old and die."

"I have so many questions," Daniel says.

"I know. So did I. But I will be at your side for as long as I can. As you know, there is a ritual we must do. We will conduct it this evening."

"Alright," Daniel replies reluctantly.

"Go home and get some rest, and meet me back here tonight."

***

I go out the back door of my home office into my private garden. A stone table sits inside a beautiful clearing of trees. Moss covers the mighty trunks, and a slight drizzle hangs in the air. A cool breeze passes me, blowing my hair behind me and revealing a shimmer of gray. I allow my mind to drift, and soon see a vision of my guides and loved ones.

"You did not keep your promise, Izzy." The voice is a tender and familiar caress in the breeze.

"Kuruks, I had no desire for anyone else."

"But you have been so lonely."

I sigh. "Those days are coming to an end. I will be home soon, my love."

THE END

About the Author

Robert W. Oliver II is the author of *Dragonfly* and *The Bravest of Souls* trilogy (currently pending re-release). He has written for numerous publications, dives deep into philosophy and comparative religious studies, and is developer, and system administrator.

Robert believes the treasured art of storytelling is vital in our modern world. No matter our technical progress, stories that speak to the heart, deal with aspirations of spirit, and delve into the mysterious realms of existence, do more than entertain us. By putting ourselves inside these stories, we learn about ourselves and further our exploration of the dream of creation.

Robert lives with his wife Marsha in the beautiful Shoals Area of North Alabama.

Enjoy the Book?
Have Feedback or Questions?

In today's world, reviews and feedback are the lifeblood of an author's public persona.

Though most writers (myself included) will tell you we enjoy the craft of writing so much that we would do it even if no one ever read or commented on their works, we all are also full of it.

Yes, it's true that writing is an incredible passion of mine. But *your* feedback is important.

I'll never forget the first time I received an email from a reader I didn't know. I was touched by their unique message about how important the work was to them. I still treasure it to this day.

It would be greatly appreciated if you left a review on Amazon or your favorite book retailer.

I appreciate ALL feedback, negative, positive, and in-between. Anything you send to me will be read. I try my best to respond to each message.

If you wish to email me directly, please contact me at
https://jeweledwoods.com/contact/

Warm Regards,
Robert W. Oliver II

Little House of Cultural Expansion

I watched an episode of Little House on the Prairie named Injun Kid last night and was struck by a pivotal moment of cultural expansion. It was subtle, but well played, and analyzing it yields a fascinating look into human psychology and spirituality.

In the episode, a half-Native American boy and his mother arrive in Walnut Grove. His grandfather is embarrassed by his presence and insists that his daughter say she adopted him. When the boy refuses to stand for prayer at church, his grandfather yells at him and informs him he must comply or be punished. The child runs away to a nearby stream and prays for peace between with his grandfather.

Laura inadvertently interrupts his prayer. He explains that he was praying.

Instead of reacting in fear or hatred because he had a different religion, she reached for common ground.

"You mean you were saying a Sioux prayer?"

In that moment, Laura's entire cultural perspective is changed. She had known nothing but Christianity all her life. In an instant, her mind expanded to see the layer above her faith – the fact that others have belief systems radically different from her own. The moment was well played by Melissa Gilbert. She caught the nuance of the exchange quite well.

Totally absorbing yourself in your culture and religion is an incredible experience – one that benefits the universe by allowing it to gain another unique perspective on the zeitgeist of your cultural paradigm. But when you step back and see other cultures, compare their similarities and differences, your mind expands.

Simply knowing other belief systems exist will invariably change yours, which is why many religions fight to keep outside influence from "corrupting" adherents. It's a shame, because some of the deepest faith and spiritual wellness one can have is by practicing spirituality in full knowledge that yours is not the only valid approach.

We all bring a unique piece to the universal jigsaw puzzle. We are singularly qualified to offer our unique channeling of spirit to others and the world. When we do this in full knowledge of what others offer, our own experience is enhanced. Our mind is expanded, and we stand on the precipice of evolving to a higher plane of existence.

Want to read more?

Visit jeweledwoods.com and sign up for my newsletter to have these and other great articles sent to your inbox.

I promise: no spam, no emails shared with anyone else - just great insights and enjoyable reads.

Made in the USA
Monee, IL
06 May 2020

29112839R00206